KIMA BLAZE

Curse of a Name

and Reflections

To the Loved Ones.
To those standing at the sidelines, watching someone you love
and care for wither away, eaten by disease.
To the second victims, the forgotten victims, of illness.
Your smiles help. You being there helps.
Thank you for standing by our side.

Contents

Introduction

The Spirit World is hibernating. No one knows why or when it happened, for no human has lived long enough to remember.

Every now and again, a minor spirit will wake and roam the quiet lands. Most live and die their lives in the Spirit World, but some find their way through the Veil and into the World Of Man. Just enough to keep some humans on their toes, but not enough to remind them all of the things that go bump in the night.

The Spirit World is hibernating, and the World Of Man has no idea how lucky they are.

1

"You're going to die, Lizzie. You're going to die, and I will have killed you."

Mom reached forward, her hands crooked like claws. Her eyes wide, pupils small. Mouth open. Her fingers touched my temple, and they were so cold it felt like ice crackled across my scalp.

I sat up with a jolt, falling away from the cold window. The woman on the seat beside me glanced my way before looking down at her book again. I drew another breath, forcing it deep into my belly before grabbing my purse. Pulling out a water bottle, I glanced at the screen over the doors at the end of the railway car — only two more stops before I was getting off.

I sipped at my water, looking at nothing through the window.

The call had come two nights ago. I'd been sleeping, exhausted after a day at work and going out with friends after. I hadn't even realized I'd answered the phone before someone was talking in my ear.

"Is this Elizabeth Key?"

"Sure," I'd answered, turning around in bed.

"I'm Dr. Altman, I'm calling about your mother, Nancy Key."

Just like that, I was awake, sitting up. "What happened?"

"Your mother was walking the train tracks. When someone tried to talk to her, she attacked them."

"Attacked?"

"Yes. They are fine, but they had to subdue her before she did any real damage, and she managed to hit her head in the process."

"How is she?"

"Fine, but we had to put her in restraints. She... She is violent."

"Yes, where was the nurse that was watching her?"

"I don't know, Ms. Key, but this is something you should talk to the nurse about."

"Ok, I'll call her. Thanks for letting me know."

"Ms. Key?"

"Yes?"

"I didn't just call to let you know what happened. Taking the nature of the incident into account, you have to sign for your mother's release."

"Why can't one of the nurses do this? They have the right to make choices for her in my absence."

"As said, because of the nature of the incident."

"I can't just pack up and leave!"

"I think you have to."

"What?"

Dr. Altman sighed. "The man she attacked... he was talking about pressing charges. Your mother is a danger to herself and others, Ms. Key. Either you take care of her or the Province will."

I'd booked my train the same night, and now I was on it. I was using some of my vacation days to go see mom and figure out what to do with her. I'd known she was violent and worse off, but she hadn't been this bad just little over a year ago when I'd seen her last.

The train pulled out from the last stop before mine, so I started packing my purse. Standing, I walked carefully past the woman in the seat next to me. She didn't even look up from her book as I tried to slide past her, and I scowled. Even if I'd been made of paper, the space between her knees and the seat in front would have been tight. I stumbled into the walkway between seats and walked to the rear of the railway car, pulling my suitcase from the compartment there.

I braced myself against the wall as the train wound down. A girl and her mother were in the intersection with me, and the girl bounced past me and started pounding on the button that would open the door even before the train stopped. The mother smiled tiredly at me, and I smiled back.

The door opened and the girl sprang out with a squeal of joy.

"Honey, not so fast!" the mother said, hurrying after her.

Grunting, I pulled the suitcase out and onto the platform.

The world smelled of the ocean, and asphalt just after a rain.

Walking along the platform to the parking lot at the side of the station, I hailed a cab and climbed in, giving the driver my address. As the cab drove away from the station, I pulled up my phone and called Mark.

"Hey," he answered on the second ring. "You there yet?"

"In a cab now," I answered.

"How are you?"

"Fine."

"Don't lie to me, hon."

"I'm..." I stopped for a moment, letting the familiar land-scape of my hometown wash over me through the window. The old cinema now turned theatre. The park. The high school.

"I'm not lying to you."

"Right."

"I'm serious."

"Right."

"Mark…"

"I'm sorry, I'm just worried. Your mother –"

"She's really sick, Mark."

"She said she was going to kill you. She attacked a man, almost clawing his eyes out."

That was partly true. "She didn't really say she was going to kill me. She said I would die and it would be her fault."

"Just as bad."

"Ok, really, you have to stop. She's my mom! She hasn't attacked anyone close to her." The lie was bitter on my tongue.

"She may. You know that!"

"I'm not having this argument over the phone, Mark. We've talked about this, and now I'm here."

"And I'm not. I wish you would have let me go with you, at least."

"No. You have your studies. I'll be fine."

"School's just started. I could take a few days off."

"Mark…" I massaged my neck with my free hand, staring at my shoes. "Meeting new people only makes it worse, you know that."

"I don't know that 'cause you've never let me meet her."

"Because meeting new people only makes it worse. Remember when I had to go home to help set up the new nurse? Mom was confused for days, even when she was lucid."

For a moment all I could hear was his breathing, then: "Any thoughts on when you'll be home?"

I sighed. "I don't know. Eric gave me this week off and is

prepared to get someone in next week to cover me as well, but I don't plan for this to take that long. I just need to figure out how bad it is and see if she can still have a nurse at home or not."

I couldn't bring myself to say anymore. To see if she could still have a nurse at home or be committed. Dr. Altman had been kind enough to give me the contact info to a facility focusing on people like my mother, but if I did that... I hadn't been there for my mother when she needed me, when she got sick, and now just to commit her? I wasn't ready for that. It may be late, but I was here now and I was going to do my best by her.

"I'll keep you updated, ok?"

"Just be careful?" I closed my eyes at those words. Opening my mouth to argue that there was nothing to be careful about, but he cut me off. "I know, I know. I'm just worried, is all. I love you, you know?"

I sighed. "I love you too."

"Good. Now, take care and call me tonight, ok?"

"Sure. Bye."

"Bye, hon."

I hung up and opened my eyes. The cab was still, waiting for a light to turn green. The driver was looking at me in the mirror.

"What?" I asked.

He shrugged and focused on the road again.

I leaned back in my seat, looking at the world as it moved past outside. I'd grown up in this town. It was big enough that someone could be anonymous if they wanted to but too small to have many of the groups one would find in bigger cities, which was why I'd moved to Toronto when I was done with school.

I sighed and turned away from the window, not wanting to think about my youth. It was both a happier and a sadder time.

Soon enough, we left the town behind. On one side of the street was a big dog park, on the other three identical apartment buildings. Then came a few smaller, older houses with small gardens in front before the plots grew more prominent and the houses changed to big ones with glass walls and double garages with automated doors. We turned down a street, leaving the modern homes behind. Woods grew up on either side of us, giving the illusion of wilderness. Too soon, the woods stopped, giving way to a new neighborhood. This one with old Victorian homes. We continued up a hill before he stopped at the top.

"We're here," the driver said.

I didn't answer, just sat in the back seat looking at my childhood home. Along the sidewalk ran a dark iron fence with an ornate gate. A driveway ran along the fence and disappeared in the shadow of old trees. Bushes and trees filled the garden in front of the three-story Victorian manor. It was painted dark green with white trimming around the windows. It looked clean enough. Most every light was on inside, except in the attic. The garden in front of the house had once been home to a multitude of plants that had grown wild over the last two years as my mother's sickness grew worse. Leaves from the almost naked trees littered the browning grass that could be seen through the bushes and dead flower stalks.

"Miss?" the driver asked, bringing me back from thoughts on the state of my home.

"Yeah, just a moment." I forced a smile and pulled up my purse to find my wallet.

I handed him the money without a word before opening the door and stepping out. The driver hurried after, giving me the change before opening the trunk and pulling my suitcase out. He didn't set it down, though, as he looked at the house.

"Do you want me to come with you?" he asked as I reached for the case.

My hands froze. "Why?"

He turned to me. "Well, I overheard you on the phone just now, and I heard about what happened on the train track."

"Thanks, but I'm fine," I answered, pulling the suitcase out of his hands. I didn't look back as I walked past the car and up the walkway toward the door. I couldn't see the grey stone path I was supposed to follow for all the leaves, but I could have walked it in my sleep.

The door stood at the top of a three-step porch and was made of solid oak. I pulled out my keys, fumbled until I found the right one and unlocked the door. It clicked familiarly. Scents of lavender, citrus, and old books filled my nose. I stepped into the foyer, hearing the cab start up behind me.

The foyer was more of a hall with coat stands, shoe racks, and a big mirror. On my right, a door led into the living room. Straight ahead was a bigger room with doors leading to the dining room, sunroom, and a library, and a staircase rounding up and out of sight toward the upper floors.

"Mom?" I closed the door behind me. "Mom, you home?"

I'd thought the house was quiet as I stepped inside, but a new kind of silence fell as I spoke. For a moment, it seemed like the entire world held its breath. For one beat, my heart sounded like the ticking of a clock, then something clattered in the room above me and steps ran toward the stairs.

2

Something slammed into the wall at the top of the stairs before footsteps sounded on the steps. A woman rounded the corner and almost flew toward the floor. Her hair was raven black with a silver streak at each temple, and her skin was golden. She was tall and thin. Her hand looked veined and sharp as she gripped the banister. As soon as her grey eyes found me, she opened her full, pink lips and screamed, hurdling toward me.

"Mom!" I lifted my arms as I yelled, grabbing her hooked hands just before they reached my face. For a second her eyes grew wide and the scream died in her throat, then she barreled into me and pushed me so hard against the door my breath was knocked from my lungs.

"Mom," I said again, lower now, as I swallowed some of her hair. I could hear her gasping, but she didn't step back.

"Lizzie?"

"Yeah."

Carefully, I started pushing her away. On the outside, a car door slammed. Mom, who seemed to relax, stiffened again. Steps sounded on the walkway, then on the porch before someone banged on the door. I could feel the wood vibrate against my back, and mom's wrists started trembling in my hands.

"Ms. Key? Ms. Key, are you alright?" I recognized the cabdriver's voice.

Keeping mom's eyes locked with mine, I answered. "Yes, thank you. I'm fine."

"I heard someone screaming?"

"Yes, I startled my mother. She's fine now."

"You sure?"

"Yes, thank you."

He stood out there for quite some time before muttering something too low for me to hear through the door. His feet were heavy on the porch as he left, but his steps drowned in the leaves and foliage. The whole time, I kept mom's gaze locked with mine. We didn't move before the cab drove away.

"There," I said when the world outside grew quiet. "It's just the two of us now, mom. It's ok."

"Who was the man at the door?"

"The cab driver, he just wanted to check that I was ok."

"But little bird, you should have said you would finish school early today. I could have picked you up."

I opened my mouth to protest, closed it, then tried again. "How old am I, mom?"

She laughed, and it was the young laugh she had when I was a child. "Honey, you know how old you are."

"Humor me."

"Humor me? Isn't that a weird thing for a sixteen-year-old to say? Or is it the latest slang?"

Something pushed against my throat and I blinked back the tears that started stinging my eyes. "I'm twenty-two, mom. Remember? I don't live here anymore."

She blinked at me before smiling. Her wrists moved in my hands and I let go. She touched my cheek. "Baby bird, I'm glad you're home early. I'll make us a snack before dad gets home"

She leaned forward and kissed my cheek before sliding her thin fingers through my hair, then turned toward the kitchen.

I watched her go. She was so thin. The nurses said she wasn't eating, but I didn't think it would be this bad. Her clothes hung on her and she looked like she was more dead than alive. Her hair, now that it had settled after her sprint, looked dirty, but she hadn't smelled, so she had to keep up with some cleaning.

As the door to the kitchen closed behind her, a man stepped into view from the sunroom. He was dressed in a green scrub set and moved to follow mom but stopped as he saw me. His eyes narrowed before widening.

"I am so sorry I wasn't in when you got home," he said, rushing toward me. "I'm Harold. I was assigned to wait with your mother until you got home." He reached out a hand and I took it. "She was asleep, so I stepped out, getting some fresh air. I didn't hear you come in." This close, he smelled like cigarettes.

I shook his hand. It was clammy and his grip was weak. "It's ok, really. I'm here now and nothing happened."

"Ok." He withdrew his hand and dragged it through his hair before turning and lifting a bag off the floor. "I need to see some ID, and I need you to sign this. Then I'll be out of your hair."

He rooted around in the bag until he found a clipboard with papers on it. I found my driver's license as I waited. Handing the clipboard to me, he took my ID but didn't look at it. He was looking around. "This is some place you've got here."

"Yeah. It's belonged to the family for generations."

"Too bad you're just using it as a nursing home for your mother. Think about raising a family in this place. You thought of selling?"

"No."

"Oh."

I focused on the papers, reading through them. They just said that mom had been delivered safely from the hospital to our agreed destination and that I took responsibility for her from here. All the while, Harold looked around, glancing at my ID now and again but never looking at me.

"There," I said, handing the clipboard back to him.

"Thank you, thank you," he said. He was past me and at the door before the clipboard was even back in his bag. As he reached for the door, he glanced at me. "You know that all the clocks in this house have stopped, right?"

I suppressed a shudder. "Yes. They unsettle her."

He nodded. "Good choice, then." And he was gone.

Letting out a relieved breath, I locked the door behind him then turned and walked deeper into the house. Setting my suitcase at the bottom of the stairs, I pushed into the kitchen. Mom was standing in the middle of the room, staring at the refrigerator. She turned when I entered, and her face lost part of the confusion that filled it. "Lizzie, what do you want for dinner?"

I looked around the room and forced a smile to my mouth. "You've just started making something, remember? If you go to the library and find a book I'll set the plates, ok?"

"My good girl," she said and walked out through the dining room.

I sighed. Pre-heating the oven, I opened the freezer on top and pulled out a frozen lasagna and some onion bread, then I found some new cheese in the fridge and cut off slices to put on top of the lasagna.

As I worked with the food, then washed the table and set the plates, I made a list in my head of what to do next.

I needed to go by Mrs. Hearth next door and thank her for stocking the fridge and freezer for me.

Had to call Dr. Altman to let him know I was home and that mom had been delivered safely by the driver.

I would also need to call the day-nurse, Lars. He'd been reassigned by the agency as mom was in the hospital and I was coming home. Needed to see if I could get him to come back and take care of her.

Then I had to talk to Mrs. Tav, the night nurse, about what happened that night. How mom got out.

And I needed to call the special needs home, no matter what Lars said.

The last thought made me shudder. I didn't want to call a home, to give mom's care over to someone else, but she wasn't herself. Or she was, but herself from another time.

When everything was done, I walked toward the library. Leaning against the door-frame, I looked at her. Mom sat in her chair by the window, an old paperback in hand. Her hair hung dirty around her face, her eyes not moving as she stared down at the words on the page. She had heavy bags around her eyes and her lips were white as she tightened her jaw.

In most ways, I was a copy of her. My hair was still all black, reaching just under my shoulder blades. I'd had bangs a few months ago, but they'd grown and now the tips tickled my cheek. I had mom's full lips and weakly tilted eyes and her strong jaw. One could clearly see she had indigenous blood with her golden skin, but my own skin was paler, making it look like I had a tan all the time. Instead, I'd inherited her body, as we were both around hundred-and-eighty centimeters tall and slim, but with strong shoulders. And I had my dad's eyes, bright green with blue spots.

This house had belonged to his family before mom met him, and he'd inherited it when his parents died, but I'd grown up here with my parents and grandmam and grandpap all raising me. Dad left shortly after mom got sick and I hadn't seen or heard from him since. Mom herself was a foster kid and didn't have any other family, so it was just the two of us.

And I'd left her too.

As the lasagna got ready and I was sure mom wasn't going to wander off, I took my suitcase up the stairs.

The ground floor of the manor was the smallest but still held a modern kitchen, a nice dining room, a sunroom, a library, and a living room. In the center of it all was a big hall with the stair leading to a landing where one of the two grandfather clocks of the house stood unwound before the stairs split and headed to the first floor. The first floor of the house held two bedrooms, one big bathroom, and dad's office. There was an opening in the story over the hallway, allowing a crystal chandelier to hang from the second floor and throw light into both the first floor and ground floor halls. A carved hardwood banister ran the length of the opening, making sure no one fell down. The rest of the story was open, a big window filling one wall and looking out over the garden, a fireplace with sitting space, and doors leading to the front balcony. The area around the window was filled with shelves and small tables holding heirlooms of my family. There was stuff on this floor that could probably sell for quite a lot of money if we needed it — stamp collections from my great grandfather's time. Crystals collected by aunt Ellie before she moved out. Old medical stuff from my great-great grandfather's time as a surgeon. An old violin that hadn't been out of its case in my lifetime.

The stair leading to the second floor was smaller and ran along the front wall of the house, just giving room to the door leading to the balcony. The second floor was more closed off than the two others, as it didn't have the chandelier or more than two places letting in sunlight. One was the glass door leading to another, much smaller balcony standing on the landing between the stairs reaching the floor and the even thinner stairs running up to the attic. The other was the big window on the other side, looking out over the garden as the window below. There stood grandmam's old piano, which had been closed and left to gather dust after she died. There was a fireplace, but only two chairs thrown in front of it as an afterthought. The other grandfather clock stood up here, trying to brighten one of the many dark corners. The rest of the floor held three bedrooms, one of them mine, mom's studio, and a big bathroom.

Over that was the attic, and I had no idea what kind of stuff filled it.

My room was just as I'd left it a year ago — a double bed along one wall, a desk under the big window. Three books lay atop one another on the small table beside the bed, and more filled the shelf on the other side, together with pictures and CDs. The door to my small walk-in closet was open, the mirror on the back of the door reflecting the light from the hallway.

I turned on the light and stepped through the door. The blue quilt on my bed seemed faint, covered with dust as it was. I threw open the window, letting the early autumn air in before lifting the quilt and hanging it over the sill. I would have to clean the whole room before I went to bed tonight, but I was going to wait until mom was in bed herself.

At the desk, I tried turning on the lamp, but it clicked and burned out. As I screwed out the bulb, I noticed the notebooks lying at the corner. They were covered in dust, just like everything else, but I picked up the topmost anyway, leafing through it.

It was my latest diary. I'd started keeping one when mom got sick, so I would have somewhere to pour out my thoughts and fears, my anger at dad for leaving, and at mom for getting sick. My fear of getting her disease.

This book was only filled halfway.

April 22

Laura's got cancer. Stage 4 Lymphoma. I'm sorry to hear that because she's been good to mom, but I can't help feeling a little anger too. Laura can't continue working with mom when she's going through treatment, meaning I have to find someone else to take care of her. Mark says he could go home with me, take a year off from school to help me with her, but I don't want that. Mom can't handle anyone new in her life, but he won't listen on that ear. Why does he have to be so stubborn? Why can't he just respect that this is a side of my life I don't want him to take part in? Is it that hard for him to respect my wishes? I love spending time with him and his normal family. No health issues or mental issues or anything. No foster kids or crappy dad's leaving. I wish I had that. Why can't I have that? I want to just not think about that when I'm with him. Not think about mom or dad or anything. Just be our own little family. So why can't he just leave it alone?

April 27

I'm home. Mom was so glad to see me she cried and hugged me. She thought last time she saw me was two years ago when we had that big fight about dad. I know it's not the last time she remembers, but when she brings it up like that it feels like it is the last real memory she has of me. What if it's the memory she dies with? A memory of us fighting. I can't have that being her last memory of me. I don't believe in life after death, but what if I'm wrong? What if I'm wrong, and she only remembers us fighting? Then again, maybe she'll remember everything that has happened since she got sick after she dies?

I hope not. There's been so many bad days. For her sake, I hope she won't remember it.

I'm home and maybe she will come around and we can make a new memory. The new nurse, a guy, comes tomorrow. I'm worried about how that is going to go. She doesn't know him. I don't know him.

I had to help Mrs. Tav when she bathed mom today. I never wanted to see mom naked, but now I have. She had scars on her arms and Mrs. Tav told me they were from mom clawing herself a few months ago. I don't know why she would hurt herself, but maybe she doesn't know she does it.

It hurts to see her like this. This is one of those moments I wish dad was here. He'd know what to do. But he's not here, the bastard, it's just us.

I wish mom was here. She'd know even better what to do.

April 28

The new nurse, Lars, is really nice. He came early so mom would still be sleeping, giving me time to know him as well.

Lars is older and has worked with people like mom before. He is prepared to take care of her 100%, but he's thankful for Mrs. Tav being here at night. He jokes that he already has a wife and she wouldn't be happy if he spent the night with another woman.

I think mom would have liked him. At least before she got sick. Not now, though. When she saw him for the first time, she screamed and threw a vase at him, yelling for him to leave me alone, not to touch me.

Lars handled it fine. He stayed calm and made me stay calm. It ended with mom grabbing me and leaving the room. She was still angry, leaving bruises on my arm, but at least she didn't throw anything else.

Maybe this will work.

I need this to work. I can't stay here. I need this to work.

April 29

Mom attacked Lars today. So now she's sedated and I'm going to Dr. Long tomorrow to see if he has any calming meds we can give her.

I don't want to.

April 30

We got some new meds and they already seem to be helping. Mom hasn't attacked Lars, but she gets weird every time he's around. Like she wants to attack him but can't bring her body to do it. She ends up crying and screaming instead.

I hate this.

I can't do this.

Tears spotted the last page.

I closed the book, remembering those days. Remembered how I grew so tired I couldn't bring myself to write much in the diary anymore. It was too exhausting, remembering mom fighting her own body, her frustration when she couldn't make it do what she wanted. Her fear for me every time she saw Lars during those first days. Mrs. Tav kept coming as usual, helping me give mom her meds and putting her to bed. She also had to take the daily cleaning as mom wouldn't trust Lars with that yet. I helped her, and that helped me.

After around eight days, mom calmed down whenever Lars came into the room. She still watched him but didn't cry or scream at him anymore.

After twelve days, Lars joined in on mom's bathroom routine at night with me and Mrs. Tav.

On day seventeen, she told me I would die and that it would be her fault.

4

Day 17

I was in the kitchen with Lars. He was getting mom's dinner pills ready while I was getting the plates out of the cabinet. It had been a good day. Mom had been calm, helping Lars and me in the garden. She loved working in the garden.

It had been a good day.

A scream split the quiet afternoon, followed by something hitting the ground. I jumped, the plates dropping from my hands and breaking as they hit the floor. I didn't stay to clean up. Lars was out the door a second before me.

The scream died. All I could hear was my own beating heart and things thumping against walls, glass breaking, heavy breathing.

Mom was in the living room. Her hands were bloody. The room shimmered in the low spring sun. Dust danced in the yellow light over the broken glass littering the hardwood floor.

Lars continued into the room, heading for mom, as I skidded to a stop in the doorway. There had been pictures on the mantelpiece, in the window frames, on one of the walls. All of them were on the floor now, broken. Blood streaked down the walls where mom had cut her fingers, dragging down the pictures.

She was standing in the middle of the room, still except for the heaving of her chest at every breath. Her dark hair hung around her face, and I could see only one eye, wide open and jumping around.

Lars reached her, stopping. He started talking in a low voice, just a whisper. I couldn't hear a word he said, and it didn't look like mom did either. She stayed in that position as he crept closer.

The glass crunched under his shoes as he moved.

A drop of blood slipped from mom's fingers and splattered on the sparkling glass.

Lars reached out a hand, touching her shoulder.

Mom snapped. One moment she was still. The next she was shrieking, moving. Her head whipped up, her eyes finding me in the doorway. In them, I saw fear, anger, rage, hate, and something else I couldn't understand. She didn't stop shrieking as she lunged for me, her bloody hands turning to claws.

Lars lunged with her, wrapping his arms around her frail body and locking his hands together.

Mom struggled against him, but he was bigger and stronger than her. It seemed that she knew within seconds that she couldn't get away, so she stopped struggling and began laughing hysterically, still looking at me. When she stopped laughing, I saw tears streaming down her face.

"Lizzie, my little Lizzie."

"Mom?"

I took a step into the room. Mom stiffened. Lars shook his head, and I stopped.

"Little Lizzie. Little Elizabeth. You're going to die, Lizzie. You're going to die, and I will have killed you."

"What are you talking about?"

She reached for me. Fingers still like claws, but her movements were gentle now, not the sharp ones of attack.

"Elizabeth, Lizzie, Elizabeth. I'm pretending it isn't your name, for your father didn't want to call you by that dark name. He wanted something else, but I didn't. I always liked his sister, Elizabeth, and was so sad when she died. She was my best friend, you know. She introduced us. So I wanted to honor her. Your father didn't, though, and he was right. Elizabeth, Lizzie, Elizabeth. My baby girl. Hair as dark as mine, eyes as green as his, and death on her lips, in her heart, from her naming day. Elizabeth, Lizzie, Elizabeth. Baby bird, going to die. Going to die, and momma bird will peck out your eyes. For a crow is a crow is a crow is Elizabeth is death."

I backed up as she spoke. Fear clawing at my skin. Her eyes never left mine, tears still streaking down her face, but her mouth showed teeth in a sneer of a smile. Her voice had turned to a song, and the tune crept through my head, along my skin, like a frosted breath.

I hit the wall in the entry with my back. The thud made mom stop singing and her smile died. When she spoke again, it was in her own voice, tears making it thick. When she spoke, it was in a whisper meant only for me:

"You're going to die, Lizzie. You're going to die, and I will have killed you."

I turned and ran.

5

I left my stuff in the suitcase and walked back downstairs. Unpacking felt like admitting that I would stay for a while, and I didn't want to be here longer than I had to.

Mom was still in the library, not looking like she'd gotten any further in the book while I was upstairs. In the kitchen, the lasagna was coming along nicely, so I put the onion bread in with the lasagna for it to heat up. Then I found what I needed for a salad in the fridge and started making it.

By the time I finished, the lasagna was ready as well, so I carried it all out to the dining table.

"Mom, dinner," I called as I put the food on the table.

No answer.

"Mom?"

I went to the door, leaning out and trying to look into the library. I could see her feet from the doorway but nothing else.

When entering the library, I found her looking out the window, a furrow in her brow. The book lay open in her lap, her hands on top of it. She was twisting her wedding ring around and around.

"Mom?"

She jumped and turned to me. Her eyes were wide for a second and she looked pale, then her expression softened and she smiled.

"What is it?"

"Dinner."

"Oh, right!"

She pushed up from the chair, the book toppling to the floor. She stepped over it and toward the dining room.

As she passed me, I closed my eyes and drew a deep breath. It would be ok. I'd get her into that home, and she could get the help she needed. I owed her that if nothing else. When opening my eyes, I walked into the library and lifted the book. Closing it, I set it on the small table beside the chair before stepping into the dining room.

Mom was already seated, still twisting her wedding ring but smiling up at me.

I sat opposite her and started putting food on her plate. She kept smiling at me, her eyes jumping over my face, and her head tilted a little. I'd seen that look on her face many times before. She didn't know me right now.

Blinked back tears, I lay a bit of the onion bread on her plate beside the lasagna and salad and started serving myself. She seemed to be having a rougher and rougher time, jumping back and forth with minutes intervals. She hadn't been this bad before. She would wake up and think she was at a particular time of her life most of the day.

"Eat, mom," I said, forcing a smile.

She started eating, glancing up at me every few seconds. If nothing else, she ate everything on her plate. I sighed in relief when she reached to take a second helping. She was so thin. I finished my meal much slower, taking my time and making sure she ate until she was full. She finished her second helping, then started on her third. Was that because she was starving or because she didn't remember she'd already eaten? There wouldn't be any food left over after her third helping, so she'd eaten enough for today.

As we ate, a key turned in the lock and Ellen Josephine Tav entered. She was an older woman with steel-grey hair pulled back in a bun. Her face was wrinkled and pale. Her hands thin but strong. She walked on silent feet into the house and stopped in the doorway as she saw us. She gave me a small nod and headed toward the kitchen.

Mom hadn't even noticed her.

I glanced at my watch. Almost six in the evening. It was almost time for mom's evening meds, and Mrs. Tav would be on until six the next day. Usually, that's when Lars showed up. I needed to call him. Hear what he thought best for mom.

Mrs. Tav entered the dining room from the kitchen, and this time mom looked up.

"Ah, hello there, Ellie. How are you?"

Mrs. Tav blinked before plastering on a smile. "I'm fine, thank you. It's been long, hasn't it?"

"Yes, it has! I'm so glad Connor decided to call you. I can't understand what the two of you were fighting about!"

"Nothing. Just siblings. We've had these fights before, you know."

Mom laughed, and the laugh was light and happy. "Yeah, I know. I don't know anyone that fights as much as you two."

Mrs. Tav smiled again and sat in the seat next to mom. She handed her a small paper cup with pills in them. Mom didn't even look at them, just took the cup and swallowed the medication dry.

"Well, I think I'll take a shower, just make yourself at home, Ellie, and I'll see you for dinner."

Mrs. Tav smiled and nodded, and we both watched as mom stood and headed upstairs. She had a smear of tomato sauce on her chin.

It was always weird for me to hear mom talk about my father's sister like that. From the moment Mrs. Tav introduced herself by her full name, mom somehow twisted her into my aunt Ellie. The old woman looked nothing like my father or my aunt, but I guess it was the name that linked it, and now that it was made, it seemed to stick. My aunt was named Elizabeth Josephine Key, Ellie for short. I could see how mom would link the names.

Letting out my breath, I slumped in the chair. "Hey, Mrs. Tav."

"Hello, Elizabeth. How was the train?"

I forced a smile. She always called me by my full name when mom wasn't around. "Cramped and late. As usual." My smile died. "She's so much worse."

"Yes. I'm glad you're looking into Midnight Sun. It's a good place. I've had other patients end up there."

"Yeah, they seem nice. It just... it seems wrong, you know? Like I'm giving up on her."

"Elizabeth, Alzheimers is a hard disease. On the patient, as well as on the loved ones. All we can do is give her what she needs when she needs it, and what she needs now is to be around people that know how to handle her at every moment of every day."

"I know. It just doesn't feel right."

Mrs. Tav didn't say anything for a second before she sighed. "How is the process of getting her into Midnight Sun going?"

A sour taste filled my mouth, but I forced myself to meet her eyes. "There's a meeting with a representative from the home tomorrow. I'm going."

Mrs. Tav narrowed her eyes but didn't break our gaze. "Who will watch her? Lars will not come."

"Mrs. Hearth said she'd do it."

"She is not trained."

"No, but mom is always calm around her. You know Mrs. Hearth, she somehow calms everyone. Even mom."

"Still, I'm not sure it is such a good idea leaving her with someone not trained in dealing with her."

"It will be fine," I said as I pushed from the table and started cleaning up. I couldn't look at her.

"I'm sorry if I upset you, Elizabeth," Mrs. Tav stood to help me. "But I am only thinking of what is best for your mother."

"I know," I growled and walked into the kitchen. Mrs. Tav followed close behind. I could feel a sneer twist my lips. "Speaking off, how did she get out?"

"What?"

I put the dishes in the sink and turned, looking straight at Mrs. Tav. She was standing in the middle of the room, the lasagna form in her hands.

"The other night. How did mom get out? You were here, weren't you? How did she get past you?"

Mrs. Tav relaxed a little and walked to put the form into the sink, but I didn't move and she ended up setting it on the counter beside me.

"I am only human, Elizabeth. Nancy had shown no signs of aggression earlier that day. She had been calm and talked with Lars at length about her little girl that was doing so well in school. When I arrived, she thought me your aunt Ellie, as she so often does, and she started telling me about your father. Giggling like a schoolgirl herself. She was having a good day."

She picked up the kettle by the stove and pushed past me to get to the water. First when the pot was on the stove, did she start talking again. "She took her medication without any trouble and went to bed without any trouble. I don't know exactly when she slipped out or how. The window was closed against the starting chill, and all the doors were locked the morning after, and your mother didn't have a key when they found her. She may have lost it, but that is not important. She must have slipped out just before midnight when I was down in the kitchen to make my evening cup of tea. She had slept peacefully until then, and I usually drink that cup every night."

"I don't care about that," I cut in, sounding meaner than I meant, but I needed to know. Needed to know how mom slipped past Mrs. Tav and outside when Mrs. Tav was supposed to have experience in how to deal with people like mom. "I want to know how she got past you, why you didn't think to check on her more often. How this could happen on your watch!" I was almost yelling, but Mrs. Tav gave me a cool look that made me shut my mouth.

Mrs. Tav started finding tea and cups in the cupboards, talking as she moved around. "I don't know. I've already told you. She probably snuck out of her bedroom when I was downstairs. She may have hidden in the hallway or somewhere else until I went back upstairs. She'd arranged her pillows to look like she was under the covers. You know how the angle is from the door. It looked to me like she hadn't moved. I didn't notice she was gone before I checked on her again a little past midnight. That was when I called the police."

I scoffed but didn't know what to say. I'd crossed my arms at some point, and my nails were digging into my flesh.

"Now, if you will excuse me, I have to take care of my

patient," Mrs. Tav said as she lifted her now full cup of tea. She didn't look at me as she walked out of the kitchen.

I looked after her and listened to her steps on the stairs before her and mom's voices, talking, drifted down to me. With a sigh so deep it almost made me cry, I returned to cleaning up after dinner.

6

I finished cleaning up after dinner. Above me, mom and Mrs. Tav moved about. Their steps and weight making the floorboards creak and speak and moan. It sounded like they were in mom's bedroom. Her meds should have kicked in and made her tired by now, so she would probably be sleeping by the time I walked upstairs.

Putting away the last plate, I leaned on the counter and drew a deep breath. I'd forgotten how draining it could be to be home. I hadn't even been here a full day, and already I felt mentally exhausted.

Shaking my head, I pushed away from the counter and started warming some water for a cup of tea. As the water boiled, I found the cleaning supplies I needed to tidy up my room in the small closet under the stairs.

I heard mom and Mrs. Tav talking above me as I stood in the hallway, and my stomach made a little twist. Mom should be asleep. Shame coursed through me, and I started biting at the nail on my right pinkie finger. The taste of nail polish made me grimace and I forced my hand away from my mouth, focusing on finding the supplies I needed.

The teakettle screamed in the kitchen. At the sound, the voices quieted. I grimaced and hurried into the kitchen, afraid the sound of the kettle would make mom nervous, then I grimaced again. I couldn't stop living just because mom was sick. Sure, I'd have to be there for her in the day, but Mrs. Tav was here now, and so I could allow myself to make a cup of tea for the evening.

Straightening my back, I finished making the cup and brought it with me. At the foot of the stairs, I picked up the duster and a small cloth before I continued up.

As I stepped onto the first-floor landing, I saw the door to mom's bedroom was open, but neither Mrs. Tav nor mom were by the bed. Usually, you couldn't see who was lying in bed because of the angles of the room and the door, but I would see if they were standing around the bed. For a moment I thought about joining them, but the thought made my stomach turn, so I pushed it away.

"Ellie?" Mom said as I rounded the banister and set foot on the first step of the staircase leading to the second floor.

"Yes?" Mrs. Tav answered, sounding a little tired.

"Who's that woman?"

"What woman?"

"The woman in the street. The one with red hair."

I was two flights up the stairs and froze. The tea splashed in the cup but didn't spill.

"I don't see anyone," Mrs. Tav said.

"Right there," mom said.

I turned and walked back down the stairs. Leaning into the bedroom, I saw the two women by the window. Mom was sitting on the sill, braiding her long hair and looking down at the street. Mrs. Tav was holding a half-folded sweater in hand and leaning over mom to look out the window.

"I still don't see anyone."

Mom blinked. Her fingers stopped working on her hair, and she just sat there, frozen. Mrs. Tav leaned back, watching her. Mom blinked and looked up at the nurse, then out at the street again.

"She's gone," mom said. Her fingers started braiding again. "You don't know who she is?"

"No. Why?"

"I've seen her before."

"Where?" Mrs. Tav finished folding the sweater and put it on top of the small pile of folded clothes in a chair standing by the window. She picked up a pair of pants from the basket at her feet and continued folding.

"Around here," mom used a band to tie off her braid and flung it over her shoulder. "Only when you're here, though."

"That's weird," Mrs. Tav answered, her voice flat and uninterested.

"Yeah."

Mom was twirling at her wedding band, still looking out at the street. Mrs. Tav continued folding clothes. I stood at the door, looking past the frame. I wasn't sure either of them had noticed me, and when mom yawned and let her wedding band go, I pulled back, ready to get to my room and start cleaning. At this rate, my tea would be cold before I got started, and I hated cold tea.

"It's just... sometimes this house gives me the creeps," mom continued. Instead of staying on the landing, I forced my feet to carry me upstairs. "I asked Connor about it, but he just waved it away as he so often does, and I don't... have you noticed anything?"

My stomach tightened at dad's name.

"Anything like what?" Mrs. Tav asked. I heard her moving

again. The sound of the creaky door leading into mom's big closet drowned out mom's next words.

"... know. Voices, maybe? Sometimes I swear I hear voices."

"What kind of voices?"

I reached the top of the stairs and stopped, torn. I shouldn't be eavesdropping, but mom mentioned dad. She did that often, but never from the time before I was born. I'd heard her talk about aunt Ellie, like now, but never dad from that time. At least that was what I told myself as I sat at the top of the stairs, clutching the cooling cup of tea in my hands, listening.

"Women voices, more often than not. But sometimes I hear children's voices as well."

"What do they say?"

"I don't know. I can't hear them that well. But I hear a woman crying at the bottom of the stairs, murmuring something. And sometimes I swear I hear children screaming in fear and pain. Sometimes they just talk, but I can never tell what they're saying. It sounds urgent, though."

"Maybe it's just your imagination."

"Yeah."

They grew silent again. I sat there, listening to them move around for I don't know how long, but finally someone turned off the lights, and Mrs. Tav walked through the door. She left it ajar before turning and looking up at me. She didn't smile, just looked at me, then sat in her usual chair beside the door. When she sat in that chair, I could only see her feet from where I sat.

Taking a sip of my tea, which was now cold and sickening, I stood and made my way to the bathroom to dump it out. That done, I put the cup on the desk in my bedroom and plugged my headset into my phone and turned up the music. I loved cleaning while listening to music, it was a way for me to blow off steam and usually calmed me, but today it didn't work. I kept glancing over my shoulder, feeling like someone was watching me. Every time I walked by the window, I looked outside. Even if I couldn't see the street from my window, I expected someone to stand in the overgrown garden, looking up at me.

The window stood open as I worked, and my flesh puckered in goosebumps even as I worked and kept warm. I told myself it was just the autumn chill and nothing else.

Even so, the wind blowing against my earbuds made me shiver, and whenever the tree outside my window moved, I had to check that it was just the wind doing it.

I couldn't understand why I was so on edge.

After finishing with the duster, I fell onto my bed and pulled my phone from my pocket. Mark had texted me. Instead of answering, I opened Snapchat and filmed a video of my childhood bedroom that I sent to him and some other friends back in Toronto. The CDs and player. The desk with the diaries and the posters on the wall. The dreamcatcher in the window, a gift from dad I strongly thought about pulling down now. I sent it, feeling a little lighter knowing I had someone waiting for me back in Toronto. A home that was all my own.

In a better mood, I finished the last of the cleaning. As I got ready to go downstairs with the cleaning supplies and the empty cup, I sent another snap to Mark. This one a selfie where I scowled at the dirty duster.

Mrs. Tav was still in her chair in the hall on the first floor, and she looked at me as I passed her on my way down. I put away everything and was bobbing my head to the music as I headed back up. I'd planned to not even look at Mrs. Tav. Just walk straight past her and up to my bedroom, get ready for bed and then call Mark. Instead, I pulled out my earbuds as I stepped onto the landing and walked over to her.

"Mrs. Tav?"

She looked up from the book, closing it around one finger to mark the page she was on. "Yes?"

"I heard what mom talked about earlier, and I was wondering about something." She didn't answer. I narrowed my eyes at her. When she still didn't say anything, I continued. "The voices and the red-haired woman. Has she mentioned this before?"

"You know she has talked about the red-haired woman before."

"Yes, I know that. I just... she's never really said she saw her in the street like that, has she? Not that I can remember, at least."

Mrs. Tav put the bookmark into her book and put it away. She pulled off her reading glasses and met my eyes straight on. "No, she has not. In fact, she has hardly talked about the Red Woman since you were here last."

"Oh."

"What I found interesting was that she talked about the Red Woman being here when Ellie was here. Do you know anything about that?"

I shook my head. "Has that happened before?"

Mrs. Tav cocked her head. "I have heard her talk about the Red Woman at the same time as talking about your aunt, but I have never heard her talk about the Red Woman actually being around Ellie. What do you make of that?"

Her gaze seemed to drill into me, and I squirmed, not able to meet her eyes. "I don't know. Maybe something about today reminded her of having that conversation with aunt Ellie?"

"What conversation?"

I chewed on my left thumbnail. "The one about this house creeping her out and the Red Woman being around aunt Ellie and stuff like that."

"You think it was an actual conversation she had with Ellie? Stop chewing on your nails."

I lowered my hand at her stern voice. "No. Yes. I don't really know. It's your job to know about these things, not mine." I was tired and angry and shameful and exhausted. I couldn't deal with Mrs. Tav's cold voice right now. Why did I even ask her? "I just don't know. I worry about her, you know? About the things she has to go through because of this shit."

"I understand."

"Anyway, I just wondered if she'd talked about the voices and so before."

"No, not that I can recall."

"Ok, good night, then."

Mrs. Tav didn't answer, but I could feel her eyes on my back as I ascended the stairs, and it was a relief when I entered the top landing where she could no longer see me. Looking over my shoulder, I made sure she couldn't see me before I pointed my tongue out at her and headed toward my bedroom to get ready for bed.

I couldn't wait to call Mark and forget about this day alto-gether.

7

My senses returned in slow motion.

I could feel the blanket brushing against my skin every time I breathed. Felt the cold on my face from the open window. Could smell the dust in the air, still lingering. Could hear nothing.

Why couldn't I hear anything? I lived in the city, there were always sounds, so why not now? Was I still dreaming?

Then the creak of an old house settling in the night.

The wind was rustling the leaves on a tree outside.

A voice singing, words muffled by closed doors.

My eyes flew open and the ceiling, grey in the weak light, came into focus.

I was home. With mom. The voice I heard was hers.

Shouldn't she be asleep? Her meds should keep her knocked out until morning. Where was Mrs. Tav?

I sat up, pushing the blanket aside. The floor was cold against my naked feet, and I hurried over to the suitcase propped up on the desk. Rummaging through it, I found my sweatpants and a couple of socks. I pulled it all on before heading toward the door.

The light in the hall was dimmed with only a small lamp by the stairs turned on, making the corners look like dark pools.

Mom's voice came from the stairs, so I headed that way. I couldn't see or hear Mrs. Tav.

The floor moaned beneath me as I walked, and I quickly started placing my steps with more care. I'd long ago learned which floorboards made noise and which didn't, and even if I couldn't remember, my body seemed to know where to put its weight so as not to make noise on instinct.

The landing was empty. Mrs. Tav wasn't in her chair, but the lights were on in the bathroom. I turned toward the stairs again, listening. Mom was singing, and I could hear her moving around down there. I walked down, making sure I didn't step on the boards that would creak. My breathing filled my head, and the feeling of the smooth banister against my hand made me shiver.

As I drew closer, some of her words reached me.

"Baby... your wings... down, down... bird."

I reached the bottom step and stopped to listen. Her voice was rich and warm, just as I remembered it, but the words, now clear to me, made the hair at the back of my neck stand on end.

I took a step, which made the floor groaned. Mom stopped singing. I froze. I didn't know why, but I was afraid of her noticing me, afraid of startling her with my presence. After a minute of quiet, she started singing again.

Baby bird; flap your wings
You are all grown up now
Baby bird; reach the sky
Blue, blue, blue, and high, high, high
Baby bird; flap your wings
Reaching for the stars now
Baby bird; grey and brown,

Falling, falling, down, down, down
Baby bird; flap your wings
Dazed down on the ground now
Baby bird; doomed to die,
All alone, say bye, bye, bye
Baby bird; you can't fly
Momma broke your wings now
Baby bird; small and spry
Cats will feast, you die, die, die
Baby bird; you can't fly
Just a broken thing now
Baby bird; momma cries,
She will eat your eyes, eyes, eyes
Baby bird; here no more
Momma killed you
Dead.

I didn't know I'd moved, but as mom stopped singing, I became aware that I was standing in the door to the sunroom, looking in at her. Moonlight fell through the glass walls, making the plants lining them into shadows. Mom was standing in the middle of the room, slowly spinning around herself, singing. It was a modified version of a song she used to sing to me when I was a child. Back then, the baby bird fell but the momma bird chased the cats away and the baby bird learned to fly anyway.

At the end of the song, mom stopped spinning. After a deep breath, she started from the top again.

As the first words hit me, I seemed to fall back into myself and took a step backward. She didn't see me standing there, her eyes were closed, but I couldn't shake the feeling that the words were meant for me. Like her chant from a year ago.

I turned and ran toward the stairs. My breath uneven and thick. My feet moved on their own, skipping the complaining boards, and I flew up the stairs without a sound.

I slammed into Mrs. Tav on her way down.

"Elizabeth? What is it?" she asked, pushing me away from her. I could feel my shoulders shake under her hands.

"Mom," I managed to push out. "She's awake, down in the sunroom. Singing." I choked on the last word.

Mrs. Tav looked at me for a moment, not seeming to understand, then it dawned on her. "Sometimes, she does not sleep through the night, but she sings that song again and again. It seems to be the only thing going through her mind when this happens."

"It's really happened before?"

"Yes. When she has had an exciting day, the medication does not seem to make her just as tired as they should, so she wakes up in the night. They are working enough to keep her calm and half asleep, so she is no danger to anyone. She started singing that song about the baby bird after you left, and that is all she does when she wakes like this. It is not hard talking her back to bed." Mrs. Tav had let go as she spoke, making to move past me. I opened my mouth to say something, but no words came out. Mrs. Tav talked instead. "Go back to bed, Elizabeth. I will take care of your mother."

I only nodded, not sure I would ever be able to speak again. My throat was too tight.

As Mrs. Tav went down, I went up. I stopped at the top of the stairs and crumbled to the floor. I'd sat like this many times, between the wall and the banister, listening to mom and dad talking at night, or when they had dinner parties with their friends, I used to listen to them talking and laughing downstairs. Now, I listened to mom and Mrs. Tav. I could hear mom's voice still, but it stopped as Mrs. Tav made the floors speak and warn of her approach. I heard her voice, old and calm, then steps. Soon, mom and Mrs. Tav came up the stairs again, Mrs. Tav supporting mom with both hands. They disappeared into mom's room.

I stayed put, listening to the old nurse's low voice, before seeing the lights from mom's room go out. Mrs. Tav moved around a little before settling into her chair in the hallway. For a while, I heard nothing before the sound of a page in a book being turned reached me.

My breath whispered out between my lips and I slumped against the wall. My hands fell into my lap, and I noticed they were shaking.

"It doesn't mean anything," I whispered to my hands, trying to calm them. "It's just a stupid song. It doesn't mean anything."

But my hands weren't listening, and I wasn't sure I believed my own words. I didn't know why I didn't believe them. It was just a feeling. A feeling of something creeping closer. Watching me, waiting for me.

I didn't sleep any more that night.

8

"Dear Lizzie! It has been so long! How are you?"

I let Mrs. Hearth pull me into her warm embrace. The old woman had been part of my life for as long as I could remember. When I was younger, she and her husband used to arrange BBQs in summer, inviting the entire neighborhood. After Mr. Jamesson died, Mrs. Hearth was left alone, but that didn't put a stop to her reaching out to everyone. She started making candy and tea, and every Saturday between elleven and one in the afternoon, she had an open house, selling her creations. I'd always wondered a little at the fact that her husband was named Jamesson, but she kept her mother's name. She'd always been a little different, which I loved about her.

"I'm fine, thank you," I answered.

The words were hardly out of my mouth before she pushed me away, but she kept her grip on my upper arms. Her hair was white and reached to the middle of her shoulder blades. Her eyes were shiny blue, and her lips painted a faint red. Her back was straight but her nose was crooked, looking like it had been broken once upon a time.

"Don't lie to me, dear. How could you possibly be ok after your mother got sick? I wouldn't be."

I shrugged. "Everything's relative. Everything considered

I'm fine, really. What about you?"

"Oh, I am good. Emma expects to get her third little girl any day now, so I am planning to visit them. Cannot cuddle those great-grand-children enough, you know." She laughed and let me go. I started finding my clothes as she began to peel off the outer layer of her own.

"What about Sara?" I asked, focusing on tying my shoes.

"Oh, dear, you know how she can be. Always up to something. But she asked me to say hi when I saw you next."

I finished with my shoes and looked up at her, seeing a glimpse in her eye and hurried to double-check my laces. She harrumphed and started rooting around in her purse. When she pulled out her hands, she was cradling a bundle of bright blue fabric, tied at the top with pale pink silk ribbons. One of her ''bundles of joy''.

"Mrs. Hearth –" I began, but she wouldn't let me finish.

"Nonsense, I made it especially for you, dear."

She pushed the little bundle into my hands as I stood, before pushing past me and into the house. Mom was sitting in the living room, drinking tea, and she let out a small sound of joy as Mrs. Hearth entered the room.

"Darling Nancy, how are you?" said Mrs. Hearth.

"I'm fine, Mrs. Hearth. Just fine," mom answered.

"You sure? I brought you this."

I followed their voices and stopped in the doorway. Mrs. Hearth had pulled another small bundle from her purse, this one a bright yellow fabric with green ribbons. She was handing it to mom as they both sat down on the sofa.

"You'll be fine, then?" I asked from the doorway.

Mom didn't look up, but Mrs. Hearth shot me a look. "Yes, we'll be fine. Bring those with you, eat one or two on the road.

They will help. I brought extras for our tea when you get back."

I opened my mouth to protest but closed it again. I knew Mrs. Hearth well enough to know I would get nowhere by arguing. She used to babysit me when I was younger, and I respected no one as much as I did her. Maybe because she let me drink soda during the weekdays and we stayed up past midnight to look at the stars. But she also always made sure my homework was done and my room clean.

Without another word, I pulled on my leather jacket and left the house, making sure to lock the door behind me. I yawned as I walked to mom's car. Before I started driving, I opened the bundle. It contained thirteen small pieces of chocolate and fudge. I pulled up a chocolate ball with nuts and chocolate sprinkles covering the surface and put it in my mouth. It melted on my tongue as I tied up the bundle again, wiping my fingers on the inside of the homemade handkerchief, and started the car.

I had a meeting to get to.

9

A nurse led me into the meeting room where a big table occupied the floor with chairs around it. Light spilled in through the windows, making the dust dance. Outside, I could see the docks. Despite the October chill, there were still boats on the water.

Four people already sat at the table: three men and one woman, all business-like.

"Ah, Ms. Key, I presume?" one of the men said, standing to take my hand. "I'm Dr. Altman, we spoke on the phone?"

"Yes, thank you," I answered, shaking his hand. "Why are you here? Is it normal for a hospital doctor to be in these meetings?"

"No," mom's regular doctor, Dr. Long, began. "But because he was the first to send a request to Midnight Sun, I asked him to join us for this meeting."

I nodded my understanding before looking to the next man, the day-nurse Lars. I narrowed my eyes at him but didn't say anything. Lastly, the woman stood and took my hand.

"I'm Meredith Hamilton. I work for Midnight Sun."

"I'm Elizabeth Key, but everyone calls me Lizzie. Thank you so much for meeting with me."

Meredith smiled and let my hand go, sitting as she spoke.

"No problem at all. Cases like this are why we're here."

"You're familiar with mom's case?" I asked as I sat.

"The good doctors have seen fit to fill me in." She motioned to some papers lying on the table in front of her. I saw the logo of the hospital where mom had stayed after she ran away the other night, the logo of the office we were in now, as well as the logo to the firm where Mrs. Tav and Lars worked.

I turned to Lars. "Why aren't you with mom?"

Lars exchanged a look with Dr. Long, before he turned to me and answered. "As per the contract we wrote when agreeing to take care of your mother, we would not be there during the day as long as you were home."

I knew that but wasn't ready to let it go. It was so unfair that I had to take care of mom on my own. I had no idea what I was doing. "But, we were both there after Laura stopped working."

"That was an induction period, and you know it. I'm sorry, but this is how it works."

Not able to answer, I nodded and looked down at my hands on the table. I was picking on my nails, scraping off the nail polish, and forced myself to stop.

"To business, then," Meredith said, seeming rather cheerful. I supposed she had to be, working with what she did. "As I understand it, your mother has been in the care of Hendrick's Helpers for about four years now?" I nodded, forcing myself to meet her eyes. "And you have not considered having her committed to a more permanent location before the episode a few nights ago?" I almost wanted to ask what episode she meant, but I knew and gave another nod in answer. Meredith wrote something on the pad in front of her before continuing, this time looking at Lars. "You and the other nurse taking care of Mrs. Key have, on the other hand, wished for her to be committed for some time?" Lars nodded. "And you have informed Ms. Key of this?"

"Yes."

"And Ms. Key has not listened?"

Lars fidgeted on his chair. "She has listened, but not wanted to do anything about it. Lizzie is young and has her own life to lead. She's done what was in her power to help her mother, but she was left alone with the care for Mrs. Key when Mr. Key left after the onset of the sickness."

"That is not important. The important part is whether Mrs. Key has shown violent tendencies for some time or not. Has she?"

"Yes."

"When was the first time you saw any sign of violence?"

"During my first day."

"What happened?"

"She threw a vase at me."

Meredith continued to write. "Have you ever seen her charge anyone? Attack them in close quarters?"

"Yes."

"When?"

"Around two weeks into my contract."

I stopped listening as Lars explained mom's attack on me, focusing instead on my nails. I was still scraping at the polish but didn't bother to stop myself. Anger and fear and shame wared inside me. This sounded more like an interrogation than anything else. What was going on? Wasn't this supposed to be a meeting to see if mom was sick enough to get a room at Midnight Sun? I wanted to speak up for mom. Tell this Meredith person that mom wasn't always bad. That she only had a few bad patches, but mostly she was ok. Like now. She was home with Mrs. Hearth, and as I'd said to Mrs. Tav, she was always calm when Mrs. Hearth was around. The irony of mom being milder with our neighbor than with me or the nurses that were supposed to take care of her, almost made me laugh, but I kept the reaction down. When I didn't laugh, I almost started crying instead, and I couldn't do that now either.

The lack of Lars's voice made me focus on the conversation again, hoping it would keep my feelings at bay.

"Dr. Altman, tell me about the episode." Meredith continued.

"I was on the night shift in the ER when a call came and told us that two people were comming our way. One had attacked the other and was currently in a violent state. She had to be restrained for the paramedics to get her into the ambulance. The other, male, had multiple wounds on his face and arms after the woman's attack."

"Who called it in?"

"The man's wife. They were out walking the dog when they saw the woman walking on the train tracks, muttering to herself."

"What happened when they tried to help?"

"Why do you ask that?" I asked, and all of them turned to me.

Meredith blinked multiple times before answering. "You do want your mother to get a place at Midnight Sun, don't you?" I shrugged. "Then let me do my job. I'm good at it. I only want to help both you and your mother, and this is the way to do it."

"But why?"

"To prove your mother's sickness. To prove that it was the sickness making her violent and not her personality."

Swallowing, I looked down at my hands again. One of my nails was utterly free of polish now.

Meredith nodded to me and turned back to Dr. Altman, motioning for him to continue.

Dr. Altman glanced at me, sympathy heavy in his eyes. "At seeing Mrs. Key, the man and woman went to talk to her. Apparently, this wasn't the first time they'd seen someone on the tracks, and they hoped to help a troubled soul. The woman, Mrs. Dean, was more persistent than her husband and reached Mrs. Key first. When she spoke, Mrs. Key turned toward them before she started screaming and attacked. Mr. Dean was able to step in the way and take the worst of it. That was when Mrs. Dean called the police."

Meredith was writing again. "And what happened in the ER?"

"I was the senior doctor on call, so I asked one of the interns to take care of Mr. Dean while I dealt with Mrs. Key. First, we thought her drunk or mad. She was screaming about a Red Woman coming after her baby bird. The police that accompanied Mrs. Key told me she was screaming at Mrs. Dean to leave her baby alone. That she couldn't have her baby. Mrs. Key was scared into aggression."

My fingers had frozen around each other, and I was staring at Dr. Altman. The Red Woman, he'd said. "Was the woman... Mrs. Dean, was it? Was she a redhead?"

The others turned to look at me as I spoke.

"Yes," Dr. Altman said. "Yes. She was. Why?"

I shook my head and looked at my hands again. Something heavy and cold had settled in my stomach and was clawing its way up my throat. I couldn't speak even if I wanted to.

Lars came to my rescue. "Mrs. Key has a great fear of

redheads, be they male or female, but clearly, the females are the worst. From the day I met her, she would shut down, from lack of a better term, when seeing a red-haired person. This shut down was always violent. She always talked about the Red Woman that was trying to take her daughter away. None of us have been able to discover where this fear comes from."

"Ms. Key, do you know anything?" Meredith asked, but I hardly heard her. In my mind's eye, I saw a woman standing in the woods, on the street, in our stairs, in our living room, our kitchen, our garden, my classroom at school, a parking lot, doorways, through windows. Even on the other side of the street in Toronto, but more seldom then when I was in Sky Harbour. Her hair was red and her eyes yellow, lips curled back in a snarl, and she was looking at me. I shook my head, trying to dislodge the images.

"Lizzie?" Lars leaned forward and put his hands on top of mine. The contact made me start and I pushed back, blinking at him. "Lizzie, what's going on in your head right now?"

The cold had settled in my mouth, making it hard to form words. I parted my lips, trying to speak, but what sounded like a sob escaped instead. The others exchanged looks. I cleared my throat, forcing the cold down a little.

"Sorry," I managed to croak. "Can I get some water?"

"Of course," Dr. Long answered. He stood and disappeared through the door.

My hands were shaking when he returned with a coffee cup filled with water and placed it before me.

"Do you need a break?" he asked, not leaving my side.

I shook my head and drank. The cold didn't budge. "No, I just... need to breathe," I managed to answer. Dr. Long nodded.

When I'd drunk half the cup, I pulled the bundle of chocolate from my pocket and opened it. Pushing one chocolate into my mouth, I offered the bundle to the others. Meredith and Lars took one, but the doctors both declined.

"One of Mrs. Hearth's?" Lars asked when he'd swallowed, a smile on his lips and his eyes far away.

"Who?" Dr. Altman asked.

Lars told him in short strokes about my neighbor as I drank the rest of the water. The warmth of the chocolate had banished the cold into the pit of my stomach. It was still there, but I could breathe again. I could speak.

"Sorry," I said as Lars finished talking. "This is just..." I couldn't finish, but the others nodded, looking sympathetic.

"Where were we?" Meredith asked after a little too long a break.

"The Red Woman," I answered, forcing myself to meet her eyes. "Yes, I know of her. Mom's talked about her a lot as she got sicker. She's scared of her."

"Do you know where that fear comes from?"

"I'm not really sure. I think scary stories, maybe? I seem to remember a red-haired woman from when I was young, but I'm not sure if she's real or not. I can't remember a name or relation or anything like that. Just an angry woman with red hair."

Meredith nodded and wrote on her pad. "Dr. Long, has Mrs. Key shown any signs of mental problems before her illness?"

"Not that I'm aware of, no. She was the perfect picture of health from the moment I became her doctor. I've treated the Key's since before Lizzie came along, and none of the family members have mentioned anything about mental breaks. She also went through therapy and a mental mapping before she was diagnosed with Alzheimers."

Meredith wrote again before folding her hands atop the pad. "So according to everyone here, Mrs. Key is sick with Alzheimers?" All the men nodded, and I did the same a moment later. "She is clearly violent because of this diagnosis?" We all nodded at the same time. "There is no proof of a mental disorder in her or her family history?" Dr. Long nodded again. It looked like he wanted to say something but didn't. It wasn't a secret that mom was a foster kid and her only known blood relative was me, but I hadn't shown any mental problems as far as I knew so the nod was correct. "And you all think she would benefit from a stay at Midnight Sun?" Collected nods again. Meredith nodded in turn and started gathering her papers. "Then, gentlemen and Ms. Key, I think I have everything I came for. I'll write up a request for her admittance. You will hear from us soon, Ms. Key." She stood, and we all followed.

"Thank you," I said as I shook her hand.

"A pleasure," she answered before turning to the others.

As she talked to the men, I pushed another chocolate into my mouth. Something about them always calmed me. Probably memories from a happy childhood.

"I'll walk you out, Lizzie," Lars said as the two doctors started packing up.

I nodded before shaking the hands of the two doctors and letting the nurse lead me outside. The sun was bright and glaring, and the scent of saltwater mingled well with the taste of chocolate still in my mouth.

"How do you think it went?" I asked as we walked across the parking lot.

"As well as we could hope. These meetings are always draining on the loved ones; that is why we don't usually invite them. The caseworker at the facility usually meets them at home. I think Mrs. Hamilton will want to come to visit with you sometime soon to meet Nancy, but I think this case is sealed and closed. If anyone needs a room at Midnight Sun, it's Nancy."

"Thank you," I said, not meaning it. It was hard to be thankful when someone called your mother violent, even if it was true.

Gazing toward the docks, Lars stood in his own thoughts for a moment. Finally, he seemed to finish thinking and turned toward me. "Lizzie, do you know what happened to your aunt?"

The question took me by surprise and I blinked at him. "She killed herself. Why?"

He shook his head, but not at what I'd said. "Just something about what Mrs. Hamilton said. About your mother's violence as a product of the Alzheimers."

"Wait, what are you really saying right now? That mom was violent before she got sick?"

Lars shrugged. "I'm not sure. But you mentioned that you didn't know who this Red Woman was, right? But she has been a part of your mother's life from before she got sick. She must have, or she wouldn't have been so afraid of her now. And, well... Your mother once said that the Red Woman had driven your aunt to her death."

"So? What does this have to do with mom?"

He turned fully to me now, meeting my eyes dead-on. "The Red Woman. Can you find out if she is real or just a figment of Nancy's imagination?"

"Why?"

"It's probably nothing."

"Lars, tell me what you're thinking!"

"It's nothing. I'm sorry I said anything."

He moved to walk away, but I grabbed his coat sleeve and forced him to stay. He was much bigger than me, even with my height, so he could easily pull away but didn't.

"Tell me what you're thinking," I begged, fear and sorrow making my voice thick.

He sighed. "Some of the things your mother said and did in the time I cared for her hasn't seemed like the things an Alzheimers patient would do." He stopped, and I shook his sleeve. Like a little girl begging for attention. "Like the Red Woman. I talked with some of the neighbors, and they've never seen a red-haired woman around your house. And your mother has talked about people like they were animals. She called Mrs. Hearth a big cat once, and Mr. Jamesson was apparently a bear. I'm a deer, and so was Laura, but Mrs. Tav was a buffalo. You can believe she got offended at that! Your mother has talked about herself as a crow, and you as her baby bird, but she never called you a crow. She never told me what you were."

"And your point is?"

"I'm just saying that maybe it isn't just Alzheimers that's the problem. Mrs. Hamilton asked if there were any mental health issues in her family, but we don't know. There's only you. And, well, maybe your grandmother gave your mother up because she had issues. We'll never know."

"Are you calling mom crazy?"

"I'm just thinking out loud."

Letting his sleeve go, I glared at him. "You're calling her crazy."

Lars sighed. "I'm just saying that you should be careful. Both of your mother and the Red Woman."

"If she really had mental problems, Dr. Long would know. I'd know."

"I know. That's why I didn't say anything in there. Maybe she's just eccentric. Or maybe there's something in her past we don't know about. I'm not a doctor."

"No, you're not."

I turned from him, heading toward my car.

"Just be careful, ok? I don't want anything bad to happen to anyone," Lars called after me, but I didn't turn back and didn't answer.

How dare he? How dare he even hint that mom didn't have Alzheimers but something else? I unlocked the car and climbed in behind the wheel. Glancing up, I saw Lars in the mirror. He hadn't moved from the spot where we talked, and his gaze was on the car. I showed my teeth at his reflection. Mom wasn't mentally sick. She had Alzheimers and needed help. I hit the wheel. Lars was the mad one, not mom. Not mom.

10

I found mom and Mrs. Hearth in the living room when I got home. They were talking and looking at photo albums. I saw a picture of myself as a baby, mom and dad both holding me, on the open page.

The two women looked up as I entered. Mrs. Hearth gave me a warm smile and mom gave me a nod before returning to the album. I wondered who I was to her today.

Mrs. Hearth stood and hugged me. "How did it go?" she asked in a low tone as she led me to the sofa and sat me down opposite mom.

"As well as could be expected, I guess. How did it go here?"

Mrs. Hearth beamed. "She was a dear, as always."

I just nodded, not able to take my eyes off mom. They'd braided her hair in two long ropes that hung over her shoulder. The grey shone like moonlight on a river in–between all the black. It made her look even more like a tribal woman, and my thoughts returned to Lars's words. The anger still shimmered inside me, but eating the rest of Mrs. Hearth's chocolates seemed to have dulled it some. Now I was just tired. But maybe Lars didn't know the whole story. Mom had once told me she tried to look for her parents, tried to find out what tribe her blood came from. Instead of doing drugs and drinking when she was a teen, she'd delved into the cultures of the indigenous population. Maybe she had a phase where she talked about everyone as their totem animal? Perhaps that was what happened when she talked about people as animals now? Did she tap into her teen mind?

"So, what did you do today?" I finally asked.

"Nothing much," Mrs. Hearth said. "We watched a movie, ate a lovely lunch, did our hair," she motioned to her hair; braided in the same way as mom's but much shorter. "And talked about this and that. You know how we old ladies can be."

Smiling, I slumped into my chair. We sat in silence for a while, mom paging through the album and smiling wistfully every now and again.

"No, I think I should head home," Mrs. Hearth finally said, moving to push herself up from the sofa.

"Why?" Mom asked, looking up from the album.

"Well, Lizzie is home, dear. You don't need me."

"Pish posh," I said, mimicking Mrs. Hearth's voice. "Why not stay for dinner?"

"I don't know..."

"Please, it's the least we can do to repay you for watching Lizzie," mom said with a smile.

Mrs. Hearth glanced at me before sinking back into her chair. "Well, I would not mind. An old woman can go a little crazy from being alone all the time. Would you know, I actually named my plants the other day."

"I've told you before; you should get a cat," mom said, closing the album and standing to put it back in its place on one of the shelves.

Mrs. Hearth shrugged. "But it is a little early for dinner

still."

I looked at the clock on my phone. She was right. It was way early for dinner. As I put the phone on the coffee table between us, I saw the chipped polish on my nails. "It is," I answered. "But I have an idea. Stay here."

Before either of them could say anything, I stood and disappeared upstairs. In my suitcase, I found what I was looking for and returned downstairs in a hurry. Mom and Mrs. Hearth were sitting in their chairs, looking at me with curiosity. I sat the small bag on the table and opened it, taking out nail cleaners, cotton, multiple bottles of nail polish, and other stuff for nail care. I lay it all out on the table in a neat order before looking at mom and Mrs. Hearth with a silly smile on my face.

"It's time I go really girly on you guys."

It ended up being a great few hours. We cleaned our nails, both Mrs. Hearth and I had old polish that needed removing, before we fixed them up. I had to help mom, as she'd never been big on nail care before we put on the polish. I went for Navy Blue from Essie. Mrs. Hearth went for the Fishnet Stockings red from Essie, even if we managed to push her to color her middle fingernails with PixieDust green from Zoya. I ended up using a good while on mom's nails. She fell for some of the art designs I'd brought. In the end, her nails were covered in Giovanna Green from Zoya, and I'd put some gold and black vine designs on top of that before. We laughed and joked and talked about boys, which was weird as Mrs. Hearth was so old and mom was... well, my mom. I even talked them into letting me share their nails on my Snapchat and Instagram account. Mom made a duck face, even if I wasn't photographing our faces, and it cracked us all up. When our polish was dry, we started on dinner and mom ate with gusto.

After Mrs. Hearth left, mom and I sat down in the living room to watch some TV while we waited for the evening to come. As mom watched, I cleaned up after our nail polish-extravaganza. When Mrs. Tav showed up, she got mom to take her meds and take a shower before going to bed, just like she'd done the night before and every night before that for the last four years.

Now, the nurse was in her customary chair in the hallway on the first floor. Mom was asleep in her bed, not visible through the cracked door, but I could hear her breathing.

"Good night," I said to Mrs. Tav as I sat a cup of tea on the small table by the chair.

"Thank you, Elizabeth, and good night to you too."

As I headed up the stairs, Mrs. Tav put her glasses on and opened her book, getting ready for a long night.

I took my time getting ready. I was exhausted after the day, and it hadn't even been that long. I'd had worse days at work or fighting with Mark. Speaking off, I hadn't called Mark today, but I wasn't in the mood to talk to him. Today had just been too full of emotions, and I couldn't deal with revisiting most of them. Especially when I knew Mark would laugh at half of it, or say it wasn't worth my energy. I wanted to go to sleep with the good feeling I still had after our girly-day with Mrs. Hearth, not annoyance and hurt from talking to my boyfriend. After brushing my teeth and washing my face, I went into my bedroom and changed. Dirty clothes were tossed in a corner, and I pulled a slim t-shirt and clean underwear from my suitcase before braiding my hair for the night. Then I texted Mark.

Me: Tired after a long day. Call you tmorrow?

I put my phone away and reached to turn off the bedside light, but stopped with my hands on the switch. My mind wandered to the day that had passed. I didn't want to think about it. I wanted to remember the time just after I got home. But that wasn't how my mind worked. The things Lars had said. Did he really believe mom was crazy? That she'd made up this Red Woman and used her to kill aunt Ellie?

Without really thinking, I reached for my diaries. I checked the different years I'd scribbled on the first page, then picked up the third book from mom's first year of Alzheimers. I leafed through the pages, skimming until finding what I was looking for.

August 30

Today was a good day. Mom's had so many bad days lately. She deserved this day, even if she got confused in the evening. I wish she just stayed at one time. It would be so much easier for everyone. But that's selfish, right? Laura said everything I wish had to come in second, now. Mom has to come first.

We ate outside today, which was nice. It's been so wet, I haven't gotten any sun, it seems like. I think mom enjoyed it until Laura called me Elizabeth – why can't she just call me Lizzie like everyone else? (Except Mrs. Tav, who is just stubborn and stupid and old and I'm pretty sure she doesn't like me) I think I hate her a little. Anyway, mom clenched her fist so hard she actually broke the hotdog she was eating. After that, she called me Ellie. Though the really weird thing happened while we were cleaning up after dinner. Mom and I were alone outside, and mom just turned and grabbed me by the arm!

"I don't care what you say, Ellie. I don't believe in curses."

I had no idea what to answer, so I only stood there.

"I know you believe there is a curse over your family, that you are going to die because of it, but you can't keep doing this to your brother. To me. We're afraid for you every time you go out the door."

Then Laura came outside again and mom let me go and headed inside without anything from the table. When I talked to her later, she was herself again.

Or as herself as she is these days. The weird thing is that mom never talks about aunt Ellie. It's like she wants to forget she ever lived. Dad talked about her a little. He has this album with pictures of only her doing crazy things. Petting lions and climbing Kilimanjaro and stuff like that. But he doesn't really like to talk about her either. I heard him yell at grandmam once, that Ellie was crazy at the end. He never talked about her again after that.

And anyway, he's gone now, so I don't know why I'm thinking about him. He doesn't deserve my thoughts.

The ink of the pen I'd used had floated out as tears dried on the page. I closed the book and picked up my phone. It had vibrated while I read.

Mark: That's OK. Everything OK over there? Miss u

I hurriedly texted back, wanting to get back to my search.

Me: Everything ok. Just a long day. Miss you too. Night

Dropping the phone on the covers, I picked up another book and started flipping through it. This was the first book of her second year with Alzheimers, and I quickly found what I was looking for.

January 3

Mom is getting worse. She seems to sink further and further into each memory as she gets them. She'd had the diagnosis for a year now, and she was probably sick a year, maybe two, before we caught it, so it isn't weird that it's getting this bad. At least that's what Dr. Long says. I think it's weird and unfair. I want more time with my mom, not this... shell.

But I've been here for over a week now, and I have to get to grips with how things are. Laura and Mrs. Tav has been trying to tell me for a while, but I didn't want to believe them. Just thought they had Alzheimers on the brain or something. But she is getting worse, and she is getting violent as well. Today proved that.

We were cleaning up after New Years and Laura called me Elizabeth and mom just snapped. I saw it in her eyes when it happened. They went from warm and a bit confused to ice-cold, and suddenly she was just there, her hands around my throat. It was only for a second, but I can't forget that feeling. Why would she do that? How could she do that?

I don't think she knew who I was, that I was me, but still.

Mom tried to choke me. I think she tried to kill m

I turned the page, but the sentence just stopped there. I hadn't been able to write anymore. Didn't want to believe it, didn't want it to be true. But I remembered her hands around my throat, and I remembered the bruise and the scratch from her nails that wouldn't grow because I kept picking at it. Thankfully, it hadn't left a scar. I don't know if I could handle a permanent reminder of mom trying to kill me.

Of her sickness trying to kill me, I amended and continued flipping through the book.

I'd left as planned the day after and not been home for a while. I'd met Mark shortly after that but never told him about this incident. The thought of telling him now made me shudder, especially after mom foreseeing my death a year ago. He would have asked me to cut her off, but even as I lived in my little bubble in Toronto, I couldn't do that.

I put the book down. I'd used a lot of space in that book to process the attack and dealing with all the new meds the doctor put her on. I wasn't home to see it, but Mrs. Tav and Laura kept me posted about everything, and the doctor needed my confirmation that he could give her the medication. They wanted to have her put in a home already back then.

I found the next book I was looking for. Some months before Laura quit and Lars took over.

October 13

Mom talked about aunt Ellie again today. She just mentioned her, all casual-like, and didn't even notice my horror. But she wouldn't know why I was afraid anyway. She doesn't remember the last time she talked about aunt Ellie to me. Or, she didn't really talk.

And then I'd scratched out a bunch of words until I tore the paper with the pencil point in one spot.

Anyway, she just started talking about her. Sitting in that chair she has in the library, all business-like.

"Ellie thinks she's cursed, but I think it's more like a self-fulfilling prophecy kind of thing, you know? She thinks she's going to die before she turns 25 years old, and if she keeps living as she does, she will kill herself."

"Maybe her living the way she does is because she thinks she will die," I said without thinking, trying to stay calm. Laura was in the kitchen and I didn't want to anger mom without Laura in the room, and my silence was just as dangerous as my words.

"That's what I mean with a self-fulfilling prophecy. Who knows, maybe we should help her along if she can't manage to die before

she turns 25. Or maybe that red-haired woman will. She's been hanging around again."

I looked up then, seeing her staring out the window. It's nothing unusual about that, but it was her hands. She usually twists her wedding ring when she stares, a sign she is confused, but not now. She was pulling her fingernails along the inside of her wrist. Again and again, along the same line, until she actually cut herself, but she didn't notice.

I let the book fall into my lap and pulled my own nails along the same line as mom had done so long ago. I didn't know how aunt Ellie died. People said she killed herself, but she hadn't left a note or anything. That much I knew.

The phone vibrated against my naked foot and shook my bones. What was I even thinking? I'd just had a long day, and Lars scared me, and mom scared me, and being back here was scary.

I wanted to go home.

I picked up the phone, fiddled with it a second, then called Mark without looking at the message. I cleaned up the books while I waited for him to answer. When he did, I sighed with relief.

Cold lanced through my body, tightening my muscles until it hurt. I forced my arms back, pushing deeper into the water, and the movement loosened the muscles. It felt like a ripple. Moving from my fingertips, up my arms, into my shoulders, down along my spine, into my legs, all the way to my toes.

I opened my eyes and saw the blurry underwater world. Then I lifted my head and pushed up, up, up. Breaking the surface, I heaved a breath, cold stabbing my lungs.

Strands of my blond hair had escaped the braid and clung to my face and chest. I pushed it back and swam toward the diving board and ladder.

The first time under was always like this — piercing and stabbing and hurting. I never felt more alive.

I was Elizabeth Josephine Key, but everyone called me Ellie.

It was early November and earlier in the morning. Frost covered the grass and rocks on land. The sky was dark violet, stars still visible. It felt like I was the only one alive in the entire world.

I climbed up the ladder set into the sheer cliff face, walked onto the diving board, and pushed off. The water closed around me again, just a small plop as I disappeared under. No one could tell I'd dived in.

Breaking the surface, I swam toward shore. One more dive, and

I'd get dressed and greet the day. Another day at work before going home to the roommate, who was always on the phone or had people over or listened to loud music. These moments in the morning were the only time I felt like myself.

I reached for the ladder, and something bit into my wrist. Yelping, I pushed back and lifted my hand. Blood lay watered out over my skin, dribbling darkly from a cut running from the base of my hand and almost down the length of my lower arm.

"Damn screws," I murmured as I covered the wound with my other hand. It was bleeding a lot and I didn't want to let go. What if I bled out in the water? I forced a laugh. This was ridiculous. I'd scraped myself on that screw a million times, stupid of me to not think of it, but it never bit deep. This was just a scratch.

I removed my hand and blood pulsed out. My stomach constricted and I felt dizzy.

"Just the cold water," I told myself and lowered both hands. The saltwater burned in the wound, but it would clean it. I took a stroke, and something grabbed my foot. My mouth opened in shock as I was pulled under, filling with water.

Trying to hold back the coughing, knowing I'd only swallow more water, I kicked out. Something soft tickled its way across my naked foot. I opened my eyes and looked down. The water was dark, but something was looking back at me. Then it was gone, and I kicked toward the surface.

It had pulled me down deep, whatever it was, but I had good lungs. I swam every day. I could reach the surface.

I had to reach the surface.

My chest burned.

It felt like small fireworks were exploding in my brain.

Breaking the surface, I gasped down air. I didn't stop to enjoy it. Coughing up water, I swam toward shore. My right arm, the one

I'd cut on the screw, felt numb and heavy, and every stroke sent pain shooting through it. I'd cut it deeper than I thought.

I reached for the ladder with my unhurt hand, still underwater and too far away, so ready to get up and be with other people, when something swam past me. The water turned black around me. I didn't have time to stop my momentum before the darkness grabbed my hand and pulled it down, away from the ladder and the air.

Before I could fight back, I was drawn under again.

I kicked, trying to dislodge whatever had hold of my hand, whatever was drawing me down, but it did no good. Whatever it was just tightened its grip and pulled faster.

The cold of the underwater currents bit into my skin. The darkness of the deep was pushing at me. The pressure made my ears pop.

I tried to pull away, tried to kick, but my movements were sluggish. As if I wasn't completely awake.

My fingers went numb and all I felt was that grip around my wrist. I couldn't move anymore. My lungs were screaming for air. I couldn't breathe. Had to breathe. Needed to breathe.

I opened my mouth and water rushed in. Cold and bitter. Biting my throat as it went down. I tried to cough, but that only gave room for more water to rush in.

The grip tightened and pulled. My fingers touched the bottom, sinking into the sand. The grip let go.

I hung there for a moment, dizzy and disoriented. My hand lifted to hover in front of me. The world was dark, but I could still make out the shape of it.

I was free.

I needed air.

Turning around, I managed to sink my legs to the bottom and push. Lifting my arms, I used them to push even higher. Kick and push. Kick and push. Again and again. I didn't want to die. Didn't want to drown. If I died here, the currents would carry me out to sea. No one would find me. I didn't want to die.

I'd forgotten to move. Couldn't move anymore. I just hung there in the water, my blond hair swimming around my face. My hands were hanging at the ends of my arms, feeling-less. Blood colored the water, still pumping from the wound on my wrist.

I needed to move. Needed air.

I lifted my eyes, raised my arms. Needed to move but couldn't. I saw the moon filtering through the surface. Saw my hand. Long and pale in the light. The light was white, then pink from the blood, then white again.

My lips parted and water slipped inside. Filling my lungs, filling me. I didn't cough. Couldn't. My eyes slid close. So dizzy. So heavy. So...

I woke with a gasp. For a second, I couldn't move, my body still asleep, then a switch turned in my head and I sat up, grabbing at my wrist at the same time as I reached for the light on the night table. It made for a clumsy move, and I knocked over a glass of water before reaching the switch.

Warm, orange light flooded the area around my bed.

I looked at my hands and wrists. Tan skin, nails bitten to the quick but painted blue, no scars or wounds on my wrists.

I was Elizabeth Key, Lizzie for short. My mother was Nancy, and my father was Connor. I was twenty-two years old. I was home and alive. I was alive.

Sighing, I slumped back against the wall. For a moment, I just sat there, staring at my wrists. The dream was slipping away for every second I was awake, but I knew I'd dreamt about aunt Ellie. Something about her dying.

Shaking my hands and head, I stood. I needed to clean up the mess. I stepped into the hall and stopped to listen. The house creaked and moaned, but I heard no steps. No singing. Only Mrs. Tav breathing and flipping pages from the hallway beneath me.

By the time I'd cleaned up, the dream was all gone and I was so tired I could hardly think. I left the towel on the floor by the foot of the bed, climbed under the covers and turned off the light.

Sleep took me as the house creaked around me. For a moment, it sounded like the ticking of a clock.

<h1 align="center">12</h1>

The beeping of the alarm penetrated my foggy mind, and I moaned as I turned over. It didn't feel liked I'd fallen asleep after the nightmare. Just like I'd laid down, closed my eyes, and then the alarm started beeping. Eyes still closed, I tried to find my phone, but it wasn't on the nightstand.

My foot hit something hard at the end of the bed and the sound of the alarm grew muffled.

Great, I'd brought it into bed with me.

I sat up and forced my eyes open. The light from the phone weakly penetrated the duvet at the end of the bed. I tried kicking the covers away, but my feet were tangled in the fabric and I only made it worse. With a curse, I lifted the top of the duvet and crawled under it, freeing my feet before turning around so I was sitting on all fours in bed, the cover over my head and back but my bottom out in the cold air.

I snagged the phone with a triumphant sound and fought my way out of the covers. When I was free, it lay in a tangled heap at the end of the bed, but I didn't care. I had the blasted alarm!

Turning it off, I groaned when I saw the time. I knew it was half-past five in the morning, but it didn't make it any better seeing it. I put the phone down on the nightstand, plugged in the charger, and stood. The hardwood floor was cold against my naked feet and I jump-walked over to the door, throwing it open and jumped from the jamb and onto the rug lying in the middle of the hallway. It was fuzzy and warm against my skin, worn down from years of feet and me sleeping on it at night while listening to mom and dad moving around downstairs when I was a kid.

The hallway was, thankfully, warmer than my bedroom, and the smell of coffee drifted up the stairs. Taking a second to draw in the scent, I went to the bathroom. I did my business and washed my hands before washing my face. Brushing out my hair, I pulled it back in a ponytail. The shorter strands left over from my bangs slipped loose and tickled my cheek. I pushed them behind my ear and walked to my room.

The floor was still cold, but I hurried to my suitcase and found a pair of socks. Pulling them on, I turned on the lights. I hummed to myself as I made the bed, closed the window, changed underwear, and found clothes for the day. When I was dressed, I checked the phone, but the battery was still low, so I left it to charge and headed downstairs without it.

Mrs. Tav wasn't in her usual spot, but I could hear the radio down in the kitchen. Stopping on the landing, I looked at mom's bedroom door. It was ajar, but I couldn't see mom from here. She moaned and moved in her sleep. I shook my head and walked down the last set of stairs. As I turned from mom's room, she started humming in her sleep.

A cold ripple ran down my back and I hurried down, away from her.

Mrs. Tav was standing in the kitchen. "There's coffee on the pot," she said.

"Thank you," I groaned and headed straight for the coffee.

"So how was mom last night?" I asked as I took a sip.

"She slept soundly through the night and should sleep a few more hours before she wakes. Almost woke when you were up an hour or so ago."

"Oh, ok." No wonder it felt like I hadn't gotten any sleep in between waking and the alarm going off.

We fell silent. Mrs. Tav had a wrinkle in her old brow. I was trying not to listen to the song playing in the back of my mind.

Baby bird; flap your wings
You are all grown up now

13

Mrs. Tav left a little before six.

I made myself a small breakfast of dry toast and headed upstairs. Mom was quiet now, still sleeping soundly, and I hurried past her room. In my bedroom, I found my computer bag and slung it over my shoulder as I checked my phone, but the battery was still low, so I left it there.

Back in the kitchen, I sat down at the table, propped up my computer and turned it on.

It booted up fast, and I opened Facebook. Nothing significant had happened since I last checked yesterday, so I moved on to checking my email. Then I got on Youtube before checking Twitter and Instagram. By the time I was through them all, I was tearing at the nails on my left hand. There wasn't much left to chew, and the nail polish made it taste like crap, but I didn't care.

The dream was sitting at the back of my mind, heavy and dark. I didn't remember much, but I remembered it being about aunt Ellie and how she died.

Forcing my left hand away from my mouth, I checked the time. Just past seven. Mark would be getting ready for school by now. For a moment I thought about calling him, but I pushed the thought away. We had talked late into the night

73

and he needed to prepare for school. Anyway, I'd have to go back upstairs for my phone, and that was such a hassle.

I stared at the small computer screen before me. Slowly, I lowered my hands to the keyboard, my fingers hovering just over the letters. I wasn't sure I wanted to look into what I was thinking about. Was afraid of what I might find. But if I waited much longer, mom would wake up and I wouldn't have time to look before Mrs. Tav came back, and I didn't want to look into it then.

My ears strained to listen. Outside, I heard someone talking, a dog barking, the wind rustling the leaves on the trees and slipping through the boards of the house, making it sound like it was ticking like a clock. Other than that, the house was quiet.

With a sigh, I let my fingers fly over the keyboard.

I opened Google and typed in the words I hoped would show me what I was looking for, and hopefully put my mind to rest.

Death of Elizabeth J. Key 1994 Skye Harbour

I pressed enter, and my hand instantly flew to my mouth so I could chew on my nails again.

As soon as the page was loaded, I started scrolling. There were multiple hits, but most of them seemed to be important events from 1994 in general or from a town in Arizona, US, with almost the same name. I had almost lost hope of finding anything, a small part of me cheering the fact when I found an article in the local paper. I clicked on the link before I could change my mind.

With my teeth sunken in my thumb so hard I thought I tasted blood, I started reading the short article.

The body that earlier this week was found in the harbor has been identified as Elizabeth Josephine Key; a twenty-four-year-old woman reported missing by her roommate four days prior.

The body was discovered by a couple, and they immediately called it in to the authorities. The police have, for the last few days, not wanted to give up any information, but the family of the deceased gave their consent last night.

The police have ruled the young woman's death a suicide so that no further investigation will be conducted.

Then followed a few commentaries from the leading officer on the case and some comments from one of the psychologists at the local office.

I tried to see if I could find any more about aunt Ellie in the newspaper, but there was little on the server. Most articles from that time weren't digitalized. This article was only on the web because it was used as a source for another, much newer article about a suicide club in the area. I could probably go to the library and see if they had the old newspapers, but I couldn't ask Mrs. Hearth to watch mom again so soon.

I went back to Google and tried again but didn't find any new info.

Standing, I walked over to the counter and poured myself another cup of coffee. Leaning my hip against the counter, I looked toward the table. My small laptop stood there, all alone, while I stared at it, hugging the warm cup to my chest. Grandmam and grandpap were both dead, and mom was no help in getting answers. The only other family I could contact was dad, and no way was I doing that.

He hadn't just left mom when she got sick. He'd left me as well. I was hardly eighteen years old when it happened. What kind of man does that to his own family?

Anyway, my phone was upstairs, so too bad.

I shook it off and walked back to the computer.

Even if I could find any contact info for dad online, I was not calling him. Not even to tell him when mom died. He chose to leave. I had nothing to say to him, and he had nothing he could say to me to change my mind. About anything.

I still sat down at the computer and tapped in his name in the search box on Google.

I don't know what I'd expected, but this wasn't it. For some reason, I thought he'd be in hiding or something, at least not easy to find, but that wasn't the case. The first link led to his Facebook page – which he didn't want while he was together with mom but clearly changed his mind about, for here it was. I also found his Myspace and Twitter page. So much for not believing in social media, dad.

Anger boiled in my stomach, but I kept it there as I clicked onto his Facebook.

He'd gone a little grey at the temples, and he'd gotten more wrinkly, but other than that, he was just as I remembered him. White of skin and blond of hair. With a straight nose and thin lips surrounded by smiling wrinkles. His forehead was creased with worry lines in contrast. His eyes, green with blue spots, were hard but had a sparkle buried deep within.

Or, he was almost just as I remembered him. In multiple of the photos, he was holding a baby in his arms, and before that, he was hugging a pregnant woman. A woman with olive skin and long dark hair, just like mom, but younger and probably healthier.

The baby in his arms was a girl, and according to the photo caption, she was baby Cornelia Key-Melman. Daughter of Catherina and Connor. She was born on May twelfth this year.

Anger and hurt coiled in my stomach and I closed the

computer screen with a snap. My hands were shaking as I gripped the table. How could he? How could he leave us behind and start over? That was what he'd done. He'd found a new woman to be with and made another daughter. It was like he tried making our family anew.

Cold froze the anger and made me sick to my stomach. What if he was really trying to recreate it? What if he wanted the house back? I had no right to it, other than him allowing mom and me stay here. What would we do if he cut the money I used to get mom the help she needed? Would he do that?

I didn't want to believe my dad could do something so cold, but he wasn't my dad anymore, was he? He was Cornelia's dad now.

Something pushed in my chest, something heavy and sharp, but I pushed it back down. I didn't want to cry. Couldn't cry now. I needed to deal with this before it actually became a problem, but I wasn't sure how.

My train of thought was cut short as the floor above me creaked. Mom was up, and I let a breath of relief fly from my lips. Mom needed my full attention, and so I could forget about dad and Catherina and Cornelia with a clean conscious.

He would not make me feel sorry for myself or sad. He didn't have that right anymore.

14

Mom was in a good mood. She ate two toasts and drank a cup of coffee, and asked me about my plans for the day three times. I answered every time, trying to stay cheerful for her.

"Mrs. Hearth came by yesterday," mom continued and I perked up. Was this a memory from yesterday or from farther back in time? "She wanted to know if you could come over and rake her lawn today?"

I kept staring at her, waiting for anything else. Mom took a sip from her coffee, smiling at me over the rim.

"Uhm, sure. Would you like to come too? It could be good for us," I said, forcing a smile.

Mom set her cup down and looked out the window. "Maybe."

I glared into my own cup. "You should come. Maybe she has some chocolate for us."

"Let's hope."

Mom finished her breakfast and ushered me to the bathroom to brush our teeth. She kept talking about maybe getting a cat, which was something she'd done before. I was a teenager, being out a lot with friends and school and activities, and dad had expanded his business and wasn't home as much, so mom was talking about getting a cat or a dog for company. This was just a year or so before she was diagnosed. Could we have caught it sooner if we'd been home more? Maybe we could have gotten her on medication and she would have stayed lucid longer. Perhaps she wouldn't have turned violent.

I spat out white toothpaste scum, rinsed my mouth with water from a glass, and walked to the door.

"I'll see you downstairs?" I asked, keeping my eyes on the carpet in the hall, feeling too guilty to look at her.

Mom gurgled a yes around her toothbrush, and I turned away. I shouldn't leave her alone in the bathroom, but there was nothing sharp she could hurt herself with, and the door was open. I would hear it if something happened.

I headed to my bedroom and got my phone. Standing at the top of the stairs, listening to mom humming to herself in the bathroom, I called Mrs. Hearth.

"Lizzie?" She answered on the second ring.

"Yeah, hi. Did you talk to mom about raking your lawn yesterday?"

"Well, yes, I did. I complained that I wanted you to move back so the job would be done properly. The boy doing it now never finish it, so I don't think he is worth paying anymore."

"Ok."

"How come, dear?"

"Mom said you asked for me to come over and rake the lawn yesterday. I think she twisted yesterday's memory into something from... just before she got sick."

"Oh, ok. Well, what did you say?"

"I said maybe we should do it together, but you know how it is, she'll probably have forgotten by the time she's finished brushing her teeth."

"Maybe, but if she has not, come by anyway, I have more chocolate for you."

I smiled at the phone before thanking her and hanging up. Mom was still humming on the floor below me, but the sound no longer held the echo of the bathroom. Walking downstairs, I found her in her bedroom, finding clothes.

Without looking up, she ordered me to get dressed. "If we finish with Mrs. Hearth's lawn early, we could go to town and eat lunch at the café."

I did as she said, not wanting to put her in a bad mood. It was rare that she was this happy. She seldom remembered the little, everyday things that gave her joy. She remembered bigger things, and many of those memories were tinged with something dark.

While dressing, I texted Mark. He hadn't answered by the time I went downstairs again, so I put my phone in the big thigh pockets of the baggy jeans I wore.

Mom was waiting for me by the front door. She was wearing work pants and boots, and a big jacket that hung loosely on her small frame. Her hair was braided and draped over one shoulder, a knitted purple headband covering her ears and pushing the few stray hairs out of her face. She also wore matching gloves and scarf. A gift from Mrs. Hearth. She was holding my matching set as well, which was a deep red color. I dressed, and we left the house, mom locking the door behind us.

"Remind me to remind Connor to take care of our lawn when he gets back," she said as we headed down the walkway and through the gate. I only nodded, and we walked in silence to Mrs. Hearth's house. She was standing at the front porch when we arrived. She smiled and talked and laughed with mom as we went to the small shed behind her house to find the rakes, and she left us to it when we started working.

It turned out to be a good day. Mom stayed in the same happy, light mood all the while. When we finished with the front lawn, all the leaves now raked into piles, Mrs. Hearth called us inside for a quick lunch of grilled cheese and tea before we were sent out again, this time to rake the backyard.

We were as good as done; all the leaves raked into piles here as well, when mom pushed me over in one of the piles. The leaves crinkled under me and flew up around me, and at my feet mom was laughing and throwing more leaves my way, her eyes shining.

I just lay there, staring at her, not sure what to feel. A part of me was afraid of her, scared that there was something else than just fun behind the push, and I was ashamed of that fear.

"Oh, honey, I'm sorry," mom said, reaching for me. "I just couldn't let a whole day of raking leaves go by without at least one of us taking a leaf bath! Remember we used to do that when you were little?"

I took her hand, made to let her help me up, but pulled her over instead. She fell with a light scream, and I laughed as she was swallowed by the leaves. She burst out of the pile in seconds, throwing more leaves at me, grinning. Laughing, I threw leaves back.

We laughed and dunked each other into the pile, threw leaves and pushed each other over, for I don't know how long. By the time we were done, leaves were scattered across the back lawn yet again.

I fell back in what was left of the pile, staring up at the darkening sky. Mom fell down beside me. We watched the clouds in silence. I heard mom's breathing calm down, getting heavier, and I didn't dare look at her. As soon as we stopped, that small fear within me came creeping back. It had been a risk, taking her outside like this. It had been fine, but her mood could have turned. She could have run away or attacked me. She could have attacked someone else.

"What have you girls been doing?" Mrs. Hearth's voice reached us, and we both sat up at the same time, looking at her where she stood at the back door, hands on her hips but a broad smile on her face.

"We may have gotten distracted," mom said sheepishly, and I relaxed a little into the leaves. She was still here and now.

Mrs. Hearth glanced at me like she noticed the shift in my mood, but she didn't say anything. Instead, she turned back to mom. "Young people today, always messing around. Well, come inside. I've got some treats for you, and even if you have made a mess of my backyard, at least the front one looks good. I took the liberty of scooping the different piles into bags."

"Thank you," mom said and pushed up.

Without another word, she helped me up, and we headed for the door.

15

The kitchen smelled of warm chocolate, sugar, and baked goods. As we entered, Mrs. Hearth pulled a tray from the oven. On it, multiple cookies rested, the chocolate chips still boiling lightly from the heat.

"Why don't you two go into the living room while I finish with these?" Mrs. Hearth said, putting the tray down.

"Thank you. I think I'll use the bathroom first, though," mom said and headed toward the hall without waiting for an answer.

"You need any help?" I asked as I untied my scarf.

Mrs. Hearth looked at me before leaning back to look into the hall. Mom's steps sounded on the staircase. Mrs. Hearth turned toward the tray of steaming cookies. Lifting a spatula, she started moving the cookies from the tray and onto a plate. It was cold, and fog covered the porcelain as soon as the hot dough touched it.

"No, dear, but I do believe you do?"

I froze. "What?"

A door slammed above us.

"I do believe you have something you want to ask me." She finished with the cookies while I just stared at her. Not once did she turn toward me. "Hurry up, dear, before Nancy is done."

"What... I don't..."

"You can't ask me about Ellie while your mother is here, so…
"

Her words hung in the air and a chill spread from my heart and through my body.

"Tick-tock," Mrs. Hearth said as she turned toward me, one cookie in hand. She took two steps, lifted one of my hands, pulled off the glove and placed the cookie in my palm. The sudden hotness, the softness, shook me out of the stupor I was in and I drew a deep breath.

"How did you know I wanted to know about aunt Ellie?"

"I know many things," she smiled and motioned for me to take a bite of the cookie. I did. "Also, I talked a lot to Lars while he worked here and know what he thought."

"Oh," I said around the mouthful of hot dough and chocolate. I wasn't sure if I was answering her or moaning from the sweetness of her baked creation.

"Now, ask away. I'll answer what I can while your mother is busy, but I will not talk about your aunt when she is around. It frightens her."

"Wait, frightens her? I thought Lars thought mom killed aunt Ellie?"

"Did he tell you that?"

I picked at the cookie. "Not directly. He said he was afraid mom was crazy. That she really made up the Red Woman she thought was the one driving Ellie to kill herself."

"Lars may think that, but he doesn't know the whole story."

"So what is the whole story?"

Mrs. Hearth tilted her head as if listening, and I did the same. A toilet flushed above us.

"I don't have time to tell you everything now, it can be a long story if you ask questions, but you should know it. I would have liked to tell you everything in one go, but I don't have the time to see you today. Can you come tomorrow night? When Nancy is asleep, and Mrs. Tav is there to look after her?"

"Sure, I'll try."

"Good." Mom was finished washing her hands and had opened the door. Mrs. Hearth reached forward and grabbed my hands, crushing the half-eaten cookie with the force of her hold. "But you must know that Nancy did not kill Ellie. She did not. But she is afraid she might have killed you."

The frost the cookie had banished flared up again, and a bubble formed in my throat. There it was again. Mom killing me.

Mrs. Hearth let my hand go as mom stepped down the stairs and onto the hallway floor. "Now eat up, dear, I need to get some warmth into those bones of yours after all the hard work you girls did for me."

Her eyes didn't leave me as she said it, and while her voice was light and warm, her face was hard. I forced the cookie to my mouth as mom entered the kitchen.

We spent a little over an hour in Mrs. Hearth's cozy living room. It was made in all brown and dark yellow and green, with plants hanging and standing on every windowsill. It made the air fresh and tasting of the plants and earth. Different spices mixed in the air, giving a sharp tang to the smell of chocolate that always blew from the kitchen.

Mom and Mrs. Hearth talked and ate cookies and drank cocoa with marshmallows. I drank little and ate even less, my mind working with what little the old woman had given me. How did she know I was looking into aunt Ellie's death?.

I shook the thoughts away. I was not in the mood for my

mind to go down dark tunnels of impossibility right now. I had enough possible dark tunnels to explore as it was.

When we'd eaten all the cookies Mrs. Hearth put out for us, we stood to go home. Before we left, she gave us a container with more cookies, now cool and hardened, but still soft and tasty. Mom talked and talked about what a sweet neighbor she was as we walked home, and what a shame it was that she was alone now, and how nice it was that I liked her. That we both needed someone good in our lives, and we could be right for each other.

I didn't bother telling her that Mrs. Hearth was way too old to be a good friend to me. She was old, but she had also been there for me since mom got sick. She had been there for mom more than me. I clamped down the feeling of shame and unlocked the front door.

"Remind me to tell Connor to take care of the garden when he gets home," mom said as she passed me, and I glanced over her shoulder at the leaf and weed-filled garden. Maybe I'd take care of it tomorrow. Or tonight. I needed something to occupy my mind from the upcoming visit with Mrs. Hearth.

Mom didn't wait for my answer but walked in and straight up to her bedroom, not taking off her boots or clothes or even putting down the container of cookies.

I closed and locked the door and turned, seeing Mrs. Tav standing at the bottom of the stairs, looking up after mom.

"Good evening, Mrs. Tav," I said, forcing a tired smile to my lips.

She looked at me. "Good evening, Elizabeth. I think your mother walked upstairs with muddy boots."

I glanced at the dirty tracks leading over the carpet and sighed. "Yeah. I'll clean up if you could help her out of her clothes? She has a container of cookies as well; you should have one."

"I will, thank you. Had a nice day?"

"Yeah, actually. Spent I don't know how many hours over at Mrs. Hearth's." I was surprised at the smile stealing across my face.

"That's good to hear. No problems?"

"No, she stayed in one place and one time."

"Good, good. Maybe she will want to share those cookies, then," the last she said in a jokingly manner before following mom.

I undressed and headed upstairs to the bathroom. When I exited, I heard mom and Mrs. Tav talking in low voices, but it sounded friendly enough, so I found the carpet steamer and some spot remover in the closet downstairs and started cleaning the carpets first.

While I worked, Mrs. Tav and mom came back downstairs, both eating a cookie. Mom shot me a look, her brow wrinkled and lower lip sucked into her mouth. She grabbed at Mrs. Tav, that carefully took her hand and patted it, murmuring soft words I didn't hear over the steamer before they both headed into the kitchen. I stared after them before returning to my work.

I was done with the carpet and had moved on to removing the stains from the hardwood floors when the smell of dinner reached me. Mom was walking back and forth between the kitchen and dining room, carrying plates and utensils and glasses. Dinner was served before I was done with the stairs, but both Mrs. Tav and mom ordered me to the table and to eat, and so I did. When we finished, mom and I cleaned up the dishes while Mrs. Tav started on the stains in the hallway upstairs.

Mom was in a good mood during dinner and after, but when left alone with me, she grew quiet and kept shooting me long looks.

"Everything ok, mom?" I asked as I put the last of the dishes in the washer.

She stiffened. "Yes, yes, just thinking."

"About what?"

"Oh, this and that."

"You look worried."

"It is normal, you know."

"What is?"

"To worry about the people you love." Her words were clipped and short.

"Who are you worried about?"

"You, Ellie. I'm worried you'll kill yourself because you believe there's a curse on your family." I narrowed my eyes, not sure what to say, but mom continued. "I'm sorry I snapped at you. It's just this house and everything."

"What do you mean?"

Mom forced a laugh. "Don't listen to me; I'm just not sleeping well."

"Because of the voices?"

She dropped the mug she was holding, and it shattered on the floor. "Voices?"

"Yes. You mentioned them before, remember?"

She lifted her hands to her head, holding it. Her eyes were jumping around the kitchen, never settling on me. "No... I don't..."

I tried to reach for her, but she stepped away, closing her eyes. "Mom, what's going on?"

"Stay out," she murmured. "Stay away from my baby. You can't have her. Not like the others. She isn't for you."

Mrs. Tav rushed through the door, having heard the cup break. She took in the scene with one swift glance; the broken mug on the floor and mom huddling around herself, clutching her head and murmuring. Me reaching for her, panic in my eyes.

"What happened?" The old woman barked.

"We were just talking, and she..." I couldn't finish and just waved at mom.

Mrs. Tav shot me an angry look and walked to mom. She put her hands over mom's, who opened her eyes and glared at the woman.

"It's ok, Nancy," Mrs. Tav said. "No one is taking your baby. Now, come with me." It wasn't a question, and Mrs. Tav's strict tone seemed to calm mom. She let Mrs. Tav wrap her hands around her and lead her out of the kitchen, neither of them looking at me.

I stayed where I was for a long time. Mom's words spinning around in my head like a snowstorm. The flakes individual thoughts that melted the moment I tried to grasp them. Above me, I heard steps against the floorboards. Someone was pacing, probably mom. At least she hadn't gotten violent. That was something.

With a sigh, I bent and started cleaning up the broken mug. I continued until the kitchen was all clean and the steps above me had gone silent. Then, still not ready to go upstairs and face mom or Mrs. Tav, I walked around the ground floor, turning off lights and checking that all doors and windows were locked. They were. Not able to put it off any longer, I headed up the stairs.

Mrs. Tav was sitting in her chair, arms crossed and foot tapping the floor in an angry rhythm. Her book lay unopened on the table. Throwing a nod her way, I hurried up the stairs, feeling her eyes burn into my back.

The glare sent a spike of anger through me. It wasn't my fault mom went weird. I was just talking to her. Maybe I'd pushed her a little, but not so much that she should start hearing things. That was what happened, right? When she clutched her head, she started talking as if someone was talking to her? Someone I couldn't hear. I stopped at the top of the stairs. I couldn't remember if mom had heard voices before, but maybe dad would know?

I snarled at nothing and headed for the bathroom. Always dad. He may have answers, and I would have to call him, but I really didn't want to. And there probably wasn't a reason to, anyway. It wasn't like anyone thought mom was crazy other than Lars, so it didn't matter.

I was still angry when I was ready for the night and crawled under the covers. I didn't want to go to sleep angry, no better way to get nightmares, so I picked up my phone and called Mark. I needed a dose of normal.

16

A scream ripped free of my throat and my hand crushed my mother's. She was murmuring nonsense words to me, patting my hair, trying to calm me.

I didn't want to be calm. I didn't want her here. I wanted Martin to be here. My Martin.

I screamed his name as soon as I'd drawn breath.

The room grew quiet for a moment before mother said: "Martin isn't here, sweetie."

"I know that!" I snapped before falling back on the bench.

"One more push, Elizabeth. One more, and you'll have your baby," the nurse between my legs said.

I didn't look at her. My eyes ran around the room, tears rolling down my cheeks.

"One more," mother said in my ear as she stroked my hair.

I wanted Martin to be here. Wanted him to hold my hand and stroke my hair.

I pushed anyway.

My eyes closed, I screamed in pain and sorrow and exhaustion.

I'm Elizabeth Sanderson, born Elizabeth Key. I'm twenty-four years old and married to Martin Sanderson. Or rather, I was widowed by Martin Sanderson. He'd died when I was three months pregnant. Lost at sea, leaving me alone with my swelling belly.

I'd moved back home to mother, father, and my younger brother. Now I was here, pushing my baby, our baby, out of my body. I didn't want to push it out. I tried to keep it inside me where it was safe.

Martin should have been here. He should have been holding my hand. I wanted Martin. The fact that he wasn't here made it all so much more real to me.

He was dead.

I wanted to die.

"One more, one more!" The nurse yelled at me.

My eyes flew open as I pushed. I was tearing in the middle. So much pain.

"Elizabeth," the voice was a whisper against my ear, cooling the sweat on my skin. I turned my head.

"Martin," I murmured.

I didn't see mother and the nurse exchange a glance. All I saw was Martin. He was here, standing at the door, smiling at me.

Without a word, he moved toward me. A shadow trailed behind him, looking more like smoke than anything else, but I didn't notice. My Martin was here to see the birth of our child.

"One more, Elizabeth."

I pushed, my eyes locked with Martin's. I didn't scream anymore, didn't complain anymore. Just looked at him as I pushed our child into the light.

A baby's scream filled the room, but I didn't look at it.

Martin was by my side now, stroking my hair, but I didn't feel his touch. My entire body was numb.

Someone was yelling for blood, for help, for a doctor.

Mother was squeezing my hand so tight it should have hurt, but didn't. I hardly felt it. I barely heard her asking me something, talking to me.

Martin leaned forward. As he moved, the smoky shadow melted together with him.

He kissed my forehead and a chill ran from where his lips touched me, across my face and into my mouth, nose, eyes, ears, down my throat and to my heart.

As he pulled back, I looked at his face, but it wasn't his anymore. It was covered in shadow. All I could see were yellow eyes.

I wanted to ask Martin what was going on, but I couldn't move my lips. I tried to breathe, but nothing happened. My chest hurt. Everything else was numb, but my chest hurt. My heart stopped beating and I stared into those yellow eyes, stared and stared and stared and stared and stared and...

For a moment I couldn't breathe, then air exploded into my lungs and I sat up, coughing. I was clawing at my chest, making sure my heart was beating, making sure I was breathing, making sure I was alive.

Those yellow eyes swam in the air around me, piercing the nightly gloom.

Still coughing, I turned on the bedside lamp and scanned the room.

Nothing out of order, no yellow eyes or creeping, smoky shadows. I was alone.

My breath steadied, and I forced myself to stay on the bed until my pulse was back to normal before I stood and walked as quietly as I could into the hallway.

The floors creaked below me and Mrs. Tav's voice floated up to me. "You ok, Elizabeth?"

"Yeah, just a bad dream."

"Ok. You going back to sleep?"

I stood in the hallway, looking over my shoulder and into

my room. The light from the bedside table threw shadows into every corner, but nothing moved. Still, I had a feeling something was watching me from those shadows. Something with yellow eyes and hate in its heart.

"Lizzie?"

"No, I don't think so," I answered, forcing myself to look around.

"I'll put on the kettle."

"Uhm... No, please don't."

"Ok?"

"I just need some air, really, and I'll be fine."

Without waiting for an answer, I headed back to my room and found some clothes. I kept glancing around while I looked through the suitcase. It felt like someone was watching me, or like I heard something just too distant to know what it was. In the end, I didn't care what clothes I ended up wearing and just sprinted downstairs, trying to outrun the sounds and feelings of my room.

Mrs. Tav was still in her chair, book closed but one finger working as a bookmark. I forced a smile, and she narrowed her eyes but didn't say anything. I rushed past her and down to the ground floor. As I passed the grandfather clock in the hall, I was sure I heard it ticking, but when I stopped and looked at it, it was as dead and quiet as it had been most of my life.

Shaking my head, I pulled on clothes and booths and headed outside.

The chilly air hit my face, catching my hair, and I inhaled, smelling wood smoke, exhaust, wet leaves and cold. Stuffing my hands in my jacket pockets, I started walking.

I'd done that a lot after mom got sick. I'd wake from nightmares in the middle of the night and couldn't go back to sleep, so I started walking. The neighborhood was safe enough, especially as long as I kept to the lit streets, so I did so back then, and I did so now.

I walked down the street, keeping to the small curb at the side. As soon as I was off our property, I started feeling lighter. Like there was a weight hanging over the land we owned that only I could feel. It was probably just everything going on with mom, but it felt like I couldn't breathe, and that ticking was making me jumpy.

I reached the end of the street, checked to see no cars were coming before I crossed and started walking back up. Somewhere, a cat meowed to be let inside, and I heard a car driving by a couple of streets over. Some of the houses still had lights in their windows, but I didn't see anyone. It was like I was the only person awake in the whole world. The only person left.

I stopped in front of Mrs. Hearth's house and looked across the street, taking in my own home. It was like a cloud was hanging over it. One I could see but not see at the same time. Like the shadows in my room when I woke. There, but not.

Folding my hands, I was about to cross the street to go home and try to get some more sleep, but instead, I turned and headed up the walkway to Mrs. Hearth's door. I didn't plan to knock or anything. Just needed to relax a little. I planned to sit on her stoop until I grew tired again. It wouldn't be the first time I sought out her house to calm myself, and it probably wouldn't be the last. Even knowing she wanted to talk to me about the very thing that was giving me nightmares, I felt calm when I was close to her. But instead of sitting down, I reached out one hand and knocked at her door.

17

I had time to regret knocking, afraid I might wake her, before Mrs. Hearth opened the door. She was dressed but didn't wear any makeup or look like she was expecting visitors. But she didn't show any surprise at my showing up at her door at this hour either.

I gave her a weak smile. She waved me inside and closed and locked the door behind me. No words were spoken. In my case, it was because it felt like I would explode if I opened my mouth. Like everything would push its way out, and I wouldn't be able to stop screaming. I didn't know why Mrs. Hearth didn't say anything. Usually, she talked a lot, but not now. Just helped me off with my scarf and hat and took my coat.

First when I was all free of my outer clothes, did she speak: "Why don't you go into the living room and make yourself comfortable, and I'll make us some tea. Do you want anything else?"

I shook my head. She gave a small smile that didn't reach her eyes. Her eyes, that usually were so smiling and warm and soft, with wrinkles spreading like roots from the corners. Now they seemed old and heavy, like she knew something she was afraid to say, or like she could see straight through my skin and into my soul. It wasn't evil in any way, but I still had to suppress a shiver from all the wisdom in those eyes.

She headed into the kitchen as I walked into the living room and sat myself down on the couch me and mom had sat on earlier that day. It felt like a million years ago, and I wasn't sure why. Nothing significant had happened since then. Not really.

Mrs. Hearth was bustling about in the kitchen, moving things around. I let myself sink into those normal sounds, and was almost in a trance when she came into the living room, carrying a tray. Not looking at me, she put out a teapot, two mugs, a bowl of honey, a small mug with milk, and a plate with homemade cookies and chocolates on it.

She sat herself down in the plush chair on the other side of the table. Her movements were stiff, and a grimace touched her mouth, but soon enough she was seated. I kept forgetting she was old. She'd always been old to me, of course, but I had never noticed how her body had gotten old as well.

As she relaxed, I poured tea into the mugs. It was a green tea, and when I lifted the lid, I saw leaves floating in the water, giving the faint color.

"What is it?" I asked as I sniffed my cup.

"A homemade mix. Some chamomile, cardamom, and marshmallow root."

"Oh." I glanced at the many plants hanging from the ceiling or standing in the windows and on tables, thinking about the flower beds in the back yard and the plants in the sunroom that we weren't allowed to touch growing up. I knew she sold teas beside her chocolates, but I'd never much liked tea, so hadn't given it much thought. "Are they all herbs?"

"A lot of them, but not all. Some are just nice to look at. I have a lot more herbs in the sunroom or garden."

"Naturally."

"Indeed."

The conversation died again and I sipped my tea. It was surprisingly good. Now that I was here, I wasn't sure how to start, what to tell Mrs. Hearth. She had been the one to ask me over, saying she had something to talk about. But that was tomorrow, and what if it wasn't aunt Ellie but something else? I was about to start talking when she sighed and leaned forward.

"Why are you out walking so late, dear?" I shrugged, not sure what to say. "You wanted to talk about your aunt Ellie and what Lars told you?" she said as she picked up her cup.

I opened my mouth to answer, but the words wouldn't come, so I sipped my tea, which helped a little. "Yes," I croaked.

"You want to know what really happened to her. If dear Nancy killed her or not."

"Yes."

"Your mother did not kill your aunt, but as I said earlier, she is afraid she might have killed you."

"Is it because of my name?"

Mrs. Hearth seemed to jump in her chair, but she didn't spill any of her tea. "Yes. How did you guess?"

I stared down into my tea. The cup was almost empty. I wasn't sure how to talk about this. When thinking about it, it seemed crazy. Mom and dad's fights when I was a kid. The dreams. Maybe I was going crazy? Perhaps I was getting Alzheimers as well? Mom had started as confused, but nothing obvious. I drained my cup and set it down, not looking at Mrs. Hearth before I started talking.

"Mom has always reacted to the name Elizabeth. And she said something a while back about aunt Ellie, which was why I thought she might have had something to do with her death, as Lars said. But there are other things. Do you remember when I left last year? Well, it was because she said something about killing me, something that scared me more than it really should." I remembered her words from that day, and as if in a trance, I spoke them. "*Elizabeth, Lizzie, Elizabeth. I'm pretending it isn't your name, for your father didn't want to call you by that dark name. He wanted something else, but I didn't. I always liked his sister, Elizabeth, and was so sad when she died. She was my best friend, you know. She introduced us. So I wanted to honor her. Your father didn't, though, and he was right. Elizabeth, Lizzie, Elizabeth. My baby girl. Hair as dark as mine, eyes as green as his, and death on her lips, in her heart, from her naming day. Elizabeth, Lizzie, Elizabeth. Baby bird, going to die. Going to die, and momma bird will peck out your eyes. For a crow is a crow is a crow is Elizabeth is death.*" I grabbed a cookie and started breaking it to pieces, still not looking at Mrs. Hearth. "I was able to forget it a little in Toronto. To live a life mostly free of mom and her weird words. Then, when I came back, I started having dreams. I dreamt of how aunt Ellie died. That her wrist was cut when she was out swimming in winter and she drowned. Then about another Elizabeth, an Elizabeth Key Sanderson, who died giving birth many years ago. I woke from that dream just now and couldn't go back to sleep. That's why I was out walking." I looked up now, tears in my eyes. Mrs. Hearth had leaned forward, her tea forgotten. "I don't know, Mrs. Hearth; I'm so confused. What if I'm starting to get sick? I don't know what's happening. I don't understand..."

My words trailed off as I started crying for real, and I buried my face in my hands. I felt more than heard or saw Mrs. Hearth stand from her chair and walk over. She sank down on the couch beside me and hugged me, shushing me and humming to calm me.

"My dear child," Mrs. Hearth said into my hair.
As my sobbing slowed, she poured more tea into my cup and pushed it into my hands. When I didn't drink, she carefully tipped the cup toward my lips, and I did as she wanted. While I drank, she dusted the crumbles of the cookie from my lap.

When I had emptied the cup, she took it from me and replaced it with a small piece of chocolate. "Eat that one," she said, smiling, and the warmth and softness was back in her eyes.

I did as she said and slumped back on the couch, grabbing a pillow and hugging it to my chest.

"I'm sorry," I said, not looking at her.

"Whatever for?"

"For breaking down like that. I don't know what that was about. I just... it's really hard to be home again, to take care of mom, and I'm not sleeping well, and there is this ticking that's..."

I stopped myself and glanced at Mrs. Hearth, afraid she was repulsed by me. But her eyes were as soft as ever, although her brow was knit in concentration. She wasn't looking at my face, however, but at my chest. I tried to follow her eyes, but there was nothing there, not even a crumb of cookie.

"Anyway," I said, and she snapped out of whatever thought had occupied her.

"Anyway," she copied and smiled a little. "You seem to have guessed that your mother is afraid she may have killed you by choosing your name, at least."

"Yeah, but that's just her being confused, right?"

"My dear Lizzie, how much I long to say that is what's

happening, but I cannot lie." I wanted to ask her about that; of course she could lie if it helped me get some sleep, but she didn't let me. "You mention the dream of girls dying and the ticking. I don't know if you remember this, but when you were very young, your parents had to toss out all the clocks that ticked in your house because they freaked you out."

"That's not true. We have two grandfather clocks."

"When was the last time those clocks were wound, my dear? And what about in Toronto? Do you have any ticking clocks there?"

I wanted to protest but couldn't. She was right. I didn't have any memories of the grandfather clocks ticking or chiming. And no, we didn't have any ticking clocks in Toronto. Mark wanted one, something about childhood memories, but I put my foot down. It was the one time I had a strong opinion of how our apartment should be decorated, so he let it pass. I'd almost forgotten that. But the ticking was so familiar to me, always there, and I told her this.

"That is because you have heard it your entire life. I remember you as a child. You were so sweet and innocent and beautiful, shining with light. But every now and again, something in you would turn dark, and you would mention the ticking and be really careful."

"What?"

Mrs. Hearth didn't seem to hear me, for she continued without pause. "I remember once, you were out in the street with some of the other kids, playing like children do, when you suddenly stopped and started looking around. It was a sunny day, but somehow a shadow had fallen over you and only you. You stood quietly for a long time before you said: "The ticking is back; we need to go." That was not the first time you said so, and it was not the last, and the other children listened to you. You all walked out of the road and disappeared into the house of the Simons'. You did not see the two cars that collided just where you had been playing a short time after."

"I remember that," I cut in. "I remember mom came and got me, and there were police and people everywhere. Two people died, didn't they?"

"Yes, and when you emerged from that house, you were all light and shiny again, like the darkness had not been there at all."

"Mrs. Hearth, what are you talking about?"

Mrs. Hearth seemed to look at me for the first time since she started talking. Then she murmured something. "Did you ever hear your parents talk about you and powers, premonitions, or something like that?"

My breath froze in my throat and my skin seemed suddenly too tight. It only lasted a second before I could breathe again. I wasn't even sure Mrs. Hearth had noticed, but when I answered, my voice was angry.

"What does that have to do with anything? I want to know what happened to aunt Ellie, and you said you could tell me. What does all of this have to do with anything?"

"You need to understand this to know what happened to your aunt. Without it, it may seem too magical to be real."

"Why not just tell me and let me be the judge of that?"

Mrs. Hearth shrugged. "I understand your anger and your fear, but I need you to trust me."

"How can I trust you when you're only talking in circles?"

"I am not, now take a cookie and another cup."

"No!"

I was about to stand and walk out the door, but Mrs. Hearth

leaned forward and grabbed my arm. Her touch seemed to burn, and the burning calmed me. When she let go, it felt like all the anger had drained out of me.

"You are scared, and I understand that, but trust me."

I nodded, suddenly too tired to speak.

Mrs. Hearth continued. "You told me about your dreams and the ticking. I have told you about your light and dark, and I want to tell you more, but I can tell you are tired and scared. You need answers, but you don't need all the backstory. I will give you the answer to your aunt's death, to the death of all the women named Elizabeth in your family, and the answer to your dreams."

She stopped, and I looked up at her, tears in my eyes again. I wasn't sure I wanted to know now. Something about the way she was speaking bore the heavy truth of something more than my own reality. I wasn't sure I wanted to know, but I needed to. When she didn't continue right away, I nodded, and she nodded back, keeping her eyes locked with mine.

"Know that I have more answers, as well. If you ever feel the need for the whole story or want to ask questions, I am here."

I nodded again, and she sighed.

"What I am about to tell you, I have gleaned from history, from you, from your parents, and from some of my own history and my own... circle.

"Before you were born, everyone in this neighborhood had lived here for a long time. Many owned family homes here, like your father, and some were sons and daughters who rented the land and built their own homes on it. My mother used to work as a maid here, for all the houses. She took the laundry, swept the porches, cleaned their homes once every other week. Everyone knew who she was and what she was. I am the same as her, and when she got pregnant with me, your great-grandfather let her rent the property I now live on. But this isn't important. What is important is that my mother knew the Elizabeth that died in 1921, and that I knew your aunt and you. My mother's mother knew a young Magdalena Elizabeth who died as well.

"So when your parents came to me and told me about your dreams, about your premonitions, as we agreed they were, and the ticking, I started digging. Your father told me what he knew, and I had other ways of learning what was going on."

"What does this have to do with anything?" I asked, but not angry this time. I was exhausted, feeling like my head was about to implode. I just wanted to know what I felt was in there; what she was afraid of telling me.

Mrs. Hearth sipped her tea. "Your father told me a story, a story of the first MacKey born in the house on this land. Of how he had a lover, a young woman who had come over with her own family early in her life. Her family was poor and she worked as a maid in the MacKey household. She got pregnant, as girls often did back then, but by the time she worked up the courage to tell Joseph, the father of her child, he was married to a woman named Elizabeth Eleanor St. Etienne, now Elizabeth Eleanor MacKey, the daughter of a rich merchant from France. So young Maud cursed Joseph. Cursed him that every child of his blood with a tie to beloved Elizabeth would die before their twenty-fifth birthday until his line was dead and gone."

A heavy silence fell. One I couldn't bear, so I spoke up. "What does that mean?"

"That mean, dearest Lizzie, that generations ago a man stuck it where he should not and brought a curse over the woman he loved, and every child born of them until the line died. At that time, a line only lived on as long as it was passed from father to son. Your father was the last son of the MacKey line, but he had a daughter, a daughter he named Elizabeth because his wife loved his now-dead sister so much. His line will die with you, but you are still of his blood, and so you are cursed."

"What?"

"You have a cursed name, dearest Lizzie, and you will die, just like every Elizabeth Key before you."

18

I wasn't sure where I was. It felt like I was sitting on the sofa, gripping the sweatpants until the fabric turned sharp and cut into my palms. It also felt like I was floating. Just outside of my body as well as far away.

Suddenly, Mrs. Hearth was in front of me. She uncurled my hands from the sweatpants and forced them around a cup. The warmth grounded me and I blinked. Everything came into focus at once. The colors, smells, sounds, and feelings. Everything.

"Oh." The sound escaped me, and I drew a shuddering breath.

"Now I want you to drink that tea, dear. It is something more relaxing than the one I gave you earlier. It should help you calm down and go to sleep when you get home. It is late, after all."

I glanced at the clock on the mantelpiece. It was almost three in the morning. It's ticking was usually too low for me to notice, but right now the sound was almost deafening.

"Oh," I said again, this time a little more planned. I felt I had to say something.

"Are you alright?" Mrs. Hearth asked as I sipped my tea. It was bitter but with a faint taste of honey. "I know this must have been a terrible shock, and I would understand if you don't believe me..."

Her words trailed off as she watched me drink. I couldn't look at her, so I looked at everything else. First when my cup was empty and my head a pleasant kind of woolly, did I look at her and speak.

"I'm not sure I do," I put the cup on the table and stood. Mrs. Hearth stood with me, wringing her hands carefully. "I need to go home now. I need sleep, but you said I could ask you questions if I needed to? That you had more answers?"

Mrs. Hearth nodded. "Yes. I have answers to many of your questions, not all, but many. I will answer as much as I am allowed."

I wanted to ask what she meant by ''allowed'', but I was too tired. It was like I was floating, but not in a wrong way. It was like my body was falling asleep around me while I moved.

"You said the tea would help me sleep?" She nodded and gave a weak smile; like she was just as exhausted as me. "Will it keep the dreams away?"

"It should if they are normal dreams."

"What's normal dreams?"

She shrugged. "Dreams. They are neither normal nor not normal, but what I mean is that some dreams are part of your brain working through things. The other kind of dreams... well, you have to be a special kind of person to have them."

I wanted to ask about that as well. Hadn't she said my dreams were premonitions? But I was tired and couldn't be bothered. I wanted to sleep a dreamless sleep.

Mrs. Hearth followed me to the hallway, where she helped me dress before she handed me a bundle of chocolate, this time in a dark red handkerchief with a gold ribbon. I'd never seen any of her bundles this dark before. I was looking at it as I walked home. Feeling the chill wind on my face, listening to it rustling the leaves.

The door was locked when I got home, and while I looked at my hand as I unlocked it, I couldn't feel the hand clutching the key. I had to ask Mrs. Hearth for more of this tea.

Mrs. Tav stood in the stairs when I locked myself in. She gave me a low welcome. I handed her my bundle of chocolate and said goodnight before heading upstairs.

I was more asleep than awake as I brushed my teeth and tied my hair up in a bun. My shoes were left at the end of the bed, but I didn't get further than to hook off my bra before I fell on top of the duvet and slipped into sleep.

19

I was running about, holding my dolly by one hand. The nurse was yelling for me to stop. Asking me what my parents would think, what the neighbors might think, if they saw me running about in my slip. I did not care. I did not want to go to that stupid party. They were always dull. Old ladies pinching my cheeks and saying I was a little angel. Saying I was a miracle.

But I was not. They told me I was a miracle for five years, then mommy got pregnant again, which no one thought she could be, and then I had a little brother, and I was not a miracle anymore. I was just Little Magdalena Elizabeth Key, a daughter.

I heard daddy talking to one of the other grown men at one of those dinner parties, saying that now that he had a son, he could die happy. I did not matter anymore. I was not a miracle child anymore. Little Matthew was the miracle now.

Speaking of Little Matthew, he was crying again, almost drowning out the nurse's yell for me to be careful as I ran toward the stairs.

I did not want to go to a party. I wanted to go outside and play with the stable boy. He was fun. He did not care if I was a miracle or not. He was kind to me even if my blond hair was not curled and pinned up. He was kind to me even if I was not in my best gown. Maybe I would shame mommy and daddy by marrying him when I grew up. I knew mommy had already started looking for a husband for me. I heard her talk to the Lady Norris from down the road about it.

I did not want to get married. I wanted to run and play and be... "Free!" I yelled as I grabbed the railing to swing myself down the stairs like I had done so many times before, but something was different.

My foot did not land on the next step as it used to. Looking down, I saw something dark covering my foot, and then the darkness tightened its hold and pulled. I tumbled over myself, hitting the next step with my neck first.

My dolly flew from my hand as I hit the wall with my face.

I tried to yell for mommy, but blood filled my mouth, choking me.

Someone screamed.

The darkness was pulling at me again, down the last steps.

I felt like I was flying. Light and not in pain and free.

As I hit the floor, all I could do was gasp as something tightened in my chest.

I could not breathe.

The nurse was there, her face white.

Little Matthew was still crying somewhere.

Mommy was asking what was going on.

I wanted mommy.

Blood filled my mouth until it trickled out, tears blending with it on the floor, and then mommy was there. She was crying, yelling at the nurse, for daddy, for anybody. She was so lovely, dressed in dark blue from head to toe, her hair, blond like mine, falling around her shoulders in curls. She used to call me her little angel, but she had not since Little Matthew came along.

He was still crying, but not here.

Mommy was here without him. I smiled, and it hurt, but I had her all to myself.

"Oh, my baby girl, my little angel," mommy said, her voice thick and strange as she bent and hugged me to her chest. I had never seen Mommy cry before, but she was crying now. Why was Mommy crying? Her scent filled me and I closed my...

I couldn't breathe. Why couldn't I breathe? Air filled my mouth and nose, pushed down through my throat. My next breath was a gasp. My eyes flew open, but I couldn't move anything else. I wanted to scream but couldn't make even the smallest noise.

Just breathe. I closed my eyes again, hard.

Staying still, I focused on breathing until I felt my muscles relax and the push in my chest lessened. I continued breathing before I tried moving a finger. It worked. Trying the rest of my fingers. They worked as well. Then my toes. Then my feet and hands. I let another breath go, a deeper one than any other until now, and sat up.

"What the actual...?" I murmured and hugged my knees to my chest.

Somewhere in the house, someone was talking. Probably the radio in the kitchen. I listened to the voices drifting up the stairs and through my door. When they grew quiet for a moment, I checked my phone. My alarm would ring in just a few minutes, so I turned it off and pushed out of bed.

I was still dressed, but my top smelled of fear, so I pulled it off. Shuddering in the cold air, I started looking for another. I had a bad taste in my mouth and was chewing on my nails as I tried to remember the dream. I knew it was like the other dreams I'd had since coming home. Something about someone named Elizabeth, and I knew it had been in this house. I recognized the banister and the stairs, the floor, the ceiling in the entrance hall. A little girl named Elizabeth had fallen down the stairs and died here.

A shiver ran up my spine and settled like a cold vice around my skull. By the time I was in the bathroom with my clothes, my head had started throbbing, and as I stood there, I realized it was throbbing in tandem with the ticking coming from the walls. I hadn't noticed it before now, as scared as I was, stuck in my own body, but now it seemed like it was coming from everywhere at once. Even from my own chest.

Fear gripped my heart and made my hands shake.

I remembered Mrs. Hearth's words from earlier that night. About a young Elizabeth dying in this house generations ago. About her tea being able to keep normal dreams away. About the curse.

The world tilted around me. I tried grabbing the counter to steady myself, but missed and fell to the floor.

20

Someone knocked on the door. "Elizabeth?" Mrs. Tav. "Are you ok in there?"

Her voice grounded me, and I drew a breath, blinking my eyes.

"Yes," I croaked. "I'm fine."

"You sure?"

I drew another deep breath, feeling oxygen filling my lungs and bursting into my blood. "Yeah, I just slipped."

Mrs. Tav was quiet for a time before she said, "Ok, if you say so."

I stayed on the floor, breathing and listening to her steps as she walked down the stairs again.

Carefully, I pulled myself to a sitting position. What happened? I looked around and saw my clothes tossed around the room at random. Saw the hairdryer where I'd pulled it to the floor with me. Warmth filled my face. Had I fainted? I'd never fainted before. A hiccup escaped me and I dragged myself to my feet and leaned on the counter. My hands were shaking as I turned on the faucet. The water splashed into the basin, the sound hypnotic. My hands gripped the edge of the counter and I leaned my forehead against the mirror. I was staring down into the basin, looking at the water circling into the drain, but not really seeing it.

I closed my eyes and breathed. I hadn't stopped breathing, that was good. My hands were hurting against the edge. They were still there. That was good. My hair hung down, tickling the naked skin of my neck and shoulders. That was real. That was good. I was real.

I couldn't believe what Mrs. Hearth had said was real.

So what was the problem? If I didn't think it was real, it didn't need to be. She had always been a little eccentric, after all. But if her story wasn't real, what had happened to Aunt Ellie? Maybe Lars was right. Perhaps mom had something to do with her death, after all?

I shook my head against the glass, my eyes still closed.

I couldn't believe mom had killed aunt Ellie. I believed that mom had loved her, both because mom said so, because Mrs. Hearth said so, and because dad said so. No matter how angry I was with him, I believed his words before mom got sick.

Mom had loved aunt Ellie. She wouldn't have killed her.

So what had? The newspaper said it was suicide.

The sounds of the water being pulled into the sink for a moment drowned out everything else. Drown. Water. Blood.

My wrist started tingling, and I opened my eyes and turned my hands to pull up the arm of the sweater. My wrist was whole. No scars or marks of any kind. Just the same, warm skin color as I'd always had. The tingling was gone again, but it had reminded me of the dream about aunt Ellie. About her wrist cut on that screw. How the wound was much deeper than it should be. About the darkness in the water, holding her down, making her bleed more than she would have if she were able to crawl onto land as soon as she cut herself.

And darkness.

The darkness had been in all of my dreams since I got home. It had been behind the birthing mother's husband. Her dead husband. It had tripped little Elizabeth in the stairs, almost dragging her down the steps.

Darkness.

Mrs. Hearth said I used to be such a bright child, but sometimes I would grow dark. When I heard the ticking. When I told the other kids to get out of the road. Or when I stopped running out of nowhere and managed not to hit my head, or run onto the almost invisible clothing line, or stopped myself from tripping in that hidden hole. Or how I knew where not to go in the woods, and then a branch would fall just there.

I remembered all of those moments. I remembered how one of the teachers at my middle school used to say I had a guardian angel. He knew no other child who was ever so close to catastrophes like me. Someone was watching over me, he used to say, then tussled my hair. I still had the little glass angel he gave me the one time I was in an accident and broke my arm. He said my guardian angel must have thought I needed to be hurt a little, so the other children wouldn't suspect and be jealous. Then he winked and snuck me the little glass angel.

It was after I had that fall and broke my arm, and my teacher told my parents about all the close calls I'd had, that dad got really scared. It was then he started talking to mom about how I was in danger. How they'd cursed me.

Cursed me.

My hands started shaking and I clenched them into fists. Pushed them into the still running water. It hurt. Steam was fogging the mirror, making my hair damp as I leaned over it, and the warm water burned, but I kept my hands under, staring at them as the water swirled between my fingers.

Dad once said I was cursed. Why? Was it the same time he and mom talked about my dreams? The time dad called them premonitions? Was that the time he also said I was cursed, or was that some other time? They'd talked about me a lot when they thought I wasn't listening, often while in their bedroom. I was always sitting between the banister and the wall at the top of the stairs. Like I'd done that first night home, listening to mom and Mrs. Tav.

I pulled my hands from the water and turned it off. As if in a trance, I pulled my head from the damp mirror and found the washcloth hanging at the wall, drying my hands on it. It was soft, and the softness almost made me cry.

I didn't want to be cursed.

I didn't want to believe I was cursed.

I wasn't cursed.

I couldn't believe it.

I was cursed.

"I'm cursed," I said it out loud, looking at myself in the mirror. My face was pale and the words didn't seem to come from my own mouth, even if I saw the lips move. "I am cursed," I said again, and this time it was a little more real.

Then I laughed. It was a hysterical sound, and I clamped my mouth shut to keep it inside. It didn't work. The laughter seemed to seep out between my sealed lips and fingers, like a broken gasket on a submarine, and I was about to drown in the noises I would make if the gasket blew.

Pulling the towel from the wall, I pushed it over my mouth and removed the hand between my lips and the softness. The fabric dampened the sounds of my hysterics. I didn't drown after all.

20

By the time I stopped laughing, my ribs, stomach, and throat were hurting so much I had to fight to keep tears from spilling from my eyes. Man, I was such a mess. I wanted to call Mark and just cry on the phone, but I didn't know what to tell him. He would say I was hysterical, tell me to come back to Toronto, to give up on mom. He'd say she was getting to me. He didn't believe in curses or anything like that. I didn't either. Or I thought I didn't, but somehow it fit.

I almost started laughing again but managed to stop myself this time.

I wasn't sure I believed I was cursed, but maybe I was getting sick, or getting pulled into the minds of two sick women? But it fit. The dreams, the ticking, mom's words, Mrs. Hearth's story, my memories, they all seemed to point to this. Even things that had happened in Toronto, things I thought were coincidences, fit. They could point to many other things, to disturbed minds and disturbed hearts, to bad luck and good luck, to old family stories and ghost stories, but none of those felt right. The curse felt right.

I buried my face in the towel again. I didn't want to admit it, but the only one who knew more about this than Mrs. Hearth was dad.

Something clenched in my chest.

I wanted to talk to mom. I wanted her to hug me and comfort me and sing me my lullaby as it was supposed to be sung. I wanted dad. I wanted my old, stable father to pull me under the covers of their big bed when I woke from a nightmare and cried them awake. I wanted him to hug me and tell me stories in a whispered voice to not wake mom after she fell asleep again. Wanted to fall asleep feeling safe.

Mom wasn't here anymore, not really, and dad wasn't here

either, but I knew what I had to do.

I needed answers, and he had them.

I had to call him.

21

I was sitting in the library, a steaming cup of coffee in my hands. It was my third cup this morning. Darkness pressed against the windows, but the sun would soon rise. The house was silent – or as silent as an old house could be. Mrs. Tav had already left, but mom was still asleep. A piece of paper lay on the table beside me. On it was dad's latest phone number, but I kept telling myself it was too early in the morning to call. Or that it was too late and I didn't want to risk talking to him when mom woke.

A book lay open in my lap, but I'd long since given up reading it. My mind kept wandering to the latest dream. The more I tried to remember it, the more I remembered the previous dreams, and the stronger the ticking became.

I took a sip of the coffee, hoping the taste would force my mind to something else. It didn't work. Setting the cup down, I stared into space, not really seeing anything, just listening to the house and the ticking, feeling like someone was breathing down my neck.

"Ouch," I drew my finger out of my mouth and watched as blood welled on the tip. I'd chewed the nail so low I'd broken the skin. "Great."

I stood and walked into the kitchen. I cleaned the wound and wrapped it in a band-aid. I was turning off the sink when the ticking stopped.

I stood still, listening, before breathing a sigh of relief when I didn't hear anything else.

Heading back to the library, my mind settled. Like it had been a hurricane until the ticking stopped. Now that I was able to think clearly, the dreams were fresh in my mind. For two nights in a row, I'd dreamt of girls named Elizabeth. The first had been my aunt, then a woman I didn't know, but she shared my surname, and then a little girl that died in this house.

Mrs. Hearth had talked about a family curse, and after this morning I was inclined to believe her. That said, I could trace the origin of all the dreams if I really tried. The dream about aunt Ellie could be blamed on Lars talking about mom maybe killing her. The dream about the birthing mother could be a product of chance. Of mom talking about the voices and so on. Then there was the little girl. Mrs. Hearth had told me about her just hours before I had that dream. They could all just be my brain trying to deal with everything going on in my life.

Lowering my hand to stop chewing on my nails, I took a sip of coffee and scanned the shelves in the library without really seeing them. This land had belonged to dad's family for generations. The original house was built in the early 1700s and was a lot bigger than this. The family sold some of the land as the years passed. Then the house burned to the ground in the late 1800s, and the family built the current house on the same lot. They continued selling off the land until my grandparents' time when they began leasing it to people instead. We owned Mrs. Hearth's property, and four of our other neighbors' as well. They paid for us to let them build and live there. Not to mention the acres of forest stretching out behind the neighborhood.

The Key-family was an old family, originally from Scotland. Dad was proud of his family history and wanted me to be too. He'd told the stories often enough.

Without really thinking, I set down the now empty coffee-cup and started walking along the shelves. On the lower shelves were children's books from generations back, and above those were shelves with newer books. Mysteries and thrillers and even some science fiction, but most of the library was filled with old books. Books that had belonged to the family for years, generations even.

I pulled out a big bible. It and many of these books had belonged to my great-great-grandfather. He went to England in his youth, where he met his wife. He returned with his wife and their firstborn after the fire, bringing his entire estate with him. My grandfather was as proud of his family-history as my dad had been and kept the bible up to date.

Carefully, I put the book on the desk in the middle of the room and opened the cover. The paper was dry and old, and the corners seemed to be falling apart, but it was well enough preserved for me to open the folded papers just inside.

Beginning on the inside of the cover, stretching over two pages, and still with a third blank page at the bottom, grew a family tree. The oldest names, those on the inside of the cover, were stamped into the leather and filled in with gold. Merida and Christian MacKey. They were the parents of Maria and Joseph. Joseph was married to Elizabeth Eleanor, and they had one son together.

At reading the name Elizabeth so far back in the family tree, my chest tightened. For a moment I couldn't breathe at all, but it let go and I drew a shuddering breath to try and calm myself.

Not touching more than the corner of the paper, trying not to smudge it with my skin, I read on.

Elizabeth died at the age of twenty-four, with a straight line of men following her, with a few daughters in-between, all seeming to live to average ages. Until 1851, when three children died on the same date, one of them a girl named Elizabeth at the age of fourteen. That was shortly before my great-great-grandfather returned, and the rest of the family was from his line. Two generations later, a girl named Magdalena Elizabeth died again, this time at the age of six. Then another in 1921, and then my aunt in 1994. No one named Elizabeth in the MacKey family had lived past the age of twenty-five.

22

After putting the bible back in its place, I couldn't sit still. I wandered up and down the stairs, checking in on mom every time I passed her room.

At the sixth of these passes, she murmured in her sleep. I wasn't able to discern the words, but when I looked in, she was tossing her head back and forth.

Without thinking, I walked inside and sat on her bed. "Mom?" I whispered, reaching for her. She froze at the sound of my voice. "Mom," I said again, not whispering, but keeping my voice low.

Her mouth opened and she breathed deeply, so deep it seemed like her chest was twice its usual size when she started letting it go. She turned around, still sleeping.

I couldn't help the small, warm smile that moved across my lips. She looked at peace now that she'd calmed down. Like she wasn't sick at all.

She puckered her lips, as if giving someone a kiss, then exhaled. She whispered something, but the only words I heard were *baby bird.*

My smile faltered, and I stood a little too fast. Blood rushed from my brain and I felt dizzy for a moment, supporting myself on her bedframe, never taking my eyes off of her. I knew, deep down, that it was a beautiful song, a song we both had fond memories of, but I couldn't help the cold grip of fear I felt now. Her modification of the song had touched me on a much deeper level than any other thing she'd said about hurting me.

When the dizziness disappeared, I walked out of her room, letting the door stand ajar so I would hear it when she woke.

I headed downstairs. If I'd been restless before, it was nothing compared to now. I couldn't wait for Mrs. Tav to return. For her to take care of mom so I could go over to Mrs. Hearth. I had questions.

Until mom got up, I busied myself with cleaning. I emptied and cleaned the refrigerator and threw out any old food that may have snuck its way to the back before I cleaned the oven.

I was about to start vacuuming when the sound of mom's voice put a stop to it. She was awake and singing as she moved around upstairs. When listening, I realized she was singing the original version of the lullaby about the baby bird. I suppressed a shudder and put away the cleaning implements and headed upstairs.

The rest of the day flew by. I helped mom take a shower, because she thought she was going to work, but by the time she got out of the shower she was sure it was the weekend. She almost walked out of the bathroom stark naked, not even turning off the water, but I managed to talk her back inside to dry up while I turned it off.

I managed to keep her occupied a little after that by helping her choose clothes. We made a game out of it, trying to find the worst combination possible. It ended up with her wearing a pinstriped skirt that reached to her knees, a bright orange t-shirt, a dark purple jacket with red roses on the hem, and pink low heels over green pantyhose. It looked horrible, but the game was fun. Then I helped do her hair, and we talked about boys. She thought I was fourteen years old and in love with one of the guys in my class. I humored her. It was actually a little fun, just talking like this. The truth was that this was around the time I got together with my first and only girlfriend, but I'd never told my mom or anyone about it.

Guilt and shame reared its ugly heads as we talked, and I couldn't meet her eyes. I'd been so obsessed with the bad things happening because of her sickness that I didn't enjoy the good things. Yesterday, we'd played with the leaves in Mrs. Hearth's garden, the day before that we did our nails, and today we were talking and playing around. If I didn't know I was older and had a different life, it would have been fun and nice.

But I knew, and while I felt guilty for leaving mom, I also felt exhaustion creeping up on me. I started having nightmares after mom got sick. Dr. Long said it was normal. Just my young brain reacting to the stress. When I stopped eating, he suggested I start seeing a therapist. I moved away instead, and my appetite and sleep got better shortly after. Now, though, the bad dreams were returning, and if not for me wanting mom to eat, I wasn't sure I'd eat anything on my own. It was nice being with mom like this, but it was also exhausting. I couldn't have my own life at all unless I found someone to take care of her.

After fixing her hair, we headed downstairs. I forced us both to eat some breakfast, even if mom didn't know I was pushing her. She just kept standing up and trying to get me ready for school.

After breakfast, I managed to sit her down in the living room with a movie. She curled up on the sofa, clutching a pillow to her chest as she always did when watching TV, and stared at the screen. I wasn't sure she was actually watching the movie, though, or just staring into nothing.

I was about to sit down with her when my phone rang. Shooting a look at mom, who was still calm and staring at the screen, I picked up the phone and walked into the library. I could still see mom from here but would have a feeling of privacy.

Checking the caller-ID, I lifted the phone to my ear. "Hey, Mark."

We flittered through the 'how are you,' me answering on autopilot before he asked: "Do you remember texting me last night?"

I rolled my eyes. "Yeah."

"That's good, 'cause I have a surprise for you."

"Oh?"

"Look outside."

I furrowed my brows and headed toward the door. I expected there to be a care-package for me. We used to do that before we moved in with each other. Sending each other packages with films or new types of coffee and stuff. I opened the door, a smile already forming on my lips, the words ''thank you'' bubbling in my throat, and froze.

There was a package there, all right, in Mark's hands. "Surprise," he said, lowering the hand holding his phone.

"Mark," I hissed, stepping outside and pulling the door closed behind me. "What are you doing here?"

Mark's smile fell. "You said you wished I was here with you."

"In a text! In the middle of the night when I was tired and alone and sad! I didn't mean it."

"What?" I groaned and massaged my neck. "You look tired,

Lizzie. Just let me inside, and I'll take care of you."

"I can't. Mom's in the living room, watching a movie."

"Let me in anyway."

"No!"

"Why not?"

"You know why not. If she sees you... there's no telling what she'll do."

"That's why I want to be here. I want to help you with this. You don't have to go through this alone."

"Yes, I do. She's my mother and I've already left her once. Not again. Not now." Mark opened his mouth to say something, but I shook my head. "I'm just... I appreciate you being here, I really do, but I can't do this now."

"Lizzie, you need to rest. You're exhausted. Don't you have a nurse helping you? That guy, Lars?"

"The agency doesn't send anyone in the day as long as dad or I am at home. There will be a nurse tonight, but not until six."

"Ok, so what do you want me to do until then?"

"Get a room at one of the hotels or something. You can't stay here."

"Fine."

"Thank you."

I turned to go back inside, but he reached out one hand and put it on my cheek. His hand was cold from the autumn air blowing around us.

"I'm sorry I upset you," he said, leaning in and giving me a small kiss on the nose. "Please call me when the nurse gets here, ok? You need to get away from all this, and I'd love to buy you dinner or something."

"Thanks, Mark."

I kissed him on the lips, and he handed me the package before he turned and headed down the steps. The wind pulled his ash-blond hair around as the sun made it glitter like molten gold. He reached the taxi still standing at the curb, and blew me a kiss before pulling off his square glasses so I could clearly see him wink one brown eye before getting in.

As I watched the car drive away, I realized he hadn't expected to stay here. He'd asked the cab to wait and hadn't even brought his luggage. Then why the argument? I groaned and walked inside. I'd started it. It was my fault, not his. I'd just gone off when seeing him. I needed to rest. Needed to get away from all this.

"Who was that?" Mom asked from the living room.

I locked the door behind me and walked in to join her. She was still on the sofa, still hugging the pillow, but she was looking at me.

"The mailman," I said, lifting the package as proof.

"What is that?"

"I don't know. Come, let's open it."

Mom and I watched one of the movies from Mark's care-package, a sappy RomCom. Just what I needed. The package also contained my fuzzy blanket from the sofa at home, which I snuggled around my and mom's feet while we watched the movie and ate some of the candy from the package. Mom ate most of it.

We ate lunch, but mom was full from the candy, so I hid the rest while she was in the bathroom. When she emerged, she wanted to draw so we headed up to her atelier, where she started making a sketch of me doing my nails. They needed tending. I'd completely ruined the design from our girly afternoon.

Mrs. Tav arrived a little before six at night as usual. She'd brought a grilled chicken, and I made rice while she watched mom. We ate together in mostly silence. Mom had charcoal on her cheek after our time in the atelier, and she was in a good mood, even if she was exhausted. Thankfully, her appetite had returned after the candy-bonanza.

I hardly ate at all, but when both Mrs. Tav and mom ganged up on me to eat more, I did. A little. When Mrs. Tav finally relented on my eating, I stood.

"Where are you going?" The old woman asked, narrowing her eyes at me.

I narrowed my eyes right back. "Out. I need some air."

Mrs. Tav only nodded and stood, starting to put away the dishes. I kissed mom on the head and said goodnight - she only smiled at me, starting to get groggy from her medication – before heading toward the entry hall.

I needed air, needed to get away, and now that Mark was here, where better to spend the night than with him. Right?

23

Mark texted me with the address to a pizzeria located down-
town as I drove. It lay close to the docks and wasn't that far
from his hotel either.

I parked mom's car along the curb and stepped out. During
the drive, I'd chided myself for not changing before going out,
but it wasn't like Mark hadn't seen me at my worst before, so
I doubted he'd care. If he did, I'd just blame the women in my
house, which wasn't a lie.

With the help of Google Maps, I found the pizzeria. It sat
on a street running along a small park. On the other side of
the park was an open view of the ocean, just barely shadowed
by construction sites and homes or businesses. The only way
to get to the park was on foot, so there was no traffic driving
by, and tables were standing outside with veranda warmers
hanging from a web of rafters, casting an orange light over
everything.

Mark was sitting at one of the outdoor tables, staring down
at the ocean as his fingers fiddled with his phone.

I stepped into his line of sight, and he blinked back into
reality, smiling at me.

"Hi," he said.

"Hey," I answered and sat in the free chair at his table. "How did you find this place?"

"The clerk at the hotel recommended it when I said I needed a quiet place to talk to my girlfriend."

"That's nice."

"Yeah."

A silence fell between us, filled with all the things that had happened to me over the last few days, with my thoughts and dreams and fears. After a moment too long, I remembered to smile.

Mark leaned forward and took my hand, and my eyes were trained on his fingers.

"What's going on up there?" He asked, poking my forehead.

"I'm just thinking."

"About?"

"Nothing, really."

"I don't believe you."

Sighing, I forced myself to meet his eyes. "It's just... do you believe in magic?"

He snorted. "Magic? Why?"

My hand curled under his, but he didn't notice. I looked away again. "Nothing, just something mom said."

"What did she say?" He sounded angry now, his fingers digging into the back of my hand.

"Nothing. It was really nothing."

"For you know you can't trust anything she says, right? You know she's crazy, right?"

I tried moving my hand out from under his, but he was still gripping it in anger. I wanted him to let go. Didn't want him to touch me after that comment.

"She's not crazy," I said, my voice hard.

He leaned back in his chair, letting my hand go. "Might as

well be."

I opened my mouth to say something, but no words came. He sensed my anger and leaned forward again.

"Forget I said anything, ok? I didn't mean it. I get so angry when I think about you all alone with that woman. I wish you'd drop it and come home." My eyes fell to my hand on the table again. "Let's just put all this talk about magic behind us, ok?"

I nodded, and suddenly I was exhausted. I wanted to tell him that I wasn't ok. That I was tired after nights of bad dreams. That I was all empty after taking care of mom. That I felt shame when looking for a new place for her to live so I could return to my own life. That I was so confused at what Mrs. Hearth had told me that I hardly even knew who I was anymore. I wanted to leave. I didn't want to drag him into the crazy that was my family. That was me.

Not that he believed in it anyway.

I didn't want to lie to him, but I couldn't tell him about the things going on in my head. Just couldn't. What if he left me? Like dad did?

"So other than magic, what's going on? You've been so vague on the phone."

"There's that whole thing with mom."

"I don't —" He was cut short as a waiter came over to take our orders. Mark asked for the same we always wanted when eating at an Italian place. A big pizza to split between us, and a beer for him and a coke for me. Mark couldn't drive, so I was always the designated driver when there were just the two of us. That was fine. I didn't like getting drunk anyway; it messed with my head. When the waiter left, Mark turned back to me. He'd left his hands on the table, and I'd grabbed one of them and pulled it to me. I couldn't meet his eyes, so I fiddled with his hand instead. Stroking his long, thin fingers and circling his short nails, feeling the hard parts where he held his pen or pencil wrong as he wrote. I'd always wanted him to learn an instrument, but he was happy with the pen as his only talent.

"I don't think that's the whole truth," he said, and it took me a moment to remember what we were talking about.

"Why do you say that?" I asked.

"Because I know you. I know how you feel about your mother, and that's part of the problem, but I think there's more to it. Something you're not telling me."

Pulling my hand from his, I looked at my nails. The fresh polish had already started to flake because of my fiddling with it.

"It's just..." What could I tell him? About the curse? He'd think me mad. Or maybe that I'd gotten Alzheimers as well. About Lars thinking mom might be crazy and not have Alzheimers at all? About the Red Woman? About the ticking? That I was probably going to die soon? Shaking my head, I settled on the least scary thing that had happened to me since I came home. "It's my dad, Connor."

"What about him?"

"You know how I haven't heard from him after mom got sick, right? And that he sends money to help with the treatment and care?"

Mark furrowed his brows. "Yeah?"

"Well, I'm really worried about what's going to happen when mom moves to a care facility. Will he take the house back? Will he want me gone?"

"Why would he want that?"

"He's got a new family: a woman and another daughter. I don't know if they even know about mom or me. And what if dad wants to move back home and raise that other kid there?"

Mark just blinked at me a few times before he remembered to speak. "Have you talked to him?"

"No, but I did look him up."

"Why?"

I shrugged. "I thought that maybe he could... I don't really know... help or care or something."

Angry tears sprang to my eyes, and I sighed in relief as the waiter returned with our drinks and a chipper ''the food will be ready shortly'' before bustling off again. The small reprieve gave me enough time to collect myself.

"Not that I can expect any help from him. I should know better."

"There's nothing wrong in wanting to talk to him. He was a good dad until recently, after all."

I snorted and grabbed my coke. Moving it aside, I started tracing lines in the circle of condensation it left on the table-top.

Mark leaned forward, retaking my hand. "If you want, I can be there when you call him? We can do it tomorrow. I can come over after your mother's in bed and we'll call him together. Hey," I blinked and looked up at him. He was smiling that sad smile of his that always made me want to hold him. "You're not alone in this, Liz. I'll help you. You know that."

I nodded and smiled in thanks. "So, how has life been without me?" I asked, trying to push everything else aside.

"Absolutely terrifying!"

I hiccupped a laugh and squeezed his hand. I couldn't talk about all this now, couldn't think about it, and Mark got that. I loved him for that, even if he didn't believe in the problems I was facing and called my sick mother crazy. I had to deal with that, but not now. Couldn't handle it on top of everything else going on.

The meal turned out to be the most enjoyable I'd had since getting the call from Dr. Altman. I ate until my stomach hurt, then we had a bowl of Italian ice cream each for dessert. It was great.

Afterward, we walked through the park and down to the pier. Once, this area had been the main docks, but as the town grew, so did the marina. When ship-traffic dwindled, part of the docks were converted to public boat space. Now, private-owned boats moored here, but a sense of what a busy place this had once been, still lingered. Especially after dark. I could almost hear the everyday bustle of sounds: Men calling and ships creaking, waves hitting wood and stone. Once or twice, I swore I saw the hull of a ship at the corner of my eye, but when I turned to look, only smaller motorboats were to be seen.

I'd always had these experiences in the older parts of town. I'd see carriages or cars from different decades moving along the streets. Hear men and women and children talking or laughing or crying while I was alone in the street. Even scented what I pictured an old harbor town would smell like before sewers were part of everyday life. I remembered thinking it was my imagination. Remembered teachers and adults saying it was nothing. Now I wondered. Maybe what I saw was actually ghosts of some sort? If Mrs. Hearth was right, that was, if I wasn't normal.

Mark tightened his grip on my hand, and my mind returned to the here and now. We were at the end of the pier, standing under a streetlight. Mark had stopped and looked out to sea.

"I always find the ocean so fascinating," he said. "I can hardly believe our ancestors traveled across it the way they did."

I rolled my eyes but didn't contradict him. He knew about my family, but he tended to forget it because I wasn't part of a Tribe and tried to look white. But it still stung a little that he forgot about a part of me.

"I mean," Mark continued. "Even now, we hardly know anything about it. You know, we've only mapped like ten percent of the entire ocean? I wonder what lives in those depths. What might have been lost with the ages?"

"I know you do," I said, suppressing a chill.

Mark noticed and pulled me against him, wrapping his arms and coat around me. It felt good to be so close to someone, and I wrapped my arms around him as well, sneaking my hands under his shirt. He yelped as my cold fingers touched him, but managed not to push me away. I giggled against his shoulder and turned my head and bit him playfully on the neck. He tasted of salt and Mark. He laughed, and the rumble ran through my body.

"Do you have to go home?" He whispered against my hair.

My smile died and I frowned out at sea. For a moment I thought about pulling away from him, but I stayed where I was.

"No," I finally said, even if my voice was a little hesitant. "Mrs. Tav will be there until six tomorrow, so I just need to be home before then."

"Good," Mark answered and pushed at me.

I moved, but before I could pull entirely away from him, he leaned in and kissed me. It was a hungry kiss, and I leaned into it. The kiss burned against my lips, and the burn spread, running up my cheeks and down my throat. It settled between my legs, another kind of hunger, as well as banishing the confusion and fear of the last few days.

I moaned and pushed against him, wrapping my arms around his throat and sliding my fingers through his hair, gripping it when his hands moved along the waistband of my jeans, slipping just inside. His fingertips were cold, and I gasped before giggling. He smiled against my lips.

"What do you say to spending a night in my hotel room?" His voice was breathy, and by the way his hips pushed against my own and the hardness that rested against my lower belly, I knew he wanted to bring me there no matter what I said.

I pushed against him again, moving my hips a little and feeling the fabric of his jeans bite into my flesh when my jacket and t-shirt pushed up.

He growled and pulled me as close to him as I could get.

I laughed. Not a giggle anymore, but a low whisper of a laugh. One of his hands found its way into the back pockets of my jeans, where his fingers slid softly against my ass before he gripped it hungrily. I laughed that same laugh again and pulled his face away from my neck, which he'd been kissing and nibbling at. When I'd managed to pull him far enough away that I could look into his eyes, I nodded.

24

It was so hot.

I did not mean to topple the lamp, but the twins were so annoying. They always were, but I was trying so hard to read this blasted book, and they kept singing and yodling, and I just wanted them to shut their traps, just for one second.

So I'd stood and started yelling at them, the book still in hand. They just mimicked my words back at me, the way they always did when mom and dad weren't around. I was the oldest, so why could they not just listen to me? But no, Jonathan loved poking in my face that I was just a girl. One would think Johana would take my side, being a girl and all, but after I became a woman she loved poking fun at me because I was not betrothed yet.

I coughed into my handkerchief and tried to see them now, but the air was full of smoke, and my eyes were full of tears.

"Jonathan! Johana!" I yelled, but the flames ate my words together with my home. Father would flog me when he learned I burned his library.

Stupid Jonathan and Johana. As soon as I stood to yell at them, they jumped toward me and started pulling at my skirts, tugging my hair out of place, dancing around me as they sang.

Elizabeth, Elizabeth

You are all grown up now

Elizabeth, Elizabeth

No man wants you in

his bed.

Then they laughed. That stupid, high-pitched laugh that was not quite a child's laugh anymore, but they wanted it to be.

God, I missed their laughter now as the flames made the house creak and moan and sound like it was screaming. I pulled down a lungful of air and yelled their names again before holding my breath, trying to listen for an answer. They had to answer. They had to.

As they laughed their stupid laugh, I swung my arms at them, trying to make them stop. It was then that the book slipped from my fingers. I do not understand how. I was holding on to it, but something seemed to grab the book and drag it from my hand and straight at the lamp on the table. The lamp fell and broke, spilling oil over mother's beautiful carpet and splattering upon father's full bookshelves. It was all burning within seconds. We did not have a chance to put it out, so I herded the twins toward the door as the smoke seemed to follow us on hot feet. We were at the door. I had already flung it open when Jonathan screamed that we had lost Johana. They were right behind me, but when I turned she was gone, and Jonathan was running into the house again, screaming for his twin.

"Jonathan! Johana!"

Where were they? Where were the servants? Where were mother and father? They were supposed to be outside, but they must have seen the shine of the fire through the library window by now. How could they not? The fire was eating its way through the ceiling as I sprinted past the drawing room for the second time, looking for the twins. I stopped at the foot of the stairs. Could they have gone up? No, they were annoying but not stupid. They knew to get out if there was a fire.

I was about to turn and run outside to see if they had somehow passed me as I searched, or maybe gotten out through the servant's door; God knew they used it enough to sneak away from lessons. My heart sank. The hallway behind me was covered with smoke. I couldn't see the door, and flames danced across the floor as I watched, blocking the way.

My breath was heavier now, and it was not all from the smoke. It was also fear. The fire was moving much faster than I believed possible. Tears slipped from my eyes as I blinked and turned. The twins were not here, so they were outside. They had to be. I just needed to join them.

Lifting my skirts, I sprang in a rather unladylike fashion toward the kitchen and the servant entrance.

As I entered the dining room, screams filled the air.

My heart skipped a beat. I could weep with joy. It was the voices of the twins. They were screaming for me, probably trying to guide me through the smoke and outside. Outside where they were safe.

I quickened my step, not thinking clearly from the joy of hearing them, and was through the door to the kitchen before I realized their voices were frightened. So frightened. And they were coughing. How could I hear them coughing from out –

The thought was not even finished when I stopped in the middle of the kitchen.

The twins were at the door, pulling and pushing at it, but it wouldn't open. For a moment, it looked like someone was holding it closed. A woman with billowing reddish hair and a sneer on her face, her piercing yellow eyes staring at me. Then I was forced to move as the fire drew closer. If it as much as touched my skirts, I'd go up in flames. I yelled for the twins to move as I sprinted toward the door, hoping my older hands could open it. At the same time, I threw a look over my shoulder. The fire was heavy and warm in the doorway, leaping across the walls, floor, and ceiling even as I looked at it.

My hands grabbed the knob. The metal was burning hot against my skin. I screamed and pulled my hand away, before wrapping the stinging flesh in my handkerchief and tried again. As the twins clutched my skirts and screamed in terror, I twisted.

It felt like the door would give, but then it stopped. I looked up through the glass and out onto the green fields beyond, but all I saw was a black fog. I thought it was the smoke billowing around me, but then the fog became the red-haired woman again. This time she smiled. There was no reassurance in that smile. It was the Devil I was looking at.

"Elizabeth! Elizabeth! It is so warm!"

Jonathan's screams broke the trance the woman's eyes had lulled me into, and I tried pushing at the door. The woman laughed soundlessly before dissolving, but the door did not move again.

"Elizabeth!"

Johana this time, sobbing into my skirts.

I gave the door one last push, but it didn't move. Tasting sot on my tongue, I turned from it and crouched with the twins in my arms.

"I am so sorry," I whispered into their hair as I tried to shield them from the smoke and fire.

So warm.

My mouth was burning.

I was so thirsty.

So warm.

I could not breathe.

So tired.

Just hug the twins. Hug them and hold them and pray.

Pray.
Pray.
Pray. Pray. Praypraypraypra...

Pray. Pray. Pray. Pray*tick.* Pray*tock. Tick*pray*tock. Tick*tock*pray.
So warm. So hot. Sweat tickling as it slipped down my nose. A drop fell onto my eyelashes and I blinked. It fell into my eyes and a weak sting followed. I moaned and sat up. It was like my body was made of lead. All stiff and gone and... dead.

With fumbling hands, I grabbed my phone and turned it on. Ten minutes to three.

I let the phone fall to the table. Mark groaned and moved beside me. I held my breath, but he didn't wake. Shuddering, I carefully pushed out of bed. I was naked, my skin feeling like I had a fever, but I was freezing. Shivers ran through me and my teeth were chattering. All the while, I could feel the flames licking across my skin, hear the ticking filling my chest, rising and wanting to push out of my mouth for the whole world to hear.

I found the way into the bathroom and closed the door behind me before turning on the lights. My pale face looked back from the mirror, and I turned away. My hands shaking, I grabbed a towel from the rack, put it on the floor and sat on it, hugging my legs to my chest and focusing on breathing, trying not to listen to the ticking.

I'd hoped to be rid of it and the nightmares if I didn't sleep at home, but they'd followed me. I couldn't get away. Why couldn't I get away?

A sob threatened to push its way up my throat, but I managed to swallow it before I pushed my forehead against my knees and closed my eyes. Just breathe.

Finally, my body calmed down. Carefully standing, I took a cold shower, the drops making my skin burn even more before going numb. When my teeth started chattering from the cold, I turned up the heat of the water a little at a time as I washed with Mark's soap and the shampoo procured by the hotel.

Showered and calmed down, I thought about the dream. If Mrs. Hearth and I were right, that meant there was only one Elizabeth in my line left. The originally cursed. What happened after I'd dreamed of her death? I didn't want to think about it, but I couldn't seem to stop myself either. The evening spent with Mark had banished my predicament to the back of my mind, I'd even forgotten it for a while, but I couldn't ignore it forever.

Another sob wanted to push free, but I kept that down as well. I was glad I'd gotten that one last night with Mark, for what if I died after my next dream? Premonition? Whatever they were? I both believed in the curse and didn't. I didn't want to believe it, but it all fit too well. It just made sense. And so I was thankful for this last night together. It was a way for me to say goodbye. He would come over tomorrow to help me call dad, Connor, and I needed him for that, but at least I'd had this last night with him. More for me than for him, to be honest. I needed it. Needed to remember myself and who I was away from all this one more time before I died.

Taking a shuddering breath, I turned off the water and stepped out of the shower. The ticking was still there, but fainter. So faint I could almost believe it wasn't real, and so that was exactly what I thought. It wasn't real.

I dried up and walked into the still dark room. I could see the light from the bathroom reflected in Mark's eyes on the bed.

I couldn't look at him, so I sat on the bed with my back to

him and started dressing. "I should go now that I'm awake. Be back before Mrs. Tav leaves."

"You still have a few hours before that..." he answered.

"If I leave now, I'll avoid any morning rush as well."

"Lizzie..."

I forced myself to turn and look at him. Forced a smile to my face. "Go back to sleep, and I'll see you again after six, ok? At my place?"

"Yeah, sure."

I leaned down and kissed him, resting my forehead against his for a second before I stood. I could feel his eyes on me as I pulled on my jacket, pushed my feet into my shoes and headed toward the door. As I closed the door behind me, I glanced back into the room and saw him there in bed, his upper body lifted with his weight on his elbows, looking at me. I smiled, and he smiled back, but even in the weak light from the hall, I could see the worry in his eyes.

I couldn't blame him.

I slumped in the driver's seat, looking out at a peaceful, sleeping world. It was so unfair. I wanted to be home in Toronto with Mark, hanging out in our apartment and talking about getting a dog as we so often did. Mark was a dog person. I didn't really know if I preferred a cat or a dog, I'd never given it much thought. Or discussing his schoolwork, or things that had happened at my job that day. Even wanted our fights, despite there being more of them than the everyday discussions as of late. I wanted everything to be back to the way it was before that cursed call from Dr. Altman. Or even better, for everything to be as it was before mom got sick. When I had a whole family and didn't feel like an orphan. For that was what I felt like. My father wasn't part of my life, he had a new family, and my mother wasn't here anymore.

My hands hit against the steering wheel so hard it sent a jolt up my wrist. I cursed and cradled my right hand to my chest a moment, breathing heavily until the pain subsided.

When the pain reseeded, I started the car and drove home.

I stayed in the car a little after parking. Just sat and looked up at my childhood home. It still belonged to dad, Connor, but I had as much right to it as that new girl of his. That Cornelia. Maybe even more right, if I played the bastard-card. Dad was always so proud of his family history, now he could regret it.

I shook my head.

He wasn't dad anymore. Even if I was to play that card to keep the house so mom could stay, he wasn't dad anymore. No. He was Connor to me now.

And did I want to be that girl? The one calling her sister a bastard?

Sighing, I stepped out of the car and walked toward the house, feeling the cold wind bite into my cheeks and make my tired eyes sting. The pain woke me some but not enough.

I locked myself in. The house was warm and smelled of home. Even now, the scent was still there.

For a moment, I just stood inside the door, unsure of what to do. I didn't dare go back to sleep. Last time I did that, I'd had a second dream, and I wasn't ready for that final dream yet. I could head back outside and talk to Mrs. Hearth, but I couldn't bear her understanding right now. I just wanted to be alone.

A yawn escaped me, and my feet started moving on their own. I headed into the kitchen. With every step, the ticking grew a little louder, as if me entering the house somehow sped things up. Thankfully, I was too tired to fear it anymore. If it was my time, so be it, but I could put it off another night.

I stifled a laugh. I was too tired to care if I lived or died, but the tiredness wasn't just in my body. I was mentally exhausted from carrying mom's treatment, and of the many memories I'd pushed out of my head when I moved to Toronto. My love for mom. The shame I felt over mom and the guilt I felt over feeling shame of her. There was just too much, and I couldn't deal with it anymore.

I'd just started the coffee maker when Mrs. Tav entered the

kitchen. She stood in the doorway and looked at me.

"Good evening," I said, forcing a smile.

"Good evening," she answered, her eyes running up and down my body. Taking in my still shower-damp hair and yesterday's clothes. "Where did you sleep?"

"My boyfriend's in town. I took a nap at his hotel room."

"Oh?"

"Mark is coming over tomorrow, by the way," I continued. "After mom's in bed, of course. He's going to help me with something."

"May I ask what?"

I met her eyes, wondering if I should lie to her. "I'm going to call Connor."

"Your father." It wasn't a question.

"Yes."

"If you need anything from me, let me know."

"I will. Thank you."

She tilted her head in what could have been a nod. "I will be upstairs."

I smiled and turned back to the coffee maker. Mrs. Tav's steps were soft, almost inaudible, as she moved, but I tracked her up the stairs and over the landing, into mom's room, then out again. She was still for a moment, but as I poured coffee into a mug, I heard her head into the bathroom. Good, I wasn't in the mood to see her again tonight.

A mug of fresh coffee in hand, I pulled out the contact to the coffeemaker and headed out of the kitchen. I hadn't turned on any lights as I moved through the house, and I left them all off now as I headed upstairs.

I already had a foot on the first step of the second stair when something made me turn back around and look into mom's room.

The door was open as usual, letting light into the darkness beyond. Mom was usually hidden from view in her bed because of the angle, but now she was standing in the middle of the floor, her back to me, looking grey in the weak light.

"Mom?" I said.

She didn't react, and I took a small step toward her. It was like her edges were smudged, not real, more like smoke. Her white nightgown reached to her ankles and seemed to move weakly in an unfelt breeze. When did mom start to sleep in a nightgown? We always put her in a full set of PJs before putting her to bed. Did she even own a nightgown?

I opened my mouth to ask what was wrong when mom took a step toward the bed and bent over the pillow. That was when I saw the shape there, mostly hidden by the angles of the room, but visible if I looked hard. Someone was in mom's bed.

I didn't think, just acted. With a scream, I threw my coffee cup and too late realized I would hit mom. But mom was gone. Or, she wasn't. It was like she parted around the cup. She turned. I saw yellow eyes and a leer on her face, red hair billowing.

Mom sat up in bed, screaming my name, and the red-haired woman was gone.

Mrs. Tav threw open the bathroom door, water dripping from her soapy hands, and rushed toward us.

I spun toward her, distracted by the sudden sound.

"What is going on here?" she asked at the same time as mom screamed: "Lizzie! Baby bird! Look out! Look out! She has her! She has her! Help her! Help me! Look out! Lizzie, Elizabeth, Lizzie! Baby bird! Look out! Look out! Lookout! Lookoutlookoutlookout!"

Mrs. Tav rushed past and grabbed mom as she lunged toward me. As I turned to follow the old woman's movement, red hair billowed into my face. Just like my own was doing at that moment, thrown around by the movement of my head. Then it was gone, and subtle darkness lifted from the hallway.

Mom's face was white, her eyes wide, her teeth bared. "Let me go! Let me go! Let me help her! My baby bird! I'm the momma bird and I need to help her! Help her! Help!"

Mrs. Tav wrestled mom back toward the bed, surprisingly strong for an old woman of her size. I stood frozen in place, hands shaking in front of me, breath hissing through my teeth.

"Baby bird! Help me!"

The sudden fear in her voice, different than the hysterics from earlier, snapped me back to reality. I sprinted into the room.

"You're hurting her!" I screamed at Mrs. Tav, but the nurse gave me one look and I skidded to a halt.

Mrs. Tav focused on mom again. "Now, Nancy, it is ok. Look, Lizzie is all right. Your baby bird is safe. You protected her. Remember? She is all right."

Mom's eyes jumped from Mrs. Tav to me and back again. Back and forth until I was almost dizzy. Mrs. Tav kept murmuring for almost three minutes before mom calmed down.

"She's ok?" mom finally asked. Her voice was husky from the screaming, low from the strain. Her breast was still heaving under the plaid fabric of her PJs.

"She is ok," Mrs. Tav said and nodded at me.

Carefully, I slunk over the floor until I was at Mrs. Tav's side, looking down at mom.

"Baby bird?" mom asked.

"Yeah, mom. I'm here. I'm fine. Really."

Mom reached for me, but Mrs. Tav held her back. Mom didn't even notice, just lay still when her movements didn't get her anywhere.

"You're all grown up," mom said. I blinked. Something in her eyes had changed. It was like she was seeing me for real for the first time in years. "What happened?" Her eyes jumped from me to Mrs. Tav, then into the hall and her breathing became shallow again. "Where did she go?"

"Where did who go?" Mrs. Tav asked, still calm.

"The woman. The red-haired woman that tried to push Lizzie down the stairs. I don't know how she got in. Where's Connor? Did he let her in? Does he know her? Where did she go?"

"There is no-one here, Nancy. You just had a bad dream."

"No, no, I know she was here. I've seen her before. She made the car swirl out of the road and onto the spot where Lizzie and the other kids had just been playing. I think the woman is stalking my baby bird, but no one listens to me when I tell them. Connor said I'm sick. That's why I see her. But I know she's real. Lizzie has seen her as well."

Both mom and Mrs. Tav turned to me now. Mrs. Tav looked tired. Mom looked pleading.

"Have you seen a red-haired woman?" Mrs. Tav asked as if going through motions she'd gone through many times before.

I opened my mouth to answer yes before closing it again. Had I really seen the Red Woman before? I'd just seen her in mom's bedroom, but that could just be memories from the dream. I remembered the red-haired woman holding the door closed so Elizabeth and the twins burned.

At the memory, fire licked at my naked arms, and I grimaced

in sudden pain, but when I looked down there were no flames.

Mrs. Tav's worried voice made me wrap my arms around myself and glance over my shoulder. The hall was empty and bright with light. Still, it felt like someone was watching me from the shadows in the stairs.

"If you are this tired, you should go to bed," Mrs. Tav said.

"What about mom?"

"She will be all right. She is calm now, are you not, Nancy?"

Mom looked at me. "I'm ok, sure, but Lizzie didn't answer me. I know she's seen the red-haired woman before. I know it. I'm not crazy."

A faint note of hysteria was creeping into her voice. Without thinking I sat on her bed. Mrs. Tav gave me a look but didn't say anything. Just moved a little so she could hold mom if she snapped again.

"I have, yes," I answered, looking mom straight in the eyes. "She's real. You're not going crazy. I'm really sorry if I scared you."

Mom relaxed against the pillows, her eyes going distant. "I knew it; I knew I wasn't crazy. You have to look out for her, baby bird. She isn't good. I think she is trying to hurt you."

"I know, mom. I'm looking out for her. I'm safe."

"Good," mom said, and her eyelids drooped shut for a moment before she blinked them open again. The feeling that she was seeing me was gone. Her eyes were confused but calm now. She didn't notice us standing around her.

I looked up at Mrs. Tav, and she must have seen the worry in my eyes, for she gave as calm a smile as she could. "It is ok. She is just going back to sleep."

While speaking, she carefully lifted her grip on mom, who didn't move. While I sat at mom's side, Mrs. Tav fumbled

around the bed and brought out cuffs hidden under the mat-
tress, tied to the bed frame. I looked away as she slipped one
cuff around each of mom's wrists and tightened them, then
around her ankles.

"This will keep her from hurting herself," Mrs. Tav said
when she saw the look on my face.

When done, she put her still damp hands on my shoulders
and helped me up from the bed and into the hallway.

When I glanced over my shoulder, mom was looking at me,
a small, loving smile across her lips, and I had to look away
because of the guilt coiling in my stomach.

26

"What happened?" Mrs. Tav asked as she led me out of mom's room and pulled the door halfway closed. The light had fallen on the bed, but when I glanced over my shoulder, it was hidden in darkness, hiding mom as well.

I shuddered and turned toward Mrs. Tav, letting her sit me down in her usual chair.

"What happened?" she asked again.

I opened my mouth to answer, then closed and opened it again. "I need to clean up. There's coffee and a broken cup in there. You could step on it tomorrow, or mom could hurt herself. I –"

"Elizabeth, it is ok. Just tell me what happened. Why is your cup broken?"

I felt like a small child, sitting there with her in front of me, her hands always touching my arm, my shoulder, my knee, as she sank to her haunches and looked up at me.

"I thought... well... it's stupid. I thought I saw someone in her room." I glanced at the door but couldn't see more than a wall through the opening: no red-haired women, no mom. Everything was silent in there.

"Saw who?"

"A woman. First, I thought it was mom, that she was awake

or sleepwalking, like when she sang that song downstairs? But she didn't react when I called for her and bent over the bed instead. Then I saw that mom was there, in the bed, and I just... I threw the cup at the other woman, but she wasn't really there anymore."

"Can you tell me what she looked like?"

"She..." Something blocked my throat and I had to swallow hard a couple of times before I was able to continue. "She was wearing a long dress, like a nightgown, white and simple. Her feet and ankles were naked, and she had red hair and yellow eyes."

"Yellow eyes?"

"Yes."

"And red hair?"

"Yes."

"So you were not lying to your mother?"

"No. But if I saw her and mom asked about her, maybe she really is here somewhere? Maybe she's hiding? Mom mentioned her, right? I didn't dream that?"

"No, you did not, but I think maybe you may have told your mom, or she may have told you, without either of you knowing."

"What?"

"I think you were partly asleep. You have had trouble sleeping since you came home, and so you are tired. You may have been half-asleep when coming back upstairs, muttering about what you were seeing. Your mother probably heard it."

"How can you say that?"

"Because I have seen you grow more and more exhausted over the last few days, and I have noticed how you sometimes blank out."

"I do not!"

"Yes, you do. You are tired and mentally exhausted because of everything happening here. I understand how that can happen; I was like that when I started working with patients like your mother. It is tiresome and hard, and it brings up a lot of emotions. What you are going through, I have seen in other loved ones as well. You are trying your best, but with your own life and everything, it is hard."

"I don't... That isn't... What?"

I had trouble processing what she was saying. Was everything just in my head? What about the curse? Was this just exhaustion talking? Believing? But Mrs. Hearth had told me about the curse... or had she? Had I been over there, talking about mom and aunt Ellie, and heard what I wanted to hear? That mom didn't do it? That somehow all the deaths of the girls named Elizabeth were coincidences?

Mrs. Tav sighed and squeezed my knee. "But this redhead, you both seem afraid of her, and your mother has mentioned her before."

I stared at her for a moment. "Right."

"Is there anything more to her than just a figment of imagination?"

I hesitated. Should I tell her everything I thought? What did I even really think? "I guess she must have been around when I was a kid. I don't really remember, but I was almost in a lot of accidents. One of my teachers said I had a guardian angel as often as I got out of accidents without being hurt."

"You told me that once."

I nodded. "I think the Red Woman was there. I have memories of her in the woods where a falling tree almost crushed me. Or standing in our garden or on the road. I think she was there, at least."

"Memories can be fickle."

"Yeah."

We both grew silent. I was still tired; my body seemed too heavy to even lift from the chair now that the adrenalin was fading. I was a little envious of mom, lying there in her bed, even if she was strapped down. The taste of bile filled my mouth and I shook my head.

Mrs. Tav saw and stood. "You should try and get some more sleep. As exhausted as you are it should keep the dreams at bay."

"Yeah," I said. I was not going back to sleep, but I needed to get upstairs so she would believe I did. How I wished for that coffee. "What about the mess?"

"I will clean up. You go to bed."

She smiled as she helped me up from the chair before almost pushing me toward the stairs. I stumbled up and into my room. Tired, but with a fire burning in my throat, I kept thinking about the Red Woman and how she kept popping up in my dreams and in mom's fears. Even in my own memories and Mrs. Hearth's story.

Slumping down at my writing desk, I pulled my diaries close.

27

I started with the first diary I'd ever started writing, flipping through the pages and skimming through the entries. Soon, the words blurred and I had to look at a couple of the last entries again. That was when I found the first mention.

May 28

Mom was so weird today. All there one moment, then I cut my finger and she started screaming at someone to get away from me. Again and again. Just those words, until the words completely lost their meaning, you know what I mean?

Thankfully, Laura was there. She practically chased me from the room and talked mom down. I stayed just outside the door, listening. This slip was my fault. I'd been stupid and clumsy, and so I'd cut myself and made mom flip. The weird thing was that when she was calm, mom blamed a red-head. Saying again and again that the Red Woman had been there, trying to take me.

Sometimes, I wonder if she doesn't have Alzheimers but some kind of double personality thing. As far as I know, Alzheimers shouldn't make you live in a fantasy but just remember your earlier life as if that was the present. So who is this red-head that mom said wanted to take me? For there was no redhead there.

I read the entry four times before I was sure I'd got it all. I felt a little sick. I'd thought the same as Lars. That maybe mom was crazy, and she'd made up the Red Woman. This was early after the diagnosis, though, and mom was mostly lucid. That was when I had hoped some medication would help her and she would return to her old self again.

I turned the pages.

The next entry about the red-head I found was in the next diary I'd started writing, within the first twenty pages.

November 13

I can't believe Mr. Tatch would give us such boring homework. I mean, the man is a legend himself, shouldn't he already know everything there is to know about the U. S. civil war? Why do we even learn about things that happened in the U. S. anyway?

Mostly a good day today. Laura was here and mom was calm. They both helped me with my homework. I'd think mom wouldn't know much, but she switched back to her own high school days and it was like I was doing the homework with a friend instead of mom. Laura encouraged it, however, saying that we should give her whatever she needed at the moment and not worry too much about everything else.

That's easy for her to say. I mean, it's not her mom that's sick, after all. And she isn't alone taking care of her. I wish dad was still here. I wish he would help. Why won't he help?

Anyway, my point here is that Laura can say it's easy to stay in the now as much as she wants, she doesn't hear her mother begging someone not to hurt me at night before Mrs. Tav gets her to sleep. She doesn't hear mom screaming at someone to leave me alone, then warn me to stay away from the woman with red hair - always that stupid red hair. What's up with that, anyway? Should

I ask her or would that only make things worse?

I flipped to the next page, prepared to read the next entry, but stopped and looked at a short entry. The page was blotched with tears, smearing the ink of my pen, but it was readable enough.

No date, just a short note.

Dad sent a letter today, in the mail, all old school-like. He said he'd opened a new account in my name where he would put in money to help with mom.

What an ass.

That was the moment I went from confusion and sorrow about Connor, to anger. And now I was going to call him? A hoarse laugh escaped me. I must be desperate.

But I was, wasn't I? I didn't really believe what Mrs. Tav had said. I wanted to but couldn't. It didn't fit. I may be exhausted and tired and mentally hurting, but I wasn't crazy, and I wasn't sick. This was the only explanation that fit. I needed answers, and Connor could give them to me.

Angry now, tiredness as good as forgotten, I flipped through a few more pages before finding another entry. Reading it, I winced in memory as guilt drowned out the anger.

November 20

I asked mom today, I couldn't help it. She's been talking about that redhead every time I hurt myself the last year. Like a ginger is sucking my soul from me or something – Adam told me that one. That old myths say that gingers don't have a soul, so they suck out others. Maybe that's what mom's afraid of, I thought, so why not ask?

I wish I hadn't.

She got all weird for a moment before she started crying. Laura couldn't calm her down, so she gave her a shot so mom wouldn't hurt herself. Mom went to sleep in the living room. It was so weird seeing her there. Not that she haven't fallen asleep on the sofa before, but this sleep seemed a lot deeper, almost as if she was dead.

I was grateful. I can't believe I was grateful, but if she were dead, she wouldn't have to go through all the stuff she's going through. I wouldn't have to go through it.

It was hours before she woke, and when she did she looked straight at me and said, as clear as ever: ''The Red Woman is the one, and she's after you, my baby bird, and I'm afraid she will use me to get what she wants.'' Then she started crying again, and when Laura tried to calm her, she clawed at her eyes and screamed, and I had to help her get control of mom again. After, mom got another shot and Laura called Mrs. Tav and she came in early. Together they carried mom upstairs, and when I followed I saw Mrs. Tav pull straps and cuffs from her bag, tie them to the bed and strap mom down.

How can they do that? Mom was just confused. It wasn't her fault. It was mine. They should strap me down, not mom.

I'm so tired. I'm not sure I can do this anymore.

This is so unfair.

Mom had known about the Red Woman, and she said she was afraid she would use mom to hurt me. Was it the same red-haired woman from my dreams? It had to be. Mom said she was the one, and I believed her. Why didn't I remember this?

I did remember it now that I'd read it. I remembered all the feelings around it — the guilt, fear, shame, and anger. The little hate I felt for Laura and Mrs. Tav. Now I knew they did what they had to do, that mom could have hurt them, me, and herself, but that didn't make it any better. Even the sight of the straps earlier tonight made me feel that same mix of feelings as that day.

Was I the reason she turned violent in the first place?

I shook my head and closed the diary. I knew I would find other entries of her, the Red Woman, in later diaries. That mom had talked about her a little. Sometimes telling me about her, sometimes yelling at her. Every time, I got that feeling of guilt and fear as the day they used the straps for the first time.

Burying my face in my hands, I closed my eyes. I didn't need to read anymore. I knew the woman was there. Like a shadow hovering just outside my field of vision, invisible to everyone other than mom. Why? Because mom was sick and somehow could see her? Or because mom had some kind of... power? Wasn't that what premonitions were? A magical power?

I laughed, but this one wasn't hysterical or hoarse. It was just a helpless laugh because I didn't know what else to do. It sounded like I was in one of those stupid comics Mark liked.

I needed to talk to Mrs. Hearth again.

Without thinking, I stood and found new clothes.

Outside, the world was still dark, but a glance at my phone told me it was close to six in the morning. I didn't even remember turning off the alarm. Mrs. Tav would soon leave. I couldn't go when Mrs. Tav was away, but how could she leave mom the way she was now?

The thought hadn't more than crossed my mind when a car pulled to a stop out front, shortly followed by a door slamming.

28

For a moment I didn't move, then I hurried over to my window. It looked in over the yard so that I wouldn't see anything out on the street, but maybe I could hear something?

As quiet as I could, I opened the window and leaned out. The cold, early morning air hit me square in the face and took my breath away. It smelled of smoke and frost, even some coffee.

I heard the leaves rustling as someone walked over them, breaking them to pieces, then low voices, too low for me to discern the words. Then the front door slammed, I heard it both through the window and behind me in the building.

Closing the window, I slipped inside and walked out of my room.

I was halfway down the first set of stairs when Mrs. Tav rounded the banister below me. She jumped when she saw me, clutching at her chest, but her composure was back in place in seconds.

She kept her voice low as she spoke. "Elizabeth, could you join us?"

"Us?" I asked as I walked down to her. My eyes jumped to mom's room, the door still ajar, and I thought I saw her shape in the bed.

"Yes. I asked for some help today, and Lars came."

"Why?"

"We can talk about it in the kitchen. Let me get you that coffee you have been wanting."

Before I could say anything else, she hurried down the stairs. I followed more slowly

At the bottom of the stairs, in the hallway, stood Lars.

"Why are you here?" I asked.

Lars pulled his hand through his hair: "Mrs. Tav called. She needed help, she said, so I'm here."

He headed toward the kitchen, glancing at me as he passed the stairs.

I hurried after him. "Needed help with what? Mom is sleeping."

Lars held the kitchen door for me. "Yes. Let's just drink that coffee, hmm?"

I stayed just inside the door, fuming. He was talking to me as if I were a child, which was not fair! I was twenty-two years old, hardly a child anymore.

The smell of coffee was strong. Mrs. Tav was pouring it into cups as we entered. She must have put on the kettle before Lars showed up.

Lars pushed out a chair for me, motioning for me to sit before he sat in the chair beside it. I did as well, reluctantly. I felt like I was being kept out of something important. Like they were plotting against me.

Mrs. Tav joined us with the cups, placed one in front of each chair before she sat with her own held between her small hands.

"What is this about?" I asked, not taking my cup.

Lars sipped his, grimaced, and poured in some milk and a little sugar before tasting again. When he lowered the cup this time, he nodded.

"Tell me about last night," he said.

"What about it?" I asked, hearing the anger in my voice.

Lars shrugged. "Mrs. Tav told me we had a situation, with both you and your mother, and that she had some thoughts about today. I want to hear it from your point of view, though, so I can make a better picture of everything and then decide what might be best for Nancy."

The anger grew until I could barely keep it in. He didn't work here anymore. What right had he to choose what was best for mom? What right had he to come in here and tell me what to do?

Forcing down a breath, I lifted my cup and took a long sip. The beverage burned my tongue, but I kept drinking anyway. Needed to calm myself, needed to get control.

When I lowered the cup, I kept my eyes on the last of my coffee and told Lars about the woman I'd seen. Lars and Mrs. Tav stayed quiet, listening and nodding every now and again. I also noticed them exchange glances as I talked, like they had discussed it beforehand.

When I was done, the clock was fifteen-minutes-over-seven in the morning. Mrs. Tav had refilled the cups, and when I drew to the end she stood and started making breakfast.

"Shouldn't you be home?" I asked as she bustled around the kitchen.

"Yes, but I left Henry a message I would be late, or early, all things considered. He won't be up yet anyway."

Henry was her husband. I knew that, but it took me a moment to remember. She seldom told me anything about her personal life.

"Oh." I twirled my cup.

Lars had been looking at me ever since I stopped talking, but he hadn't said anything. His brow was furrowed and he kept chewing at his bottom lip. Now and again, his eyes would glaze over, and he kept stroking his fingertip across the surface of the table. Like he was writing.

Finally, Mrs. Tav put plates of bacon and eggs before us and poured fresh coffee before sitting with us.

Lars sighed as soon as she'd scooted under the table. "Mr. Michaels, our boss, called me last night about what to do with Nancy. You have done a good job taking care of her, as good a job as anyone could expect from someone so young." I bristled. "But after last night... we don't feel comfortable with you having to take care of her after that."

"But she's fine now. She's almost always fine after sleep, as long as we don't start talking about the thing that upset her."

"Yes, I know, but in this case... She became violent toward you."

"No, not me. The Red Woman."

"Who was not there," Mrs. Tav said.

Lars sighed. "I know you love your mother, but as far as we know, you might be her trigger this time. We wouldn't feel safe leaving you two alone. So, I will be staying after Mrs. Tav leaves, and she will return earlier than normal. Have you heard anything from Midnight Sun yet?"

I wanted to argue with Lars staying here, but a part of me was thankful. The part of me that was scared of mom. The part that had made me run a year ago. "No," I finally answered.

He nodded. "I'll make a few calls today, see about that room."

"I haven't been there yet."

"I know, but we're not comfortable with this situation

anymore. We want her in an institute, for her own and everyone else's safety, and Midnight Sun is among the best."

"What about what I want? What mom wants?"

"Nancy is not well, and if you fight us on this I can take it to court. I only want what is best for her, and you, and everyone, and Midnight Sun is the best."

I wanted to fight him. The anger was fizzling inside me, but it was small. I was so tired, and I needed to breathe, and mom… "So, what? You plan for them to come and get her today?"

"I don't think that will be possible, but maybe after the weekend. I will do my best to make this happen quickly." He put down his knife and fork. He and Mrs. Tav had been eating, but I hadn't, now they shared a look. "Until tonight, though, I want to keep your mother sedated and in bed."

I slammed my hands onto the table. "What?!"

"I think sleep will do her good." Mrs. Tav hurriedly said. "She has been restless after you came home. Has not slept well, has been waking a lot."

"You think it's my fault?" I asked.

"Yes," Lars answered. "And I think what is best for her now is being kept in bed. She should be waking around now, so Mrs. Tav will help me get her cleaned up, feed her, and then back to bed again. I want you to stay out of our way while we do this. I don't want her to see you."

"But…"

"Elizabeth, this is what is best for her," Mrs. Tav said.

I wanted to argue, but couldn't. Instead, I stood, food untouched, and walked upstairs. I heard Mrs. Tav and Lars talking in hushed, hurried voices that disappeared as the distance between us grew.

When Mrs. Tav found me, I was standing in mom's doorway,

looking at her and crying.

"I was wondering," I started as Mrs. Tav chased me out of the room and closed the door behind me. "Why are you doing this now? Last night isn't the first time mom has attacked me."

"It's the first time you have instigated the attack. The other times, there was something else. Last night, you were the main cause of the attack."

"So, what's the difference? Why does that matter?"

We were halfway up the stairs, but Mrs. Tav grabbed my arm and forced me to stop. "In light of the incident on the train tracks, it matters."

I pulled my arm from her grasp without looking and hurried up the stairs.

Mrs. Tav followed me up to my bedroom where I grabbed my notes about Connor, pushed my computer into a shoulder bag together with the diaries before she followed me downstairs again. Lars was in the hall outside mom's room. I could hear her moan groggily as we passed. They wouldn't let me see her even to say goodbye. Or more accurate, wouldn't let her see me. I didn't have a choice.

I pulled on my jacket and stuffed my feet into warmer shoes before pulling the scarf, cap, and gloves Mrs. Hearth had knitted for me from the shelf and let Mrs. Tav push me out the door.

I stood on the stoop and listened to her lock the door behind me. She had reassured me she would call when mom was back in bed so I could come home. But I didn't want to come home. I wanted to *be* home. I wanted to help her.

With a sigh, I hugged the diary to my chest, clutched the strap of my shoulder bag with my free hand, and headed toward Mrs. Hearth's place. It was still early, but I could see smoke rising from her chimney.

I concidered taking mom's car to town and shop or something. Shopping for new nail polish always made me feel better, I'd even thrown a few bottles into the bag before being pushed out the door now, but the thought of being around other people didn't sit well with me. I needed answers, and I knew how to get them, I couldn't just push that aside. Not if time was as pressing as the ticking from my chest indicated.

Climbing the stairs to Mrs. Hearth's door, I knocked and heard movement within seconds from the other side. As the door opened, the smell of a wood fire, coffee, toasting bread, cheese, and something sweet baking seemed to hug me.

Mrs. Hearth was dressed and ready as usual, and she didn't look surprised to see me. Instead, she just stepped aside and let me enter. She took my coat and asked if I wanted breakfast. I answered I'd already eaten.

"Join me in the kitchen anyway and tell me your troubles," she said, heading that way without a second glance at me.

I sat down in a chair at her small table as she bustled around before joining me with her own breakfast, setting a plate of cookies between us. At the sight, a sudden rage toward the cookies engulfed me. All these stupid cookies everywhere. Instead of throwing the plate through the room as I wanted, I grabbed one of them and took a bite. The buttery dough and warm chocolate soothed me as soon as it hit my tongue.

Stupid, tasty cookies.

As I ate, I told Mrs. Hearth about everything that had happened. She stopped me when I talked about the new dreams, asked me questions, then sat back as I told her about scaring mom.

"What does it all mean?" I asked when I was done, reaching for my sixth cookie, but stopping it on the way to my mouth. I was starting to feel sick but couldn't stop myself from eating either.

"I think you know what it means," Mrs. Hearth said. She was long done with her breakfast, her coffee cup empty, but she hadn't once stood to clean or refill. I appreciated that.

"Can you tell me?"

"You have to ask the right questions."

When I didn't ask, she stood and started cleaning, giving me time. I crumbled the cookie in my hands, breaking it to pieces and eating only the chocolate chips within. The act of doing something helped.

Mrs. Hearth sat a cup of green tea in front of me before she sat in her chair again.

"What am I? Why do I have these dreams? Why do I hear the ticking? How does mom know of the Red Woman?" I asked.

Mrs. Hearth smiled as she sipped her tea, but it was a tired and sad smile, not reaching her eyes. "Those are the right questions."

"So, what are the answers?"

"What do you know about your family?"

"The Keys? A little, I've got dad's info with me, I thought of calling him, getting more answers."

29

"That is good, but I'm talking about your mother's side of the family."

"She doesn't have any."

"She does. Everyone has a family, their blood comes from somewhere, and sometimes blood is thicker than even our feelings about said families."

"What does that mean?"

"That means you have some of your mother's family in you. What do you know of it?"

I turned the cup of tea between my fingers, a little too sick to the stomach to drink it yet. The steam was calming to look at, however. When I spoke, I didn't look up. "We both have the look of the Natives, so I guess we must have some of that blood in us, not that far back, by how much mom looks it. But usually, First Nation children without parents would be picked up by a tribe. I've read that somewhere, so maybe not? Maybe some other tribal folk from other parts of the world?"

"Or the tribes did not know about your mother when she was a child."

"How is that possible?"

"Her mother may have been white and had a fun night with a native, and made your mother. It is not unheard of, dear." She hurriedly said when I blushed. "That way she may not have known even the name of the father to put on the birth certificate."

"And that way, they may not have known about her, as she kept quiet and just wanted to get through her childhood years. She slipped through their fingers." Even if she researched it, I added to myself, she may never have tried contacting any of the local tribes.

"Yes. Also, considering her grey eyes, her father probably

isn't pureblood either. Maybe he wasn't part of a tribe."

"But what does that have to do with anything?"

"What do you know of ingenious culture in this country? Or any tribal people culture, for that matter?"

I shrugged. "Not much. They worship nature, have shamans and stuff like that. The stuff everyone knows from TV."

She pointed at me and smiled, like a proud teacher. "There you have it."

"What? Worship nature?"

"No, the shaman bit. Shamans are known to commune with spirits, to talk with nature, to help the dead move on."

I laughed. "But that's not real. It's just supernatural mojo."

"So you don't believe in the curse anymore?"

My laughter died. The ticking filled the silence. At least for me, I wasn't sure Mrs. Hearth could hear it.

"So, what," I finally said. "I've got shaman blood or something?"

"I think both you and your mother are shamans."

"Ok," I pulled the word as long as I could, taking my time absorbing what she was saying. "What does that mean?"

"I think your dreams are warnings. Your shaman spirit talking to the spirit of the woman that cursed your family, talking to the spirits of those she have killed. I think the ticking you hear is the spirit of the curse talking to you, maybe even warning you. This is why you had the premonitions about what the curse wanted to do to you when you were a child. This is why you hear the clock of your life. This is why your mother saw the red-haired woman every time the curse almost got you. You probably would have seen her as well if you looked for her, and not been so distracted from the ticking and the upcoming accidents. Not so distracted at keeping yourself and others alive."

I wanted to laugh at what she was saying. Wanted to say she was crazy. That mom was crazy. Even that I was crazy for believing in the curse, to begin with. But I couldn't form the words, couldn't push the air through my throat to laugh. I didn't want to be crazy, better a shaman that was going to die than crazy, but I didn't want to be that either. I didn't want to be here at all. I wanted to be in Toronto, living my life. I wanted mom to be healthy. I wanted some guy in the 1700s to keep his dick in his pants and not scorn the maid.

Instead of the laugh, a sob escaped me, and tears soon followed. I bent over the cup, weeping into it. I was so tired. It was like I was hurting all over.

Mrs. Hearth leaned forward and took my hand. She talked in a low, soothing voice until I calmed down, then she bade me drink my tea, and I did. It roiled in my stomach before settling, pushing the heaviness of the cookies deep down to a place I wouldn't feel them.

"So what do I do?" I asked when I could speak again.

"That is up to you."

"Please," I begged. Fear gripping my heart at the thought of being left alone. "Please help me."

"I'm not a shaman. I don't know how to help you with that."

"But you know the curse. You can help me with that, right? That wasn't put there by a shaman after all, but by a…" A what? A witch? "A woman," I finally said, my voice empty.

Mrs. Hearth was smiling that crooked smile again. "You can say it, dear."

"Say what?"

"That it was put there by a witch."

"Witches don't exist."

"Neither did shamans a few minutes ago, but here you are."

I blinked at her. "So the red-haired woman with the yellow eyes, she's a witch?"

Mrs. Hearth nodded. "The yellowness of her eyes is her using magic."

"How do you know?"

Without saying a word, she leaned forward and put her hand between my breasts. I jerked in surprise, but didn't pull away. Her fingers seemed to burn through the fabric of my shirt. Then her eyes started glowing. It was a muted yellow, more like the moon than the angry yellow of fire I'd seen in the Red Woman's eyes. The warmth spread through my chest, and as it spread it seemed to pull a cold I hadn't even known was there, with it. When Mrs. Hearth pulled her fingers away, it was like she pulled the sadness and insecurity and anger right out of me. It seemed to hover in the air before disappearing like smoke. Her eyes stopped glowing.

"I know because I am a witch myself."

Falling back in my chair, I touched my chest where Mrs. Hearth's fingers had rested just a moment before. It felt like fear was trying to grab hold, but it didn't find anywhere to grow. I wasn't really afraid, just shocked.

"What?" I finally asked.

"I am a witch, as was my mother and her mother before her, and as is my daughters and their daughters will be."

"A witch," I croaked.

"Yes. Like you are a shaman."

"Ok."

"Now, about that curse of yours. Shamans cannot place curses, as far as I know, but witches can. It is hard for the body, and it does something to your blood. It turns you. That is how a dark witch is born. The witch that cursed your family became a dark witch when she placed the curse and probably lost her child because of it."

"Ok," I said again, too stunned to say anything else.

"The reason I mention this, dear, is because the way to break a curse is by using the blood of the one that placed it. But if the witch lost her child from placing the curse, which I think she did, there is no guarantee she has any descendants."

"Ok."

"I started looking when you came home. I talked to my coven and asked them to ask others. We are looking, but I am not sure we have the time."

"They haven't found anything?"

"No."

"Ok." I tasted the finality in that ok. I was going to die. I was sure of that now. After dreaming the next dream, the last Elizabeth, I would die before my next sleep. I wanted to weep but was all dried out. "So what do I do?"

"There are ways to freeze a curse for a while, but it is not a solution, and I don't think it will help you."

"Why?"

"Because I have never tried my potions on a shaman before. You are a rare breed. The fact that both you and your mother have the powers is amazing. It does not always breed true."

"Breed true?"

"Not everyone born of the blood has the powers."

"Ok."

"I would think other shamans would feel your powers, actually, but maybe they are so far away they don't notice, or they think you are in a tribe, as you are together and of the same blood. Or maybe they are not like witches at all and cannot sense each other that way."

"Ok." I was starting to hate that word.

Mrs. Heart was looking at me but not saying anything. Her brows furrowed, her lips pressed thin. It was easy to see she was thinking. I wanted to know what was on her mind. The quiet made the ticking so much more prominent, and I didn't like listening to it.

"So what do I do?" I asked after what felt like forever.

"I don't know, dear. I am not sure how I can help you."

"Ok."

"Stop saying ok."

"Ok."

"Lizzie…"

"O… I'm sorry. Fine. But I really don't know what else to say. It's all so much. I'm not even sure I believe it. But if I don't, I'm crazy, and I don't want to be crazy. I don't know, ok? I don't know."

"Ok, dear"

I grinned at her, and she cracked a half-smile in return. I could taste the desperation in the air between us.

"Should I try calling Connor?"

"You don't call him dad anymore?"

"No. He has another kid to call him that."

"Oh."

"Yeah."

"Are you ok?"

That hysterical laugh escaped me. It was almost like a friend now. "Yeah, I'm ok. Why shouldn't I be? I mean, my mom is sick and we need to have her committed before she hurts anyone. My dad has made a new family while his oldest daughter is trying so hard to help his wife. He sends money, though, what a Good Samaritan he is. So he knocks another woman up, making the curse live even longer. At the same time, that curse is about to kill me. And there is a curse, and witches are real, and I'm a shaman, and so is mom, and the ghost of a wronged dark witch is haunting me. Yeah, I'm fine."

My voice grew in volume with each word until I was almost screaming the words. Mrs. Hearth sat quiet, unfazed by my outburst.

"Drink your tea," she said, still calm.

I scowled at her but drank the tea and immediately felt calmer. Was this a potion? She said she wasn't sure how the potions worked on a shaman. Maybe that was why her sleeping potion hadn't helped me the other night?

"No, dear. I don't think Connor can help you. I will contact him and give him a proper flogging, though."

"You will?"

"Oh yes. Men at that age, I swear. They are like teenagers all over again."

I laughed, but it wasn't as hysterical this time. It was more hollow, almost not real. "My boyfriend isn't like that."

"Good." Her eyes fell to my hands. "But if you want to talk with your father, you should call him before you go to sleep today."

"Why?"

Her eyes were sad. "Because I am not sure how I can help you."

"Ok."

We didn't say anything else. Her words were slowly sinking in. She couldn't help me. I was probably going to die. Maybe tonight, surely tomorrow. There wasn't any question about it anymore. It felt right. I was going to die, and there was nothing anyone could do to help me.

I was still sitting curled up in Mrs. Hearth's living room when a car stopped outside.

"Your man is here, dear," said Mrs. Hearth from where she stood by the windows, looking at the street.

"Yeah," I answered flatly, pushing up from the sofa.

"What will you do?"

"I don't know. Just... be with him, I guess."

Mrs. Hearth left the window and walked to me. "I wish there was something I could do."

"Yeah," I answered, letting her wrap me in a hug. I could feel her heart beating through her entire body and into mine. "So do I."

I pushed away from her, unable to look her in the eye.

She followed me into the hallway and watched as I got dressed. As I tied my shoes, she opened the door. A cold blast of autumn air rushed through it, hitting me in the face. I pulled it into my lungs, hoping the cold would shock me back to caring, but nothing happened. So I stood and walked out.

As I passed her, Mrs. Hearth grabbed my hand. I forced myself to turn to her, feeling something heavy move in my chest. "Keep your phone on, dear. I may still be able to help."

"Don't," I said, wrapping my hand around hers and squeezing. "Don't try to give me hope when you just crushed it. Please."

"Lizzie –"

"No. Just let me go, ok?"

Tears were forming in Mrs. Hearth's eyes, and she looked at me like she'd never see me again. Maybe she wouldn't.

Without another word, I pulled my hand from hers and looked away.

Mark was standing at the curb in front of my house where I'd asked him to wait. He turned as I walked down the porch from Mrs. Hearth's front door. He smiled as he saw me, but it was soon replaced by a frown as his eyes wandered to the house behind me.

Wrapping me in his arms, he kissed me on the nose. I buried my face against his chest. Without a word, I wrapped my hand with his and pulled him down the street. He followed, keeping pace with me so he wouldn't be left behind. I only glanced over my shoulder once, looking at Mrs. Hearth's house. She was standing on the porch, arms wrapped around herself, crying. I prayed Mark hadn't seen and walked a little faster.

On the other side of Mrs. Hearth's neighbor, I turned and walked along a small path moving between two hedges. This was where my family's land stopped, and the house owners lived on their own land. I'd discovered the shortcut when I was a kid and showed it to the other kids in the neighborhood. It didn't look like many used it anymore, for wilted brambles seemed to be everywhere. I pushed through them, not letting go of Mark.

"Where are we going?" he asked as he moved to keep up with me.

"Just someplace where we can be alone," I answered. He

didn't ask anymore.

Through the wilted hedges, I could see the fence at the end of one piece of land. A few steps more and I saw the other fence. Our part of properties stretched a little farther than the self-owned, and so there wasn't room for much at their backs. Another house sprang up on my right, another self-owned piece of land, but on my left were woods. Thin and scraggly in the autumn, but still there. I followed the path until the end and walked onto the curb on another street. The houses here weren't Victorian in style but typical Canadian homes. The little piece of forest stretched along the road on our side, down until the road took a turn. There was a small playground for the neighborhood kids, and that was where I was headed.

The gate squealed as I pushed it open, but I didn't care. Mark closed it as he walked in behind me and I let his hand go. The sudden cold of that move sent a shiver through me, but I suppressed it and headed for the swing set, sitting down on one of them.

Mark walked slower, looking around. The forest pressed at the fence at the back of the grounds, stretching all the way to the next neighborhood. It was the same forest I'd driven through to get home.

"Was this place here when you were a kid?" Mark asked as he sat down on the other swing. He pushed back and forth a little with his feet, building momentum.

"Yes. But they've redone it some since then. That jungle gym wasn't here when I was little, and they changed out the swing set after the old one fell apart."

"Pretty neat."

We sat in silence for a while, the only sound Mark's swing as it groaned with his movement.

"So what's going to happen to your mom now?" he asked after a while.

"Lars is looking at getting her into Midnight Sun faster. Trying to push it and stuff, but they probably won't do anything until next week."

"And until then?"

I shrugged. "Keep her drugged, I guess? I really don't know."

Silence again. Mark let his speed die until he was sitting beside me. "And what will you do?"

I could feel his eyes on me but couldn't look at him, so I shrugged instead. "Dunno. I can't go back to Toronto until this is over, at least."

"And after that?"

I couldn't answer. There would be no after. This was probably my last day alive.

That heavy thing in my chest moved again, and I drew a shuddering breath.

"Hey, it's going to be ok," Mark said, mistaking my ragged breathing for tears.

Mark stood from his swing and walked over to me, pulling me to my feet and wrapping his arms around me. Restlessness moved in my stomach, and I pushed away from him. Let my hands slide up his back and to his neck, his hair. He looked at me, just a little taller than me, and I leaned into him and kissed him. He kissed me back. I parted my lips, wanting to take him in and pushed up against him, grinding. I wanted to use him to forget, like last night.

"Lizzie," he whispered against my lips. I kissed deeper, pushed harder, tried to make him shut up. He kissed me back, wrapped me in his arms, and for a moment I did forget before he pushed me away. "Lizzie, what's going on?"

I pulled all the way from him, turned my back on him and walked to the jungle gym. He was right behind me, his feet sinking into the sand that covered the ground.

"Lizzie, talk to me."

I climbed onto the jungle gym, sat on top of it and looked across the street to the houses there. Many looked empty at this time of day. The occupants at work and school, but I could hear a dog barking in one of them. A cat was sitting on a fence, staring back at me.

"Lizzie." Mark was beside me, sitting as close as he could on the bars of the gym. "Please, tell me what's going on."

I couldn't tell him everything. Couldn't tell him why Mrs. Hearth was crying when we left. Couldn't tell him why I wasn't able to look at him. If I told him everything, he would try to talk me out of it. Would call me crazy, or sick, or he would do everything he could to keep me alive. He would stir the fear that had finally died in my stomach until it blazed hot yet again. Then I would be afraid to die, and I didn't want to die in fear. I just had to get through today and tonight, and if I survived until the day after tomorrow, then it would all have been for nothing. It would all have been a bad dream, and I could forget everything about the Red Woman and the Elizabeths and everything. I could go back to my life.

Mark had taken the risk of falling through the bars and was sitting against me, his arms wrapped around me, smelling my hair.

"You're scaring me," he whispered against my head, and I leaned into him. This way, I didn't have to look at him.

"It's Connor," I managed to say. Not a lie. What would happen to mom if I died? Would he pull the money he used to support her treatment? Would he take back the house? I started shaking.

"Maybe you should just call him now?"

"What?"

"We talked about calling him tonight, right? But I'm here now, and this way, you'll get it over with."

I sat for a long moment, just leaning against him. Feeling his heat creep into me, feeling how his breath made my hair move. It made me feel both restless and safe. The safety came from the known, the fact that I knew Mark and his body and his mind. The restlessness was also part of that. The things about him that I didn't like. The things I'd really noticed for the first time yesterday. How he flung the word crazy around. How he forgot about a part of me. How he didn't listen. But despite that, he was safe, and I knew that I finally had the security I needed to call Connor.

"Ok," I breathed, pulling my phone from the jacket pocket where I'd stashed it as I left Mrs. Hearth's place. "Ok," I said again, finding the info I'd saved.

"Key-Melman resident, Catherina speaking."

Everything was silent. My head and my voice. Everything I'd thought to say dried up as if it had never even been there.

"Hello?" the woman said, voice uncertain now.

I cleared my throat. "Yes, hello." She breathed in relief. "Is Connor home?"

"Yes, just a moment. Who should I say it's from?"

"Lizzie."

The woman, Catherina, gave no indication she knew who I was, but gave a chirping ok and put the phone down. I just sat there, listening to a child babbling somewhere on the other end. Mark stroked my hand and I jumped, having almost forgotten he was there. I leaned into him.

Someone breathed heavily on the other end of the line. "Lizzie?"

The voice stabbed me in the chest and I had to draw my own deep breath.

"Lizzie, are you there?" Connor asked again.

"Yes," I finally managed.

The line was silent for a moment. "Can I... Is it Nancy?"

A glow of anger burst to life in my stomach, but I kept it there. I wouldn't give him the pleasure of knowing he got to me.

"What happens to mom is none of your business," I answered, voice even and cold. "You lost that right when you left."

"Lizzie, I –"

"No, you listen to me. Honestly, I'm not really sure why I called, it's clear you've started a new life." Mark squeezed my hand again, reminding me to stay calm, to not give Connor my feelings. I closed my eyes. "I need some answers."

"Anything."

"What really happened with aunt Ellie?"

Mark moved beside me, trying to meet my eye but I didn't look at him.

"She drowned," Connor answered, voice cold.

"Just drowned?"

"Yes. Lizzie, what is this about?"

"Why didn't you want me to be named Elizabeth?"

He was silent, but I heard movement on the other end. Like he was walking. A door closed, and the babble of the child and Catherina grew muffled.

"I don't understand," he finally answered.

"Don't play dumb with me. At least give me the courtesy of being honest. That's the least you could do."

"Lizzie." It was the exasperated voice he'd used on me when I was a child and pestered him about something I wanted or something I didn't understand. Before he'd left, when he used that voice on me, I reverted to a three-year-old child that had gone too far. Not anymore.

"Don't. You knew. Maybe you didn't believe it, but some part of you knew. That was why you didn't want mom to name me after aunt Ellie. You let her anyway, I don't know why, but you let her. What happens is just as much your fault as hers." My voice grew thick with tears and I blinked hard to keep them from falling.

"Now, you listen here," he started the moment I stopped to draw breath. His voice was angry now. I could almost feel the emotion vibrate through the phone. "You will not speak to your father this way. Especially not about something as stupid as that... that... curse." He spat the last word like it tasted foul.

"Oh, yes I will," I snarled back, tears and sadness forgotten. "If this is my last night, then I can speak to you as I damned well please. Why should I even spend this time on you? It's not like –"

"Elizabeth Key, that's –"

"No! No, it's not enough! I won't have you telling me what I can and can't do anymore! You've always done that. Tried to get mom and me to fit in a set, but we never did, did we?"

"What are you insinuating?"

"I don't really know, but I've had it. You always wanted something from mom and me that we couldn't give, and it destroyed us. You destroyed us."

"Is that truly what you think I did to you?"

His voice was calm now. Not hurt, as I'd tried to. Not angry, like I'd hoped. It was empty, and for some reason, that was so much worse.

"Honestly, I don't know and I don't care," I said.

"So, what do you care about?"

"Mom."

"Ok, so is there something I can do for the two of you?"

His calm voice was not what I'd expected, but now that I'd moved over the first shock of it, I was getting angry again, so I snarled into the phone.

"Officially give me the house. Sell it to me, give it to me, I don't care, but I want it. You left it behind, just as much as you left us. You have no right to it anymore. Everything that belongs to it as well. It should be mine by right, not that other daughter of yours. She is, after all, born out of wedlock."

He drew a sharp breath. What? Did he think I wouldn't know? How did he think I found him?

"By the way, congratulations, good thing it wasn't a boy, right?"

"Lizzie," he began, but I kept talking.

"Please don't. I'm glad you moved on, really. I've lived a whole life since you left that I'm glad I got the chance to experience. Even with all the bad, which bring us back to aunt Ellie and my name."

"This is not something we should talk about over the phone." He was using his business voice now, and I wasn't sure if I should be sad or happy he decided he had to treat me as an equal rather than as his daughter.

"I don't think I have much of a choice."

He gave a dry laugh that sounded forced. "You don't truly believe it, do you? You don't think a curse will kill you?"

"Why shouldn't I believe it? Some strange stuff has been happening, and mom has been saying some thi –"

"Are you taking her word over mine? That woman is sick, Elizabeth, you can't believe what she says."

"That woman," I spat back, "is my mother, and she's been more honest with me than you ever were. Even if she's sick now, she isn't making any of this stuff up. She told me about the voices, about how afraid you were for aunt Ellie's life when you were younger. So, if you were really so afraid your sister would die from a curse, how could you name your own daughter by the name that was said to trigger the curse?"

For a long moment, silence reigned over the phone. Mark had moved his hands to my shoulders and was squeezing them. For a heartbeat, I wondered what he thought of this conversation, at least the part he could hear. I hadn't planned to talk so openly about the curse, but Connor got under my skin. And, I noticed, I didn't care.

Finally, as I began to fear he'd hung up, Connor spoke: "Because your mother said it wouldn't kill you."

"What?"

"Nancy... she said she could protect you, somehow. That such a curse couldn't get her baby bird." My mouth was open, but I couldn't find any words. If this was true, then why had mom said she would kill me later on? "Happy now?" Connor said. "Did you get what you want?"

I licked my lips, trying to moisten my mouth enough to speak again. "No," I croaked. "You didn't promise me the house."

"Elizabeth..."

"Don't Elizabeth me. I asked for the house, but you didn't promise it to me. I want it."

"Why?"

"So mom has somewhere to stay if something should happen to me. No matter what mom said when I was a baby, you should have known better. My blood will be on your hands if something happens, no matter what you tell yourself."

Before he could say anything else, I hung up the phone. For a heartbeat, all I heard was the rustling of the wind through the trees behind me. The phone started ringing in my hand, and I stared down at the number I'd just called. A sob clawed its way up my throat, and I slumped against Mark's chest.

He didn't say anything. Didn't ask anything about my

questions to Connor, but I could feel them hanging in the air beside us. Instead of asking, he took the phone from my hands and turned it off before wrapping one arm around me and letting me cry it out.

33

Mark held me until I stopped crying. When my sobs died, he let his arm fall from my shoulders and leaned back, his body stiff against mine.

"You want to tell me what that was about?" he asked, his voice heavy with feelings, but I couldn't tell which ones.

"What was what about?" I asked, not moving.

"That talk? With your father? There was a lot there I haven't heard anything about."

The emotions in his voice became clearer now. Part of it was anger. Another part was disgust.

"You remember I asked you about magic yesterday?" Yesterday, I'd been afraid of what he would say, but that feeling of not caring was still heavy in my chest. Whatever he said, whatever he called me, it didn't matter anymore.

"Yes."

"The reason for that is because I think there's a curse on my family. A curse that will kill me soon."

He stopped breathing for a second. "Ok. And where did you get this idea?"

"Mom and Mrs. Hearth."

"The old lady you were with just now?"

I nodded and pushed away from him, sitting up and looking

at nothing. His leg was still touching mine, and it was vibrating with tension.

"Yes."

A long moment passed.

"Ok," he repeated and sat up, wrapping one arm around me again. It felt tense and unnatural, but he still did it.

"You really believe me?"

"No." My heart sank. Ok, I cared a little. "I don't believe in magic or curses, and neither do you. I do believe in the effects of stress on the psyche, and you've been under a lot of stress for the last week. I believe you're exhausted and that you need help." I tried to push away from him, opened my mouth to deny it, but he tightened his arm and talked over me. "What you're calling a curse sounds a lot like depression, and the talk of it killing you makes me think you're suicidal. I love you and want to take care of you, so I will stick with you through this and get you the help you need. But that means we're going back to Toronto as soon as your mother is committed, and I'm not leaving you alone until then."

"That's not what's going on!" I said, still trying to push away from him. "Why can't you just listen to what I have to say for once and believe me?"

"I believe you, Lizzie. I believe you're sick."

I wanted to scream at him, to rage, but I was too tired. Instead, I leaned against him again. What did it matter? Come tomorrow, he would know that it wasn't just depression. I would be dead. And if I wasn't? Well, then I'd let him take care of me. He loved me, after all. What did it matter what I felt, if it wasn't real anyway?

We just sat there, watching the street. Saw families coming home from work and school. Heard that dog again, barking happily as its pack returned. Soon, the scent of dinner was on the air and Mark's stomach growled.

I giggled, unable to help myself, and the sound broke the spell we were under.

Mark moved away from me, and I stretched my back, hearing it pop in the cold, quiet air.

"When can we go back to your place?"

I checked my phone. It was half-past-five. "Now? Mom is probably still asleep. Why?"

"Because you need to rest, and you do that best in your own bed."

I wanted to argue that I was fine, but sighed. "I can go in and check beforehand to make sure."

Mark only nodded. His eyes were heavy with concern, and I knew the conversation about my psyche wasn't forgotten and probably never would be.

Not meeting his eyes, I climbed down from the gym. He took my hand, and I squeezed it before walking home, following the same route we'd taken to get to the playground. The sun was as good as gone, but we weren't alone on the street. People were walking their dogs, some with their whole family in tow, others alone. I greeted some of them, and they greeted me back. I saw that a couple of the older people wanted to stop and talk, but I couldn't bring myself to any more than a greeting, so I pulled Mark along.

At home, I pulled the keys from my pocket. "Stay here," I told Mark as I unlocked the door and slipped through.

Inside I could hear voices coming from the kitchen. Pulling off my outer clothes and walking as quietly as I could, I snuck forward. My first thought was that the voices were Mrs. Tav's radio, but no. It was her and Lars.

"... anything," Lars said.

"I'm not surprised," Mrs. Tav answered.

"I know you don't agree with me, but you've got to admit something is off."

"There are many things we do not know about Nancy's past, Lars. Some of the things she says, some of the things you are so hung up on, may have a natural explanation. The only one that can tell is Nancy, and I do not want to push that on her good days."

"Fine, but what about Lizzie? You have to agree she's falling apart?"

"Of course she is! You have seen what is going on with her mother, and she is all alone with her care, and she is so young. How would you react if this happened to you?"

"That's not what I'm talking about."

I pushed through the door. "Hey."

Lars jumped a little where he sat in his chair. Mrs. Tav was by the fridge, putting something away, not seeming surprised at all.

"Hello, Elizabeth. How was your day?" she said, shooting Lars a look. He wasn't looking at me.

"Ok. I was at Mrs. Hearth's, and then my boyfriend came over."

"Really?"

"Yes. He's outside. I was wondering if mom was still asleep so I could sneak him up."

Lars cleared his throat. "Are you sure that's such a good idea?"

No. "Yeah. I'll sneak him up and hide him in my room. Mom will be too drugged to even think about going upstairs, right?" My voice was odd and sharp, even if I tried to joke about it.

Honestly, it wasn't funny, but I didn't want to spend my last night alive fighting with Mark, or to care about prosperity.

Lars looked away, guilt on his face. I felt a small stab of satisfaction at that.

"Most likely. Remember to eat," Mrs. Tav said. Her eyes were as calculating as ever, but there was something there that I couldn't remember her ever looking at me with. Warmth, maybe?

"Yeah, thanks. Do we have any pizzas?"

Mrs. Tav guffawed. "I will take a look. Take the boyfriend upstairs, and I will bring up the pizza when it is ready. Nancy should be waking soon."

"Thanks."

I left the kitchen, not looking at either of them. I wasn't sure what I'd heard. Was Lars claiming I was going crazy too? But Mrs. Tav didn't think so. At least not that mom was crazy. Me, though? I didn't know. I'd interrupted them before she could answer. Hadn't been able to hear more. What if they were right? What if there was no curse and I was just crazy?

I shook away the thought and opened the door. Mark was leaning against the wall, looking at the street. Mr. Norris was standing on his porch on the other side of the road, arms crossed and looking at Mark. I gave the older man a wave, and he grudgingly waved back before I pulled Mark inside.

"Don't mess with Mr. Norris. He's an old Green Cap."

"Really?"

"Yeah. He's the bane of any young punk walking these streets. Come on, mom's still asleep but won't be for long. We should get you hidden away. Mrs. Tav will bring some food so we won't starve."

He gave a small nod and pulled off his jacket. I pulled off my shoes and put away his as he stepped out of them.

I took his hand. "This way."

I pulled him along as he looked around, wonder in his eyes. Up the stairs and almost onto the next flight when I stopped. Mom's bedroom door was fully open.

"Lizzie?" Mark whispered in my ear.

"Yeah, I just need to do something. Head up the stairs. It's the door with tape on it."

"Why tape?"

I forced a smile. "I used to have a poster there. Just go."

He gave me a worried look before letting my hand go and moving away.

As soon as he was up the stairs and out of sight, I turned toward mom's room again.

After standing there for almost a minute, I walked inside and turned on the light. I heard Mrs. Tav walk out of the kitchen downstairs, so I closed the door behind me. When I turned, I couldn't look at mom right away. I didn't want to leave her. I wanted to help her. But I'd done all I could do. At least she wouldn't grieve me. She wouldn't even know I was dead. To her, I would always be her little bird.

Mrs. Tav had cleaned up the coffee and cup from the floor and wall. I studied the clean spots a long time before I was able to look directly at mom.

Her hair was shiny and pulled back in a loose braid. Her arms were lying on top of her covers, and I could see that Mrs. Tav had dressed her in the yellow PJ I'd gotten her last Christmas. The sight of it made my chest hurt.

"Oh, mom," I breathed. When she didn't answer, I walked to her bed and sat at her side.

I reached forward and brushed her cheek. She smiled in her

sleep and turned her head into my touch.

Still looking at her calm face, I took her hand. Absentmindedly, I fiddled with her wrist cuff, tearing at the fabric until I couldn't stand it anymore and pushed it under the duvet, out of sight.

I wanted to remember her asleep and at peace.

After a long time, the door creaked open behind me. "Elizabeth?" Mrs. Tav asked in a low voice.

I stiffened, afraid the use of that name would wake mom, but she kept sleeping.

"Yeah," I said, wiping my face for any tears before giving mom's hand a final squeeze. For a second, it felt like she squeezed back, but when I looked at her face, she was still asleep. I stood and walked to the door.

Mrs. Tav gave me a sympathetic look, but when she opened her mouth to say something, I turned away from her. This wasn't part of the plan.

A tray was standing at the table by her chair. Two glass bottle cokes and multiple slices of pizza rested on top of two plates. She'd even remembered some of the seasonings I liked on pizza.

"Thanks," I said, not looking at her as I grabbed the tray and headed up the stairs.

34

Usually, the bed was soft. I normally sank into it, as if into warm water, and felt a little like I thought it must feel to be in Heaven. Not today. Today, the covers scratched my skin until it burned. This must be Hell, I was thinking now.

It had not been Hell. Not when it started.

I had felt the weak pain in my stomach since waking up and told my maidservant about it. She said it was the early signs of labor. She had seen it in her mother and sister enough times. I knew that. I had seen it in them myself. I had envied them every time. I always wanted my own child. I wanted to feel the joy of giving something life, something of me, the way my mother had given me, and I had seen my mother's servants do multiple times in my life.

My maidservant was just a few years older than me and had been with me my whole life. Now, she would be with me as I brought my first child into this world, and I was so happy to share this with her.

It had started as Heaven.

That felt long ago. I knew it had been almost two days. Two days since the pains started.

The maidservant had run for the midwife as the other servants got everything ready. My water had not yet broken when the midwife arrived with her apprentice, but that was ok, she said. It gave us time to prepare.

The pains got worse around lunch, and my water fell just before dinner, tinged with blood. I had been in Hell ever since.

Joseph was outside the door. I could hear him walking back and forth, back and forth, murmuring to his sister or someone else that also cared for me.

Then his steps slowed and I heard a new female voice. Fear gripped my heart and twisted. I screamed as another wave of labor pain shot through me at the same time.

"S'il vous plait," I begged, unable to remember the proper English word.

The midwife patted my leg and pulled up my dress to look. She gasped.

"Quelle?" My maidservant asked, too worried to speak English herself, and pushed the midwife aside. I could see the top of her forehead as it grew pale, and she took two steps away from me. The midwife waved her apprentice over and gave the girl a low command before walking briskly toward the door.

"What?" Finding the English words were hard, but I managed to asked the apprentice as she motioned for me to drink. "What is it?"

"I cannot say, milady. Please drink something. It will help."

"Not before you tell me what it is!"

I tried to sit up but could not move my body without pain. The door was ajar, and I could hear voices but not the words.

"Joseph!" I screamed. "Joseph, what is happen –"

My question was cut off by another wave of pain and I screamed as my body ripped in half.

When my scream died, the sound of a scuffle outside the door *pulled my attention.*

"...be here," Joseph was saying to someone. "Get her out and make sure she does not return!"

I could see his back through the crack in the door, and hear someone talking low and fast, then Joseph turned and pushed into the room. He opened his mouth, about to say something, when someone yelled in the hallway. He had barely turned when a woman crashed into him, throwing him against the door and into the room. She had wild red hair and almost glowing yellow eyes.

I gasped in fear, grabbing at my stomach to protect it.

I had seen this woman, this girl, before. She showed up shortly after Joseph and I were married. She was pregnant, claiming it was Joseph's child. She was not pregnant now. Her body showed no signs of the child she carried back then.

"You," she hissed before her eyes fell to the blood on the covers, and her sneer turned to a smirk. "You are Elizabeth Eleanor MacKey, and my curse is complete." She spun on Joseph as he pushed off the door, servants flanking him. She pointed at him and laughed. "You did this to her, to me! You took my child from me, and now I am taking yours."

The servants rushed forward, grabbing her, and she laughed and laughed as they pulled her out. Just before the door closed between us, she turned and stabbed those yellow eyes into me.

"This is his fault, you know. All his fault," she spat toward Joseph.

I did not see what happened next, as another wave of pain almost made me lose consciousness. It felt like the scream ripping from me lasted...

...forever.

I clapped hands over my own mouth to still the screaming,

but nothing happened. It wasn't coming from me.

Then another yell was heard, and the scream stopped.

It came from within the house.

I didn't think, too afraid and tired to even consider the fact that I was still alive, that the ticking was almost deafening, that Mark was tossing beside me and sighing in his sleep. I just pushed out of bed and sprang through the door.

Someone was moving on the floor below and I rushed down the stairs, almost stumbling when I tried to stop before reaching the landing.

Mom was standing at the foot of the stairs. She had blood on her fingers and leached into the yellow fabric of her PJs at her wrists and ankles. Behind her, on the floor with the table lamp by her head, was Mrs. Tav. She wasn't moving.

35

"Mrs. Tav? Mom, what's going on?"

I took the last few steps and stopped two steps above her, one hand clutching the banister. Something felt wrong.

"Mom?"

It didn't look like she heard me. She only stood there, her hair hanging like a curtain in front of her bowed face, breathing heavily.

I let the banister go and reached for her. "Mom?"

My fingers were centimeters from her face when she exhaled. The breath made her hair puff into my fingertips.

She moved so fast I didn't even have time to think. With a shriek, she jumped forward, bloody fingers shooting for my face.

I stumbled back, hitting the banister with my shoulders and gasping at the sudden pain. My gasp was cut short by mom's fingers closing around my throat.

My hands flew up and grabbed at her wrists. They were so thin I was afraid of breaking them, but I couldn't breathe. I tried pulling at them, but she wasn't letting go, and my fighting only made her dig in harder.

I could hardly see her through the hair. Just her mouth, snarling. The hard wood was digging into my skin, hurting.

The ticking filled my ears, almost drowning out the *thump thump thump* of my heart. Using one foot, I pushed away from the banister, pushing mom with me.

We almost toppled down the last steps, but mom spun me around, like we were dancing, and slammed me up against the wall beside the stairs. I couldn't breathe. My vision was becoming splotchy, dark fog creeping in, creeping around mom.

I blinked and focused on her. The struggle had thrown her hair out of her face so I could see her eyes. Something red reflected in them.

"M...mom," I croaked, barely audible, digging my fingers into her wrists, feeling the blood on them make my own skin slick, but there was no strength left in my muscles. I was empty.

My legs gave way less than a second after my grip faltered from her wrists, and I slumped. Mom slumped with me, and we sat down on the floor — her pushing me up against the wall, cutting off my breath, crying and whispering something.

"No!"

Mark sprinted down the stairs and crashed into mom, throwing her off me. I gasped for air, filling my lungs and coughing all at the same time. Blinking away tears, I looked around.

Mom and Mark were entangled at the edge of the stairs. Mom was snarling like an animal, her hair wild around her face, her fingers clawing at Mark's eyes. Mark was trying to hold her off of me, but she kept slipping out of his hands. She wasn't looking at him, though, she was looking at me. Or something behind me.

Still heaving for breath, I turned my head. My shadow stretched across the wall, bigger than it should be, and it blinked with yellow eyes. A shadow can't smile, but I swore this one did.

Someone thumped to the floor, and I turned just in time to see Mark thrown toward the stairs.

I tried to scream, but my throat was too raw. Scuttling across the floor, I tried to reach him before he started falling, but I was too late. He tumbled down the stairs and crashed into the grandfather clock on the landing below. Sliding to the floor, he left a smear of blood on the wall where his head had hit.

I pushed to my feet, but before I was completely standing, mom was there again. She grabbed my hair and pulled, one of her clawed hands reaching for my throat. I tried to tear away from her, but she had a grip long before I even realized what was happening. Her painted nails dug into my skin until it broke.

"You can't have her," mom said as she pushed me back against the wall, leaning into my face. "You can't have my baby bird."

I couldn't see her anymore. The dark fog from my dreams was covering everything. The fog with the yellow eyes. That was stupid. Fog didn't have eyes. Mom had yellow eyes, but that wasn't right either. Her eyes were grey. What was she saying? Why was she holding my throat like that? Why couldn't I move? What was she saying? Singing? Was she singing? No, not singing, chanting... something... what?

I couldn't move anything anymore, couldn't see anything except the dark, and couldn't feel anything either, but I could hear. The ticking was winding down together with my heartbeat, and mom's words seemed to creep in between the sounds, like water through cracks, filling up the silence.

"You can't have my child, you demon. You can't have her,

even if I have to kill you to keep her safe. My baby bird will be safe from you. You can't have my child. You can't have her. You can – "

Her voice was cut off by something breaking inside me, and then I heard nothing, felt nothing, smelled nothing. Couldn't move, couldn't breathe, wasn't... alive.

36

I never believed in life after death. I thought that when you died, it was like going to sleep and then there was nothing. It's a bit hard to wrap my mind around, even if I believe it, so I don't think about it much. The point is, I never believed in life after death. Not until mom got sick and I started hoping she would get another chance in a new life or an afterlife, but even then I didn't really believe.

The last few days may have changed my mind. The ghost of a scorned woman was going to kill me, and I believed that. I was ready for her to kill me, to die, but I always thought that when I died, it would be over. It would be me, darkness, nothing, and a deep sleep with no thoughts or memories or dreams or anything.

I was wrong.

I can't speak for people dying from natural causes. All I know is that people that are killed by family curses don't end up alone, and they don't end up in nothingness or darkness either.

The first thing I saw as I woke was a grey fog, almost black in some places. I moved to sit up but noticed that I was already standing. Floating would be more like it. I was floating in a kind of fog, and I was naked. The only thing I could feel was a push on my throat, like someone was squeezing it, but I knew I didn't need air here. Still, it was uncomfortable.

Then I noticed the others.

The woman beside me looked like me, but not in the obvious ways. She was pale where I was tan. She had blond hair reaching to the middle of her back where I had shorter, black hair. But our eyes and noses were the same. Even without the likeness, I would recognize aunt Ellie anywhere.

The woman beside her was our age. She had short brown hair, and she had a little more color than aunt Ellie. Like she'd loved working in the sun. Her stomach had a pregnant look to it, but I knew there was no baby there. It had been born just before she died.

Next to her was a little girl. She had golden ringlets spilling over her pointy, cream-colored shoulders, and her eyes were big and blue.

Beside her stood four children.

The first one was also the youngest, maybe six years old with blond curls spilling across her pale shoulders and the biggest blue eyes I'd ever seen.

The oldest of the children came next, and she was in her early teens, with ashen hair and pale green eyes and freckles on her torso and face. She was hugging two young children to her, a boy and a girl, with the same color hair but with brown eyes and no freckles. I recognized those twins.

Farthest away from me was a woman a little older than myself. Her blond hair hung in weak waves around her face and down her back, and she was heavily pregnant. They were all as naked as me.

They were all looking at me with sadness in their eyes, the youngest crying.

"I'm so sorry," aunt Ellie said, at the same time as she didn't say it. I saw her mouth move, but the grey fog swallowed the words. I heard them inside my head.

"What is this place?" I asked.

"This is the place where she keeps her trophies," the pregnant Elizabeth said with a heavy French accent. "This is where she comes to gloat while she waits for another to be cursed."

"What? She's real?"

"As real as us, here, and real to the cursed, but not real in any other way."

"That makes no sense."

"We know," aunt Ellie said, smiling a small smile. "But that is our lives... or deaths, now."

As she said it, I noticed the cut on her wrist. It wasn't bleeding, but the skin was pulled back, showing flesh. Her hair was moving as if she was underwater, and now and again water dribbled from her nose and mouth. I looked down the line and saw the way of death in each of them. Saw the blood glistening between the legs of the two that had died giving birth. The youngest Elizabeth turned so I could see her bashed in head, and the three children that had been killed by the flames had shadows of fire dancing across their skin, never resting.

"So what now?"

"Now we wait for her to return."

"What then?"

"Then we wait for the next cursed child to be born, and her game stars all over aga –"

The pregnant Elizabeth's words were cut short by a scream that seemed to shake even the quiet greyness that trapped us. It was a scream filled with sorrow and rage and fear, and I recognized it as mom's voice.

"Mom," I whispered, looking around. I couldn't move much. It was like something was holding me in place, but of what I could see, mom wasn't here.

"That's new," aunt Ellie said beside me, and one of the other Elizabeth's asked something, but I wasn't listening.

"Mom?" My voice, like the others, was swallowed by the greyness, and I wasn't sure the others could hear something not directed at them, but I had to try anyway. "Mom!"

I pulled against the powers holding me. I needed to get to her. I couldn't be dead. She couldn't have killed me. It would kill her. It would hurt so many. If I'd died any other way, that would be fine, but not like this. Not by her hands.

I cursed under my breath.

From deep within the fog, ticking started.

The other Elizabeths grew quiet and listened, looking around for the source.

"I. Can't. Be. Here." I gritted through my teeth as I pulled. The ticking grew louder and louder, and something was pushing on my chest. Not like before, not like the press of choking, but something else, something filling it.

Something that was pushing out.

I stopped struggling against the bonds long enough to feel something struggling within. Something wanting out. Something alive.

I closed my eyes and listened. The ticking was stronger now, coming from all of us and none of us at the same time. I could feel the spirits at my side, taste their emotions, smell their deaths, and I could hear steps in the fog. Someone coming toward us.

In-between all that, I heard wings flapping.

When I opened my eyes, a red-haired woman with the yellow eyes was standing in front of me. She wasn't naked like the rest of us, but the dark smoke form she'd taken in my dreams flowed around her like a living dress.

The Red Woman.

She smiled at me and opened her mouth to say something, probably to gloat, but didn't have the chance.

A white crow flew out of the fog-filled world, screaming as it turned in the air, claws out. The Red Woman sprang back but wasn't fast enough to avoid the crow. It landed on her face, clawing and pecking.

For a second, I believed whatever it was, wherever it came from, could help us, then the Red Woman grabbed it with pale hands and flung it aside.

The crow thudded to the ground that wasn't really ground before it sprang to its feet again. It was keeping one of its wings close to its body and I could almost taste its pain.

But the Red Woman was also in pain. She was screaming and clutching at her face. Blood leaked through her fingers and ran down her uncovered chin, dripped from her parted lips. The crow cooed happily and started wobbling toward me. On the way, it stopped above a small object on the ground and pecked at it. The thing spun away from the crow, revealing one of the Red Woman's yellow eyes.

The woman was on her knees, but as the crow hopped past her, she stopped screaming and lowered her hands. Where her eye had been was only a black hole. Blood leaked from it like tears, blending with the blood spilling from scratches on her face. The blood moved like the fog composing her body in my dreams. Thick and thin all at the same time. The crow froze as the Red Woman moved.

"Fly!" I yelled, my word swallowed by the greyness and too late.

The Red Woman reached out and grabbed the crow as it tried to fly with its broken wing. The bird screamed and tried to get out of her grip, pecking and clawing, but the Red Woman didn't let go. Snarling, she grabbed the bird's head and twisted. The small body went limp in her hands.

A keening sound filled my chest and throat and head. It took me a moment to realize it was me screaming.

"Meddlesome shamans," the Red Woman said as she stood, turning her mangled face toward me and dropping the crow's body. It landed with a sickening sound, head twisted at an impossible angle. "Always trying to save the lost, but not this time." She reached toward me with a bloody hand. "An eye for an eye, they say, and I will have my price."

"But it wasn't me," I said, trying to pull from her but not able to. My voice was hoarse from the screaming and I tasted blood and tears on the air.

"Oh, but it is close enough. That was your mother, trying to undo what she has done." I stopped breathing and felt my chest tighten as something moved deep within me. "She was such a meddlesome woman. Able to see me as I tried to get my price but not able to stop me. That was all you, but none of you were strong enough. No-one are strong enough to stop me now!"

I closed my eyes as she reached for me. Her fingers were cold and wet against my brow, like mist coated in blood, not flesh. Her nails dug into my brow and the soft area under my eye.

"Ironically, her protective instinct was the very thing I used to kill you. I just put my face over yours, and in her state, she killed you to protect you." Blood pooled around the cold spots on my skin and ran down my face. I felt it at the same time as I didn't. "Such a shame for her, but not for me." A scream built in my chest, and something in there moved. "And now, who knows what kind of power she has given me in you? I really should have let her live, but that is life. Or death, for us."

She cackled.

The thing in my chest pushed, and I pulled. It was fear and sorrow and shame and regret. It moved and formed, trying to push through my skin, and I let it. I pushed at the thing beneath my breasts, pushed and pulled it out, letting it free, believing in it, embracing it.

Something sprang from my chest. The cold spots around my eye disappeared as the Red Woman screamed in fear and fury.

I opened my eyes, blinking away the blood.

A white owl was flying around the Red Woman's head. Claws out and beak parted in a scream that made my spine shudder. The Red Woman had her hands out, trying to catch the owl, but had trouble locating it with one missing eye. She spun around, growling and snarling like an animal.

The owl took its time, spinning and diving, staying just at the end of her reach. Then, seemingly out of nowhere, it dived. Like a white streak, it passed the Red Woman's hands and landed on her face.

She screamed and fell to her knees as the owl flung its wings wide and flew up. As it circled over me, it dropped an eyeball before my feet.

The bonds holding me fell away. I stepped out of them, feeling like I was walking through water, but it wasn't holding me back anymore.

The owl landed on my shoulder, claws digging into my skin but not hurting. Not in this form.

36

I grabbed the weeping woman before me. She jerked, trying to get away but not able to. As I turned her face toward me, I saw only black pools of shadow where her eyes used to be. She was weeping blood, not tears.

"The curse ends now," I said, and the owl flew from my shoulder and straight into her chest, just like it had emerged from mine.

Letting her go, I stepped back. The woman screamed and clawed at her chest, spilling her own blood as she tried to get to the owl inside her. I could see the shadow of it under her skin, but there was no way to pull it out if it didn't want to leave.

"It is not enough," she cackled in-between her screaming. "I am stronger than you!"

And I knew I wasn't enough. My soul wasn't strong enough to break the curse, to kill the Red Woman. I had no idea what to do. If I didn't get rid of her, I'd be dead. Mom would be dead. The other Elizabeths and I would be trapped here forever.

A hand touched my shoulder, and I turned.

Aunt Ellie stood behind me, her eyes on the screaming woman at my feet.

"I have an idea," she said and stepped forward.

Reaching out with the same hand she'd used to touch me, she gripped the Red Woman's flailing arm. Blood was flowing from the claw marks on her chest as well as from her ruined face.

The world seemed to stop for a heartbeat as aunt Ellie made contact, then a wound sprang up on the Red Woman's arm, matching the injury on aunt Ellie's. The Red Woman coughed, and blood-colored water splattered from her lips.

Gurgling, she clawed at aunt Ellie's grip, but her bloodied

fingers didn't make contact. It was like they dissolved when they came too close.

The pregnant Elizabeth Eleanor came next, gripping the clawing arm and pulling it to the side.

The Red Woman screamed in fear.

Magdalena Elizabeth stepped in-between the spread arms and grabbed the Red Woman's head with both small hands.

Then came Elizabeth Key Sanderson, followed by Elizabeth MacKey and the twins.

They all gripped the Red Woman, and as they made contact, something happened to her.

Blood was pooling on the floor beneath her and springing from between her legs. Brain matter was making the back of her head sticky, and her skin was burning and cracking from a fire none of us could feel. Water was still bubbling from her mouth as she screamed and screamed. And the shadow of my owl was spread wide within her chest, clawing at her heart.

Finally, the screaming stopped. The woman slumped forward. She hadn't even fallen over before she started to disappear like the fog she was. The owl flew from the blackness, just as white as before, and landed on my shoulder. I turned away from what was left of the Red Woman and fell to my knees by the white crow. Carefully, I lifted the body and hugged it to my chest. I was weeping, but the fog ate every sound.

"Thank you, mom."

When I opened my eyes, I was lying in the hallway at home. My throat hurt, and I was dizzy. Mrs. Tav was talking on the phone and at the same time, telling me to stay down, don't move or speak or do anything. She was crying.

I stayed down as she told me but turned my head. It hurt, but I saw what I needed to see. Mom lying beside me, eyes open and empty. Chest not moving. Dead.

37

Mrs. Tav was still on the phone, and I heard her ask for an ambulance. I blinked, for a moment expecting mom to blink back at me, but she didn't. She was as dead as the crow had been in my dream.

Tears pricked at my eyes, and I turned my face away from her. My chest and throat hurt, and the thought of sobbing scared me. If I hurt like this from just breathing regularly, what would I feel like from sobbing?

Something moved at the edge of my vision, and I continued turning my head to look. I wasn't sure what to expect, but a small fear gripped my stomach. What if the Red Woman was here? Waiting for me? Ready to finish what she'd started?

But no. Women were standing at the top of the stairs, out of the way from our bodies and Mrs. Tav, but they weren't the Red Woman. It took me a moment to recognize them.

Elizabeth Eleanor MacKey was standing in front of the small crowd, eyes locked on me. Her hair was as curly and pretty as it had been when I last saw her, but she wasn't naked anymore. She wore a flimsy, white gown that blew in its own weak wind, and she was stroking her big belly.

My eyes flew from her to the fourteen-year-old ghost of Elizabeth by her side, dressed in the same gown as she'd died in, but no longer with flames burning against her skin. The twins were standing just behind her, dressed as they had been in the dream I had of them as they died.

Six-year-old Magdalena Elizabeth was holding my aunt Ellie's hand, both of them dressed as well: Magdalena Elizabeth in the slip she'd been wearing as she ran away from her nurse, woolen stockings on her feet, and Aunt Ellie in her swimming suit.

Elizabeth Key Sanderson was in her hospital gown and kept glancing at Elizabeth Eleanor's belly with hunger.

I blinked before turning my head away from them.

Mrs. Tav was sitting between mom and me. She cradled the phone against her chest with one hand as she closed mom's eyes.

"Don't," I managed to croak.

Mrs. Tav jumped and turned to me. "Elizabeth, how are you feeling?"

"Don't call me that," I hissed. That name was the reason all of this happened. The reason mom was dead.

Mrs. Tav flinched as if I'd hit her. "I am so sorry. Nancy... she... I do not know what happened."

I shook my head and looked away from her, staring into the ceiling for a heartbeat. My thoughts were slow and sluggish, as if half-frozen. There was something I should worry about. Someone. Not mom, but...

"Mark." I turned back to Mrs. Tav. She was still looking at me. "Where's Mark?"

Mrs. Tav's eyes flicked up toward the gaggle of dead women and kids, and for a moment I thought she saw them as well, then I remembered they were standing at the stairs. Remembered Mark falling over the edge before mom grabbed me again.

"No," I hissed and started to push up.

Mrs. Tav was there in a flash, grabbing my shoulder and pushing me down.

"Stay," she said, some of the cold professionality of the nurse back in her voice. "Your heart stopped beating. I was able to bring you back, but you need to stay put until the ambulance arrives."

I was contemplating pushing against her, forcing her to let me up, but decided to stay. My body felt like one big bruise.

"What about Mark?" I asked.

"He is knocked out but alive. The ambulance is on its way. They will help."

I wanted to argue with her but couldn't find the strength to bother, so I just turned away, looking at the ceiling. There was nowhere else for me to look. I didn't want to look at Mrs. Tav and mom behind her, and I didn't want to look at the women by the stairs. The fact that they were here...

No. I closed my eyes. They were probably just a part of my imagination. Something I'd dreamed up when my mind was lacking oxygen — a hallucination.

When I opened my eyes I expected them to be gone, but they were still there.

"Why are you here?" I whispered, scowling at them.

"What?" Mrs. Tav asked, but her voice was like a bug or something as unimportant. I couldn't deal with her now. I had to get my mind back on track.

Aunt Ellie pushed past Elizabeth Eleanor and came over to me. She sat down by my side, stroking one hand over my forehead and hair. I swear I could feel her flesh against mine, even if I knew she was dead. The wound was gone from her wrist, but her hair was still floating around her face and shoulders as if in water.

"We don't know," she said. "I hoped we'd move on when the witch was gone, but we haven't, and we don't know why."

I looked away from her, glancing at Magdalena Elizabeth as she huddled behind teen-Elizabeth, standing together with the twins.

I closed my eyes again, unable to keep them open. I heard Mrs. Tav breathing at one side, and knew aunt Ellie was on my other, still stroking my hair. She was like a small spot of light behind my eyelids, the same as the others by the stairs — the other ghosts. I could sense them. Like something inside me was pulling them toward me, connecting us by a cold thread anchored in my chest.

Finally, the sound of sirens pushed through the tense quiet. I opened my eyes and saw the flash of red and blue on the ceiling as they parked outside.

"I need to let them in," Mrs. Tav said. She didn't move. It was like she was waiting for me to answer, but I didn't, didn't know what to say. She pushed up and headed down.

I looked as she started on the stairs, seeing the women step back to let her pass, but she still stuck her hand through one of the twin's shoulder.

Closing my eyes, I turned away again.

<h1 style="text-align:center">38</h1>

Everything after the paramedics showed up was a blur of people and movement and emotions.

Mark was rushed to the hospital even before they'd started on mom or me.

I watched as two of them perform CPR on mom for a while before giving up. They kept glancing at me as if they only did it to keep me happy. Before they gave up, I was on a stretcher and on my way downstairs. The paramedics that took care of me tried to get me to talk, but I couldn't bring myself to do it. It was like I'd used up all my words before they arrived. Mrs. Tav told them that I'd talked and seemed confused, so they needed to take me in to check for brain damage or something like that.

I lay backward as they moved me down the stairs and had an ample view of the gaggle of ghosts. Murder of spirits? I didn't know what to call them. They stayed at the top of the stairs but followed as I was carried away. As if they didn't have a choice in the matter.

I leaned against the stretcher and closed my eyes.

At the hospital, Dr. Altman came rushing to meet me at the ambulance bay. Machines and tests I didn't know anything about followed. I just did what they said, not thinking about anything.

Not until he was going to take an x-ray of my chest to see if I had any broken ribs from Mrs. Tav's CPR.

I'd pulled off my t-shirt and was turning toward the board when the young technician in there with me smiled and said: "That's an interesting tattoo. I've never seen that style before." He'd been chatty since I came in, possibly trying to stay awake or perhaps trying to be helpful. I hadn't answered but considered answering now, to tell him I didn't have a tattoo.

Then I saw myself in the glass separating the room I was in from the place where the technicians and other personnel waited as the x-ray machine did its thing. One thing was the bruises on my throat and how tired I looked. I'd expected that. I hadn't expected the shadow on my torso.

Almost in a daze, I walked closer to the window to get a better look, then looked down.

It was the shadow of an owl in flight seen from the front. As if trying to break from my chest. Wings and tail feathers spread wide. The wings reached up over the lower parts of my breasts, the tips disappeared under my arms. The feathers on the head, standing up like two small horns, were up on the insides of my breasts, and the tail feathers stopped just over my belly button.

"Wha..." I began, but couldn't speak anymore as the world tipped around me.

"Shit," the technician said and sprang forward, grabbing me before my legs gave way. "I'm so sorry if I'm touching anything I shouldn't right now, but I reacted on instinct," he said in a hurry as he lowered me to the floor.

Dr. Altman, that had been standing in the security room, sprinted through the door.

"What happened?" he asked, crouching beside me and grabbing a pen-light from his front pocket. "Ms. Key, can you hear me?"

He shone the light into my eyes, and I gave a small nod.

"Please speak," Dr. Altman said.

"Yes," I answered, almost in a whisper. From the way I was lying on the floor, I could see the owl. It was grey and looked kind of like a scar but smooth. "Sorry," I said, tearing my eyes away from the mark. "Just... my throat."

"Of course," he said. "You think you can get up?"

I gave another small nod, and with their help, I was on my feet again.

Things went as smoothly as they could after that. They got their pictures and saw that yes, I had some broken ribs. I hadn't gotten any brain damage from the lack of oxygen, though, and my throat was just bruised and should heal nicely. I'd been lucky, the doctor said, and I was released.

When I asked about Mark, a nurse told me he'd gotten a concussion and was driven to the hospital in Halifax to be kept over-night, but he was awake and responsive.

They also told me that mom had hit Mrs. Tav in the back of the head with the table lamp, but she'd only had a wound that needed stitches.

I had to answer some questions from the police before I could go. They asked about what had happened, and I told them a modified version of events in-between yawns. I'd gotten some pain pills, and they were making me drowsy. When I'd told them everything, they let me go but asked me to be available in case they had more questions. I only nodded and left.

Mrs. Hearth was waiting for me in the lobby. When she saw me, her face split in a smile of relief as her eyes brimmed with tears.

"Oh, Lizzie," she said and wrapped me in a careful hug. I just stood there, letting her hug me. "I am so sorry. Mrs. Tav told me what happened. Are you ok?"

Her eyes were serious as she pulled away, and I could see the question in them. What had really happened? I only shook my head in answer, and she gave a small nod before leading me out of the hospital.

We didn't say anything on the drive home.

Night had turned to day, and the day had turned to early evening again before I was let go, so the world was as dark as it had been when the ambulance drove me away. The hours I'd spent in the hospital were a kind of limbo. The things that had happened could hardly touch me there, but now I felt them creeping closer and catching up with me.

As Mrs. Hearth parked in front of her house, I couldn't help but look at my own in the rearview mirror. My home stood empty and innocently, but a shiver ran through me at the sight, and I almost started crying.

Mrs. Hearth saw. "You can stay with me for a while if you want."

I nodded and let her lead me into her house.

I stood in the hallway outside one of her spare bedrooms as she made the bed. Finally, when the room was done and Mrs. Hearth stood in front of me, I said: "The Red Woman tried to kill me, but she couldn't. Mom gave her life to save me, and then the other Elizabeths killed the Red Woman."

"Oh," Mrs. Hearth said, as if unsure how to respond. I couldn't blame her.

"And the ghosts of the other Elizabeths and the twins are here."

I pointed at the gaggle of ghosts standing behind me. They'd been close all the while. That feeling I had of them not able to leave my side had gotten stronger and stronger as they followed me around.

Mrs. Hearth looked at where I pointed but I knew she couldn't see them. After a few seconds, she sighed.

"Let us just get some sleep, and we will figure this all out tomorrow," she said.

"But you believe me?"

"Dear, I am a witch. Of course I believe you."

She gave my shoulder a small squeeze before she went to her bedroom. I just stood in the hall for a long time. Finally, I sank down on the carpet covering the floor and curled up there.

Epilogue

I wanted it to rain so bad, but it didn't. The sun was shining from a clear autumn sky dotted with a few white, puffy clouds here and there. There was a sour wind, pushing through the layers of clothing and to the bone, where it nestled together with that cold spot that never truly left me these days.

A leaf blew by, and I reached out and grabbed it. My nails were black today, with a faint sparkle of dark purple. My clothes were black as well, and I had trouble seeing for all the tears.

I turned my hand so I could look at the leaf. It was red with a few spots of brown, like dried blood.

Something white flashed in the corner of my eye. I turned to look, hope building in my chest and falling just as quickly. Sitting in the top of the tree that had once given the leaf life, sat a white dove. The tree was almost naked now. The dove turned its head to look at me with its other eye before it flew away. I had half a thought about it being alone here in the autumn, and how cliché it was to have a white dove at a funeral, but it was soon forgotten to the sorrow of it not being a crow.

"Lizzie?"

Mark's arms snaked around me and pulled me to him. I

forced myself to rest against his warm chest, hoping his warmth would flow through my skin and into that cold spot even as I knew it wouldn't.

"You ok?" he asked against my hair.

"No," I answered and pushed away from him. "We just sent my mother to cremation. I'm not ok."

"I'm sorry, I didn't mean..."

"I know. I just... I need a moment."

Mark pushed his hands into his suit pockets. He didn't look at me as he spoke. "I'll wait by the car."

"Thanks."

"Don't take too long. The others are waiting for us at the wake."

Without an answer, I turned away from him. I could feel him standing behind me. His heat, and his eyes on me. Then he sighed and started walking away, feet crushing dead leaves.

I was alone outside the church now. I could hear the faint whisper of people talking up at the road. Mark joining them. I wanted to join them. To sprint after my boyfriend, burrow into his chest, let him hold me and comfort me. But I couldn't.

Curling my fists against each other to keep from chewing on my nails, I looked up at the tree again, hoping for a white crow that wasn't there.

Something moved beside me, but I didn't need to turn to know what it was.

"What am I supposed to do with you?" I asked, not looking at the ghosts. "Why are you even here if the curse has been lifted?"

Elizabeth Eleanor shrugged. It looked weird on her. It was a movement she'd picked up from me and still hadn't perfected. The first time I'd done it, she claimed that ladies didn't shrug.

Now she was trying to make the movement her own.

"We do not know any more than you do, Elizabeth. If it were up to me, I would like nothing more than to be with my Joseph again. Instead, I am here."

"I know," I growled and turned to look at them.

Magdalena Elizabeth was playing with the twins, running around the church chasing leaves. They didn't move the leaves as they ran, but they chased them anyway. Her angelic face split open in a wide grin that made Elizabeth Eleanor huff with indignation.

"Proper ladies do not grin," I murmured under my breath and had to stifle a laugh. "You can't stay here, though," I continued a little louder. "I can't have you floating around me like this. Mrs. Tav and Mark both think I'm going crazy already."

"They should respect a lady's need to mourn her mother," Elizabeth Eleanor said, and I sighed, not looking at her.

"I really need to find each of you a new name. I can't keep thinking of you as Old Elizabeth, Teen Elizabeth, Child Elizabeth, and War Elizabeth."

"What about me?" aunt Ellie said, smiling a little.

"You're aunt Ellie," I answered, smiling back.

"Why do we need new names?" Teen Elizabeth asked.

"If you're going to stick around it will drive me crazy not having individual names for each of you."

She shrugged as well, owning the movement a little more than Elizabeth Eleanor.

"But that will have to wait for another day," I sighed. "I'm tired, and have living people waiting for me."

Shooting a last look up at the tree, I turned and walked toward the cars. I could feel the ghosts trail after me, tied to that cold spot within my chest, but I didn't turn to look at the spirits and didn't listen to their low voices. I would deal with them later when I knew what I could do to help them. For now, I needed to decide what to do with myself.

Connor had left a multitude of voicemails on my phone after the accident. Someone had called to tell him what was going on, and now he was wondering what I was going to do. Two days ago I'd called him back, forbidding him from coming to the funeral. He'd lost that right. And I still wanted the house. He'd wanted to argue that I didn't need it, that Cornelia deserved to know her family history. I played the curse card, and he relented. He still wanted to meet up to talk things over, but I felt secure enough that I could make the house mine.

I hadn't told Mark or anyone else what I planned. I wasn't sure it was the right thing to do before today.

I reached the road where Mark was waiting. He reached out a hand, looking uncertain. I looked at the hand and took it. His shoulders relaxed a little and he kissed my nose as he opened the car door for me. I let go and climbed in.

As he climbed into the car on the driver's side, he reached over and retook my hand. Keeping our gazes locked together, he lifted the hand and kissed it. A small smile pulled at my lips, but I knew it didn't reach my eyes.

I didn't know what to do. I would have to tell him I was staying here, that I was leaving the life we'd had together behind. I wasn't the same girl that left him less than two weeks ago to help her mom. She was dead: Killed by her mother.

I was Elizabeth now, the survivor of a family curse that had killed so many. I was a shaman that needed to get to know my powers. I was a young woman that could see and talk to ghosts. A woman with a gift, a curse, and a new purpose. A woman

Mark had called crazy.

Sighing, I leaned back in my seat.

For now, just for now, I let myself rest against the safety of what I knew compared to the uncertainty ahead.

REFLECTIONS

1

I was playing with a rat in a tutu, waiting for someone to bring me my kiwi bush when something changed. I couldn't quite put my finger on what it was, but there was something... the rat jumped forward and bit my finger. I shrieked without making a sound and flailed my arm, trying to dislodge it. As I flailed, the rat started growing. Its fur turned to smooth skin, and its sharp front teeth started spreading, growing, loosening their grip. I grabbed my chance and slipped my finger away. Without waiting, I turned and ran. The corridor was growing darker for every step, somehow stretching longer and longer. Gasping as I ran, I glanced over my shoulder to see if the rat was following. The rat was gone, but a shark in a tutu was in its place, steadily catching up to me. I tried to run faster, but couldn't. My pulse was hammering in my ears, the walls pulsing along to the uneven rhythm. Ba-ram. Ba-ram. Ba-ba-ba-ba-ba-ba-ba-rum. Ba-rum. Ba-rum. Ba-ba-ba... I could feel the shark breathing cold on my neck, I...

"Sara, come on! Your phone is ringing!"

Jake was pressing his cold hands to my neck, trying to wake me from my dream. I groaned for a moment, listening as my heartbeat dissolved into the *Jaws* theme song.

I scrambled away from Jake and lunged for my phone, pressing it to my ear before I remembered to push the screen to answer. Cursing, I pushed the button and tried again.

"Emma? Is it happening?" My voice was a tad too high, almost spilling over with joy. The line crackled. Someone was breathing, but not speaking. "Emma?"

The person on the line drew a deep breath. "You need to get involved." It was Emma's voice, but it didn't sound like she was really there. The words were flat and empty. "Right now."

"Emma?"

The breathing hitched. "Sara?"

She was back.

I breathed a sigh of relief. "What did you see?"

For a heartbeat, she didn't answer. "I can't tell you."

"Aw, come on! Not this again!"

"If I tell you, you might change it in an even worse way."

"Change what?"

When she answered, her voice was so low I could barely hear it, sounding almost hollow again. "Everything will change." She cleared her throat, forcing her voice back to normal. "I just called to tell you to get involved, ok?"

"Involved with what?"

"That's up to you."

"Sometimes, I hate what pregnancy does to your powers."

She laughed without joy. "Me and you both. This round has been even worse than the other times. This last week..." she drew another shuddering breath. "Everything sets me off. Like right now? I was in the bathroom and turned too fast, and I saw the futures in the shapes my hair made!"

"That's new."

"Yes. It's usually worse when I get close to popping, though, so hopefully, I'll have this little one out within the week."

"I thought she was on her way already," I said, leaning my back against the wall. Beside me, Jake had sat up and was looking at me. I couldn't see his expression in the dark of the bedroom, but his eyes glinted with the light from my phone. "You made me dream I was being chased by a shark in a tutu. I don't think I'll ever sleep again!"

Emma chuckled, and this time it was a real sound. "That's what you get for putting the *Jaws* theme as my ringtone every time I get pregnant. I won't even apologize."

I stuck my tongue out at the phone. "Neither will I. I love my nieces, but they're little biters, just like sharks, so *Jaws*'s what you get."

She laughed again, and I could picture her body relaxing. She always got tense when her power took over, and it could take days to work out the knots in her back. Laughter and a hot bath were the best remedies.

I could feel my own neck tensing up just thinking about what her power taking over meant.

Emma, my older sister, was something called a Pathfinder witch. All witches have one active power that's unique to us, and being a Pathfinder is one of the worst of them. These witches see the futures. They're good at divination even before they reach puberty, when their power sets in, which is also when most Pathfinders either kill themselves or go insane from all the possible futures they see. Even if they avoid things like tarot cards and scrying and crystals, the power will out. It starts pushing its way into their everyday life, and they can see the future in raindrops, fires, the clouds, or even the shadows cast by sunlight. Or like now, when the power got so strong, it manifested through the movement of Emma's hair. Emma was twenty-seven years old, and the oldest living Pathfinder in Canada to this date. She'd only been able to hold the visions at bay because of modern medication, but she cut back on those when she's pregnant, and so her power grows stronger and stronger. This was Emma's third pregnancy, and I hoped it would be her last. Her power got stronger for each one, and what if her pills didn't work this time around? What if the power was stronger than the medication, and this was the beginning of a downward spiral? I didn't want a world without my sister in it.

Jake twined his fingers with mine, knowing how afraid for her I was and giving silent comfort.

Sighing, I continued talking with Emma. She'd just finished taking a shower when the vision hit, so at least she didn't have to risk the drops now that she'd already slipped away once. I did make a point out of asking why she was awake and showering at three in the morning, which she joked away before we finally said our good-byes.

"Don't call me again before the little one is coming," I said.

Emma made a non-committal sound, but I heard her chuckling as she hung up.

I stared at my phone. She'd sounded cheerful enough, sounded like herself, and I'm sure I heard Thomas', her husband's voice in the background before we disconnected. He would take care of her, and keep her away from triggers for the rest of the morning.

"What did she say? I guess the baby isn't on the way yet?" Jake asked, squeezing my hand as he spoke.

I forced a smile before telling him what Emma had said. Both about what I needed to do, and what little she'd let slip about the future. That everything would change.

"What do you think that means?" I asked as I put my phone away.

"Maybe Trump will attack North-Korea?" Jake said.

I grabbed my pillow and hit him with it. "Don't even joke 'bout stuff like that!"

He laughed and tried to grab the pillow, but I hit him with it again. Lunging forward, he grabbed me around the wrist and held my hand still. He was pushed up against my chest now, and I could feel his breathing on my cheek. Bending a little, he placed a light kiss on my lips. As he moved to pull away, I followed and nipped at his bottom lip. For a second, we sat like that; him over me and our noses touching. He let my wrist go and trailed his fingers along my arm and down my naked chest, cupping my breast. I smiled and nipped his lip again, glad for the distraction. As he kissed his way along my jaw and neck, I let the fear go. Emma would be ok, and how much could the world change anyway? Emma saw multiple futures based on multiple choices. Chances of things changing drastically were minimal, especially if Emma was doing what she could to minimize the event, like including me.

I spared half a thought to what an unimportant witch like me could do in the grand scheme of things before I let myself get lost in Jake and his touch.

2

We didn't get any more sleep that night, so I was tired but happy when we left to eat breakfast. Usually, we ate at home, but considering we were up so early, we made a date out of it. Jake even brought his computer bag to try and get some work done after I left.

In the light of day, we always drew some looks when we walked side by side. Not that we were that hot or anything – although I think so – but because we looked so different. Jake was hundred-and-ninety centimeters tall and too skinny for his own good. His brown hair was always a little too long and kept falling into his cloudy grey eyes. He usually wore a dark t-shirt with some stupid pun on it – today it was a science pun. On top it said: ''I am a'' and then it had the periodical placements of germanium, nickel, uranium, and sulfur, spelling out the word ''genius'' – with a light grey jacket over it, and well-worn jeans. He could blend into any crowd looking like that. I kind of envied him for it.

I was hundred-and-sixty-five centimeters tall, meaning I was a lot shorter than Jake, and I had broad shoulders and a big bosom, but thin hips. Unlike Jake, I had some extra padding, and I was more than happy about it. My hair was kept in a long pixie cut dyed blue – although now so faded it looked more like ice-blue - and my arms and upper back were covered in tattoos, none of which showed now. It was October, and too cold for me to walk around flashing my art. People looked at us because we didn't match. While I wore mostly black or darkly colored earth-tones, I always made sure to have something flashy on me. I liked showing off, and that only made Jake's casual look seem stranger. At least according to the barista at our favorite café, where we were now heading.

We ordered and sat down, losing ourselves in conversations about everyday life – Jake was currently working on translating some old German text for the Library of the University of Dartmouth, and trying to learn Japanese on the side. Not that he had any problem learning new languages, he already knew eight of them and planned to expand even more after he finished his Japanese studies. Our food arrived as he tried to teach me a Kanji, and I happily consumed the pancakes and muffins I'd ordered.

I was so focused on my food and the company that I didn't notice time running by. It was Jake, eating more calmly and enjoying the food with each bite, which pointed out that it was almost eight in the morning. I gulped down the last of my smoothie and nabbed the muffin off of Jake's platter as I stood. He chuckled as I hurried out the door.

My first charge, Midna, didn't live too far away from the café, and I was already dressed in work-out clothes, so I jogged, ringing the bell just two minutes after eight. The intercom clicked.

"Almost late this time," Nadia said.

"Just almost," I answered, trying to keep from breathing too hard. "Let me in, will you?"

The door buzzed and I walked in. I took my time up the

stairs, trying to calm my breathing. I may walk around all day for work, but my stamina had never been the best. Not that I planned to do anything about it either.

The door to the apartment was open, and I walked right in, more than happy to greet my first charge of the day. Midna, a black German Shepherd and Husky mix with the brightest blue eyes I'd seen on any dog, came bouncing out of the living room. She flumped her ass down a meter or so away, her tail swishing over the floor as she waited for my cuddles. I sat and gave her just what she wanted.

Nadia, Midna's owner, leaned against the doorframe between the living room and hallway, a cup of steaming ramen held in one hand, her other tapping against the doorway. Her golden ring flashed, and the diamonds scraped against the wood. Wincing, Nadia wrapped the hand around the ramen cup. She had heavy bags under her eyes, and her hair stood every-which-way.

"You look like crap," I said as I stood to grab Midna's harness.

"Deadline coming up," Nadia answered with a yawn. "And an impossible client. I've changed the picture at least three times for that ass-hat."

I chuckled and tried to coach Midna into the harness. She was a rescue from an abusive home, and things like harnesses were scary. We'd been working on her wearing one for months, and while she now didn't mind having it on, getting it on was still a little scary. Nadia stood still as I worked. Midna kept turning her head away from the opening, and finally, I used my magic. It coursed through my blood, and instantly I was able to slip the harness over the dog's head. I handed her a treat, and Midna seemed mollified.

My active power was luck. If I didn't concentrate, I had an aura of luck around me. It gave me an extra edge in everything I did, but it also took the luck from someone else. My coven wanted me to bind my powers, afraid it would corrupt me, but I refused. It was a whole thing.

I kept my eyes down so Nadia wouldn't see the gold in them until I'd secured the harness, then I clamped down on my magic and finally looked up with a smile.

"Gets easier every time," I said.

Nadia chuckled. "If you say so. Have a nice walk."

"Good luck with your client."

Nadia snorted as she headed to her office. I clicked the leash onto the harness and made sure it was connected to my stomach belt before we headed out the door.

We walked across the street and through a park. Almost twenty minutes after we set out, I pulled a set of keys from my pocket and let us into a townhouse. No-one greeted us at the door, so with Midna in tow, I walked into the house until I reached the living room at the back. A bloodhound lay sprawled across an antique sofa, making it look small in comparison with his huge body.

"Hey, Sherlock," at my voice, he lifted his head and took us in. "It's time for your walk."

With a sigh that seemed to vibrate through his entire body, he slid his way out of the sofa and lumbered toward us.

"You know you're not allowed on the furniture, right?" I said as he snuffled his nose into Midna's ruff. I bent and pulled his flesh away from his eyes. "You don't care, do you?" He snorted, which made Midna shake her head to make him stop.

Laughing, I led the two dogs into the hallway. Getting Sherlock into his harness was much faster than with Midna, and we were soon out the door. I double-checked that it was locked before we headed back into the park.

We lumbered around for an hour or so.

Sherlock was an elderly guy, almost nine years old, so he didn't make too much noise or want a lot of playtime. Midna was younger, just over a year old, but she had never been a playful or loud dog. As far as I could tell, her previous owners had punished her whenever she did anything other than lie in her cage. That's why I walked her together with Sherlock. He was an old, steady man that could be a safe harbor for her. In the months I'd walked them together, I'd seen her come more and more out of her shell, daring to take more space with him at her back.

I walked Sherlock back home first. He'd started dragging his paws, which was a good sign he was tired, but at least he'd gotten his business done, and got some treats and cuddles as well. He would sleep until his owners came home at the end of the day.

Then I headed back through the park. I made sure to walk past the fenced-in section for dogs this time around. Midna stayed close to my legs, but she watched the other dogs play with interest. That was more than she had done before. Maybe in a month or two, we could consider stopping by in the morning when there were fewer dogs there?

Nadia didn't answer the buzzer when I called, so I rang the bell to her neighbor.

Old Mama, a drag queen that never gave me any other name, no matter what guise I saw her in, answered in a drawling voice. "Nadia cooped up with work again?"

"Asshole client," I answered. "Let me in?"

"You should ask for a key, darling," but she buzzed me in.

"I will," I said before hurrying through the door.

The door into Nadia's apartment was unlocked, and I got Midna out of her harness and collar. Reaching for the door, I gave myself a once-over in the full-figure mirror beside it.

"I need to dye my hair again. Purple, green, or maybe orangy-red in celebration of your name-sister?" I winked at Midna in the mirror, and she thumped her tail twice. "Green it is!" I blew Midna a kiss and hurried out the door. I had other clients waiting.

I walked a couple of Pomeranians that would never go with any of the other dogs I walked. They didn't need much time, as they were both old, and tired within half an hour. Then I headed to a neighborhood at the edge of town. Here, I had five dogs waiting for me, and I could walk them all together. They were of varying ages, but they never seemed to tire. Probably the effect of living somewhere where they could be let out to play any time they got restless. The more action a dog got, the more action the dog would need. I spent two hours walking and playing with them.

I'd just dropped off the first one when my phone rang.

It was the *Charmed* theme, so I knew it was Grams. "What's up?" I answered.

Grams sniffled, and I stopped in my track. The dogs pulled at my stomach belt, surprised at my sudden stillness

"Sara, dear, are you busy?" Grams sounded strange. Like she'd been crying.

"You ok?" I asked, not answering her question. Of course I wouldn't be too busy to hear what was going on if she were crying!

"Yes, dear, I am fine." My shoulders relaxed. "Are you busy?"

I forced my feet to start moving. "No, just out with some dogs. What's up?"

"I... I don't know how to say this... It is about Nancy."

My heart seemed to grow two sizes too big. "Lizzie ok?"

"Yes. She had a scare, but she is fine."

I closed my eyes and breathed a sigh of relief. "What 'bout Nancy?"

Grams drew a deep, shuddering breath. "She is dead."

I drew a shuddering breath of my own and blinked away the sudden tears filling my eyes. "What happened?"

"I don't quite know yet, dear. There must have been an episode of some kind. Everyone in the house were taken to the emergency room."

"Everyone?"

"Mrs. Tav, Lizzie, and Lizzie's boyfriend. A man named Mark."

My heart was still too big, and now it fluttered painfully. I shouldn't care about Lizzie having a boyfriend, but I did. "Are they ok?"

"Mark was driven to Dartmouth Hospital." The emergency room in Sky Harbour was well equipped, but any serious injuries were sent to Dartmouth. "But they kept Mrs. Tav and Lizzie here, and as far as I can tell, Mark will be all right. I just got a call from Lizzie asking me to pick her up when they are done with her, so I thought now would be a good time to let you know what was happening. I know you loved Nancy very much."

The tears threatened to spill over again. I'd spent a lot of time over at Lizzie's place. Her mother and father practically raised me at times. When Nancy got her diagnosis, it felt like someone tore out my lungs and stepped on them. Now, knowing she was dead, I could suddenly breathe again. It may sound cruel, but she was so bad the last time I saw her, I couldn't help but think that she was better off now. At least she wasn't hurting anymore.

We talked a little about what would happen next. I knew Lizzie had been going through a lot this last week, and I wanted to be there for her any way I could, but as Grams pointed out, that wasn't my place anymore. She would keep me updated about everything. When I asked about how things ended with Lizzie and her nightmares, Grams again shot me down.

"If it went as we feared, I would think it is Lizzie's story to tell, not mine," Grams said with a hint of steel in her voice.

"Fine," I mumbled.

We said our good-byes after that, with Grams promising to call when Lizzie was back home.

I rushed through delivering the dogs to their respective homes, almost mixing up the two labs that were mother and daughter and lived two houses apart, but I got them all settled and could finally drive back. I had two more stops to make, but my heart wasn't in it. I kept playing through the two phone calls I'd gotten this day. First, Emma calling to tell me to ''get involved'', and now Grams calling to tell me that Nancy was dead, and I knew Lizzie was going through something. Was this the thing I was supposed to get involved in? If so, when? Should I message Lizzie now? Let her know I knew what had happened and tell her I was there for her if she needed it? Or should I take Grams' advice and wait? Let Lizzie tell me if she wanted to?

By the time I was done with my walks for the day, my head felt like it was full of wool, and all I wanted was a hot bath, a cup of tea, and a hug.

3

I was in a dace when I came home. Jake called hello from the library, but I didn't answer. Just walked into the bedroom and started undressing.

"Sara?"

When I didn't answer this time either, I heard him move. The next thing I knew, he was standing in the doorway, watching as I pulled out of my leggings and stood in just my underwear. I stared at the closet, unsure of what to do next.

Jake walked all the way into the room and wrapped his arms around me, resting his chin on top of my head. "What's bothering you?" he asked, squeezing his arms just a little.

I opened my mouth, closed it, before pulling out of his arms and leaning my back against the closet door.

"Nancy died," I said.

It took a moment before recognition sparked in his eyes. "Mrs. Hearth's neighbor? The one with Alzheimers?" I nodded. He sighed and reached out his arms again. I walked into them and let him envelop me. "I'm so sorry. I know you were close." I nodded and buried my face against his shoulder. We stood like that for almost a minute before he spoke again. "Why don't you take a bath while I prepare dinner? I know 'tis your turn, but I'm more than happy to take it off your hands."

He knew me too well.

"Thank you," I sniffled.

He kissed the top of my head. "That's what I'm here for."

I squeezed him tight before pulling out of his arms again. He bent and kissed me at the corner of my mouth before leading me toward the bathroom. I sat on the toilet as he started the water running and found a vial of lavender oil Grams had made. He poured a few drops into the swirling water before he dimmed the light until they were just an orange glow.

"You'll be ok?" He asked. I nodded, and he closed the door, leaving me alone with the sound of water and the scent of flowers.

I sat on the toilet until the bathtub was half-full, then I pulled off my underwear and crawled into the bathtub.

As the water rose, I returned to my thoughts from earlier. What did Emma mean? And what should I do about Nancy and Lizzie? What could I do? And should I do anything?

In moments like this, I almost envied Emma's divination powers. It seemed like such an easy way to get answers. Even as I thought it, I felt bad and forced my thoughts to something else. Planning where to walk my charges tomorrow was calming enough.

When the tub was full, I turned off the faucet and sank even deeper, inhaling the lavender smell and letting the warm water wash away my worries.

I must have dozed off, for the next thing I knew the water was cold.

Getting up, I dried off and emptied the tub. As I turned on the light, I glimpsed myself in the mirror. The bags under my eyes, always visible because of my pale complexion, had spread to cover my entire eye, making it look like I had matching bruises. I grimaced and headed to the bedroom, where I dressed in a long knitted sweater and stuffed my feet into my unicorn slippers.

The smell of pizza filled the apartment, and I followed my nose to the kitchen. Jake sat at the table with a piece of paper and a pencil. I walked over and looked at the paper. It was filled with kanji.

Jake put down the pencil and grabbed me, pulling me into his lap. "How are you feeling?"

I rested my head on his shoulder. "Tired. But pizza will help. Where did you order from?"

"It's homemade."

I almost sprang out of his lap and turned to the stove, but he pulled me back down again, laughing. "It's not done yet! Patience."

"I hate that word."

"Yet, you use it on your dogs almost daily." I bit his shoulder, and he yelped. "Doesn't mean you have to act like one!"

I smiled and kissed the spot I'd just bit. He grumbled but didn't push me off his lap. As we sat there, I noticed my phone lay on the table next to Jake's, the charger plugged into the wall. A small light blinked on the screen. I stiffened.

Jake noticed and squeezed my arm. "It was just a message, no call. So it can't be more bad news, right?"

"Yeah."

I reached for the phone and unlocked it. There was indeed only one message, and it was from Grams. A small spark of pride lighted in my chest. She'd just learned how to send messages, and while she preferred to call, she was trying. That made me happy. The message was short and to the point:

Lizzie was ok and would be staying at grams' place for a while, not wanting to go home. Grams still didn't know what had happened, but she would call me tomorrow if she learned anything new. She again asked me to stay in Halifax until the funeral.

I let Jake read the message with me before I put the phone away. Before either of us could speak, the alarm on Jake's phone went off.

"Pizza," he said, and I scrambled out of his lap before he could ask me to move.

He chuckled and stood, saving the pizza from the oven as I set the table. His home-made pizza was the best, and just the smell of it seemed to calm my aching heart.

We talked about everything and nothing, and by the time we went to bed, I'd almost forgotten about the two phone calls that had shaped my day. Even as I remembered them, I buried my face in my pillow and pushed the thoughts aside. Emma had said I would know when to get involved, and it wasn't yet, so I should just forget about it and try to live my life.

4

The night was filled with fitful dreams and restless sleep. I kept waking up, and when the alarm finally rang, I was grateful the night was over. Even if it felt like I hadn't slept a wink. I chugged down a cup of coffee and ate a left-over slice of pizza as Jake started making himself toast and an omelet.

"You sure you don't want any?" he asked, casting a disapproving glance at my slice of pizza.

"Don't have time," I grumbled. I wasn't a morning person on the best of days. Today was not one of those days.

Jake sighed and returned to his breakfast.

I stole a sip of his coffee before I left.

The sky was grey with clouds, and a cold wind snuck its way past my clothes and seemed to chew its way into my bones. I huddled deeper into my scarf and grumbled at having to spend the entire day outside. I usually loved my job, it was diverse and fun, and I loved dogs, but on days like this, I envied Jake for being able to work from home or anywhere else he wanted. As long as he turned in the translated pages by the deadline, his bosses didn't care if he did the work here or in Spain. Maybe we should just move to Spain? I could walk dogs anywhere, after all. Even if I would miss my pack of weirdos.

The car hadn't even warmed up properly by the time I

reached Nadia's place, and I stayed behind the wheel for a moment, praying for some heat to dispel the cold. When it became clear it wouldn't help, I grumbled some more and left the car at the curb.

I rang the doorbell before stuffing my hands into my pockets, flexing my fingers in hope of heating them up.

Nadia didn't answer, so after half a minute, I rang again, this time bouncing up and down to stay warm.

Again, she didn't answer.

"Oh, come on," I grumbled and rang again, keeping my finger on the button a little longer than necessary. Maybe she was still asleep? I knew a lot of people slept with earbuds, so maybe that's why she didn't hear the bell? Or she was so wrapped up in her work that she didn't notice.

When she didn't answer this time either, I rang for Old Mama.

The intercom crackled before I'd lifted my finger from the button. "Dog girl?" Old Mama said, sounding gruff.

"Good morning to you, too," I answered, equally blunt.

"Get up here and make that dog shut it."

The lock buzzed and I opened the door. "What do you mean?" I asked, but the intercom was silent.

Not that I needed her answer. The moment I stepped into the building, I heard a high-pitched barking. I'd never heard Midna bark before, but I instantly knew it was her, and she was scared out of her mind.

I took the stairs two steps at a time, letting my magic loose so it would keep me from tripping or slipping.

When I got to the right floor, Old Mama greeted me. She stood in her own doorway, clad only in a silken dress that reached to her ankles, and without a hint of makeup. There was even stubble on her chin, which I'd never seen before.

"How long's she been barking?" I asked as I crossed to Nadia's door, keeping my eyes away from Mama. I didn't want her to see the gold of magic in them.

"Since just before six," Mama answered, walking to stand by my side. "I tried knocking, but Nadia didn't answer."

"Did you check on her?"

Mama scowled at me. "With her dog going off like that? No way, darling. I figured I'd wait for you. You can handle the dog."

I glanced at her but quickly looked away. I couldn't blame her for not wanting to risk a frightened dog on her own, but I wish she'd called the police or someone to help her and not waited two hours for me to show up. What if Nadia had fallen or cut herself? Or someone had broken in and hurt her? Two hours was too long to wait when someone might be hurt on the other side of the door.

As I reached for the knob, I knocked and called for Nadia. At my voice, Midna quieted down for a second before she started up again. This time she sounded more frantic. As if she'd hoped to get someone's attention with her barking, and now that she finally had, we had to hurry. Something was wrong. I could hear it in the tone of her bark. She was so scared she'd even forgotten about her abuse.

The door was unlocked, and I pulled it open, preparing to grab the dog as she sprang out, but nothing happened.

The hairs on my arms rose, and my neck started tingling as I stared into the hallway. Midna was standing in the living room, her fur on end and tail tucked to her stomach. Her ears lay so flat they were almost hidden by her ruff. Her blue eyes didn't once look at me but were glued to the mirror by the door.

Or where the mirror had been. Just the frame stood there now, the glass lay scattered across the floor. Like it had exploded from within. I stared at the reflection of my golden eyes in one of the shards for a second before moving. I needed to get to Midna and check if she'd cut her paws.

Before I could walk through the doorway, Mama grabbed my arm. I spun on her but stopped my words as I saw she had her phone to her ear. As I watched, she rattled off the address and informed whoever she was calling that there might be someone hurt in the apartment.

"I need to get to Midna," I mouthed.

Mama growled and answered something the person on the other line asked.

"If you tell them –" I began, but Mama lifted her hand.

When the person on the other end of the line finished talking, Mama met my eyes and nodded. "Try not to disturb the glass."

I nodded and turned to the apartment. Keeping my eyes on Midna, I stepped from clear spot to clear spot. Something about my reflection in the shards made my neck tingle even worse. Like it wasn't my own eyes looking back at me.

My luck was still running free, and with its help, I was able to step through the hallway without breaking or moving any of the mirror-shards.

The moment I was by her side, Midna whined and pushed herself up against my legs. I crouched and curled my fingers into her ruff, mumbling nonsense, and trying to comfort her. She calmed down a little, her frightened barks turning to a low, whining growl. She wouldn't look at me, never taking her eyes off the frame. A few shards still clung to it at the edges, and I tried to see what she saw in them, but there was nothing there but our own reflections. Somehow, that didn't make me feel any better.

After a bit of mumbling, I was able to talk Midna into lying down. It was clear she wouldn't leave her spot even if I ordered her to, so I hoped my command would keep her in place even as I looked for Nadia. Midna might not have walked onto the glass yet, but now that the door was open and someone she trusted was in the apartment to look for her mom, there was no guaranty that her instincts wouldn't take over, and she'd try to flee.

I gave her one last pat on the ruff, mumbled reassurances that I would be back, then hurried into the apartment. Where to look first? As I stood there, insecurity roaring in my stomach, I remembered something from the show *Station 19*. They followed the wall around a room. Sure, there was no smoke here to make it harder to see, but the thought stuck with me. Follow the walls.

The apartment was built as a square, with the hallway and living room in the middle, and four doorways leading from the living room and into the rest of the apartment.

To my right was the opening leading into the kitchen, and I went that way first. It was small and without any hiding spots, but I checked under the table and in the corners anyway, making sure to follow the right-side wall around the room. A cup stood on the counter, grounds of instant-coffee filling the bottom. The water-boiler was filled with water, but it was cool when I touched it.

Moving from the kitchen, I glanced at Midna to make sure she was still in place and walked to the next door, which stood ajar. It was Nadia's office. The lights were on, showing the empty room, but I still followed the wall and checked under the desk and in the closet.

"How's it going, darling?" Mama called from the doorway when I left the office.

"Haven't found her yet," I answered, turning toward the next door.

"The police and an ambulance are on the way."

I mumbled something about it being good and opened the door. Something flickered on the floor, reflecting the light from the living room, and I rushed to turn on the overhead lights.

The bathroom was empty. The mirror that had once hung on the wall was gone, broken, the shards lying across the floor. Some had even flown into the shower, slicing through the curtain as it went. Just like in the hallway, it looked like the mirror had exploded from within.

I didn't dare enter the bathroom. It was smaller than the hallway, and the mirror had been bigger, so there was no chance I wouldn't step on any of it. I called for Nadia, but there was nowhere in that room she could have hidden. My eyes swept over the glass again, noting that there was no sign of blood. If Nadia had been in there when the mirror exploded, she would have been cut. Even if she'd broken the mirror herself and flung the shards around, she would have cut herself.

The lack of blood should have calmed me, but instead, it made that prickling feeling at my neck intensify and spread down my spine. Something was wrong here. Wrong in a way the police and other officials wouldn't be able to fix.

Shaking away the thought, I hurried to the last door and pushed it open.

Again, the light of the living room reflected off a mirror, but this time it was whole. As I turned on the overhead light, I stared at the three mirrors facing me. They were part of an antique vanity, the wood dark and chipped with age. I walked to it and let my fingers slide along the silver brushes lying in a neat line just under the center mirror. Both the vanity and the brushes were antiques, and I remembered the ring Nadia always wore. Gold with two diamonds and a sapphire. An heirloom from her grandmother, she'd once told me. Maybe this set was also an heirloom? But why weren't the mirrors in here broken like the others?

I stared at my reflection for a long time, waiting for a chill to creep down my back, or some other feeling of wrongness, but nothing happened. These three were only mirrors. Old and pretty, but not dangerous. So why were the other mirrors wrong? Why had they broken and not these?

At Mama's questioning call, I tore my eyes away from the mirrors and hurriedly checked under the bed and in the closet, but there was no sign of Nadia. I hadn't thought there would be. The longer I spent in this apartment, the surer I got something magical was going on. Would I have noticed without my power? I had no idea, but I trusted my luck, and it was letting me know something was wrong here. It told me this was magical, even if something like this had never happened in Halifax before. At least not in my memory, but Jake would know.

I left the bedroom and told Mama what I'd found. She informed me that the police had arrived and asked me to stay in the apartment with Midna until they had a proper hold on the situation. Confirming I'd heard her, I sank onto the floor beside Midna and stroked her back. Her fur had flattened a little, but she was still growling low in her chest. She cast a look at me as I touched her and whined.

"I know, girl," I murmured. "I know you're worried 'bout

your mom, but we'll find her."

The sound of men's voices reached me from the hallway, and I sighed. Who knew how long this would take. I reached for my phone and called in my temp to take care of my other charges for the day. Even if this didn't take long, I couldn't just wander around with dogs and do nothing. If I was right, Nadia needed my help now, not in a few hours.

Marianne, my temp, was more than happy for the extra work, and we agreed to meet outside Nadia's building so I could hand over the keys, and she'd drop them off at my place when she was done for the day.

By the time she arrived, the police had taken pictures of the hallway and the mirror-shards there, and finally let me and Midna out. The officer I talked to was less than happy about the dog that wouldn't leave my side, but he only commented once.

I'd turned off my luck before the police arrived, not wanting any comments about my weird eyes. That would only keep me here longer, and I feared Nadia didn't have any time to spare. The mirrors were the thing that worried me the most. Ghosts and minor spirits wouldn't do something like that.

When Marianne arrived, Mama went down and handed over the keys, as I was in the middle of questioning. There wasn't much I could tell the police that they wouldn't see for themselves, so in the end, the officer handed me his card and told me to call if I thought of anything else.

"What about the dog?" Mama asked. She'd thrown on a wig and shaved at some point, and it seemed to give her a little extra piff.

"Part of my agreement with Nadia is that I'll watch Midna if something happens," I said, tightening my grip on the leash, afraid the police might take her away from me. "I have her contact info, so I can call her parents and –"

"Please don't," the officer talked over me. "It would be better that the news of their missing daughter comes from the police, rather than a dog-walker." He said the last with a sneer, and both Mama and I lifted our eyebrows in return. He cleared his throat and looked away.

"Sure," I said. "I'll call tomorrow, then. They might want Midna 'til Nadia's found."

The officer grumbled something and disappeared into Nadia's apartment.

"What a prick," Mama murmured, and I snickered.

"Can you watch Midna for a sec?" I asked, growing serious again. "I need to grab some stuff from the apartment."

Mama looked down at the dog. Midna had stopped growling and whimpering, and instead looked as miserable as a dog could manage. My heart hurt every time I looked at her.

Mama nodded and took the leash. As I started toward the apartment, Midna whined and tried to follow, so I spent a few seconds telling her I'd be back. I allowed my luck out again, hoping it would keep the dog in place when I left. It did.

A police officer stood just inside the doorway, and I told him what I needed. He called over another officer that then proceeded to follow me around the apartment as I put together a bag of Midna's stuff. I had hoped they would let me do this alone, for there was something I needed if I wanted to help Nadia, but even my luck didn't seem to affect the officer enough for him to leave me wandering around alone.

I packed Midna's harness, a few of her toys, a blanket from

her crate, and scooped some food into empty boxes I found in a cupboard in the kitchen. I'd hoped my slow meandering would do what my luck had not, but the officer stuck to me like a burr to fur, so finally, I had to do my thing with him tagging along.

"What do you need in the bedroom?" He asked as I pushed open the door and walked in. A woman was taking pictures of the vanity and just barely glanced up as we entered.

"I need something of Nadia's," I answered and headed toward the hamper in the corner.

I would have preferred something more personal. Some hair, or even better, a few drops of blood, but there was no way I could get my hands on neither without seeming like a stalker right now. Not that I knew where to get any blood. If Nadia had bled on the shards, that would have been one thing, but she hadn't, so I had to improvise.

"Why?"

"Midna, that's the dog, was abused by her previous owners. She trusts me, yes, but being in a new house without her mom for who knows how long might trigger her, so bringing something of Nadia's will help to avoid that." I pulled the t-shirt I'd seen Nadia wear yesterday from the top of the hamper. "A-ha! This'll do."

"I'm not sure you can take that," the officer said. He was looking between the photographer and me as if afraid she would tattle on him.

"Just note it down on the report," the woman huffed. "Dirty laundry is hardly evidence."

"As far as we know!" the officer answered.

I rolled my eyes and pushed the t-shirt into the bag. "I don't need anything else, so I'll be outa your hair," I said and hurried past the officer before he could ask any more questions.

In the hall, Midna met me with half a tail-wag before plastering it up between her legs again. I took the leash and said my good-byes to Mama. She looked older now than when I arrived that morning, even after shaving. I considered hugging her, but we weren't close enough for that, so I just waved and hurried down the stairs, Midna sticking close to my feet.

Midna went in the back of the car. I didn't have a cage for transport, but the space was big enough for a large dog to stand, and there was a screen between it and the rest of the car so that a loose dog wouldn't cause an accident. I got her settled with the t-shirt I'd borrowed before I climbed into the front seat and started the car, turning the heater on full. The cold of the morning was still in my bones.

Leaning my head back and taking a deep breath, I shut down my luck. It was always hard after using it on and off like I had today. Almost like it was fighting me to stay on, but I got it under control. When I opened my eyes and glanced into the rearview mirror, the gaze meeting mine was blue and not gold. Sighing, I started the drive home.

6

Jake's first reaction to seeing me home early was a smile, but it faltered when he saw Midna.

"Sara?" He didn't need to say anymore. I knew what he was asking and why he asked it.

With a sigh, I kicked off my sneakers and unleashed Midna before I started telling Jake about my morning. As I did so, I walked around the apartment, finding the dog-bed and bowls we stored in the hallway closet for just such occasions. Midna stuck to my heels the entire time, throwing long looks at Jake.

"You think this is magical?" Jake asked when I finished.

"Yeah, although I can't remember nothing like it. Spirits are usually much more down-low. Breaking a few mirrors, that's fine, but a disappearance as well?"

Jake pulled a hand through his hair as he nodded. "Yes, 'tis indeed strange. I can't remember anything like this off the top of my head, either. I could Read?"

"No. Not yet."

He narrowed his eyes. "What will you do?"

"I'm gonna scry for her."

"Scry?" he crossed his arms.

"Yeah," I said as I coached Midna into the bed. She walked carefully around a few times before settling down, her eyes never leaving me.

"How? There is no spell for scrying after someone that's not family. You know that."

I shrugged. "I'm modifying it."

Jake's arms fell to hang limp along his sides. "How? Other witches have tried before, you know? It didn't work for them, so why should it work for you?"

I tapped the side of my nose. "Because I'm lucky."

He groaned and rolled his eyes as he crossed his arms again. When he looked at me, his brow was furrowed, and his eyes seemed darker, somehow. More like storm clouds than rain clouds.

"I was wondering if you'd spot me," I said, making my eyes big and pleading. "You don't need to be in the circle with me. Just be in the room in case it goes wrong?"

He sighed. "Even if you think it'll go wrong, you're going through with it, aren't you?"

"Yeah."

"Fine," he flung his hands in the air before settling them on his hips. "What do you need?"

I gave him the list of tools and herbs I'd need before I walked into the library, Midna at my heels, to write down the spell so I wouldn't forget it. I re-wrote the last verse three times before I thought it would work.

When I came back to the living room, I saw that Jake had moved the table, sofa, and rug to clear an open space on the hardwood floor. In the middle of the open space stood jars with herbs and a small mortar, two white candles and matches, a small cauldron and a pitcher of saltwater, a besom, and a piece of chalk. I put the paper down together with the things and went to get the t-shirt. I wasn't lying when I said it would help

Midna calm down, but I also had another reason for needing it.

When I entered the living room again, Jake was reading the spell. "It might work," he said without looking up. "'tis simple, but it might work."

I kissed him on the cheek.

Before I could start, I needed Midna to accept Jake. With my luck and bond with Midna, it didn't take long before she was ok with Jake. She didn't want him to touch her, but it was ok that he sat beside her bed. That would have to be good enough. After I threw the circle, I couldn't speak to her, and if she walked into the circle, she'd break it and the spell, which could be bad. If she tried to do that, Jake would have to hold her in place until I undid the circle. I hoped that wouldn't happen, for it would set back our training by months.

Pushing thoughts of the dog from my mind, I picked up the besom and started making my way around the stuff on the floor. I moved clockwise around and around, spiraling outward, until I'd formed a big enough circle, brushing as I went. When that was done, I put the besom in its original place and picked up the chalk. Throwing one last look toward Midna to make sure she was calm, I let my luck loose. Bending, I put the chalk to the floor.

Instantly, I felt magic spark in my fingers. The magic only grew as I walked around, drawing a perfect circle with me inside. The circle complete, I stood, facing North. Putting out a finger, I began murmuring Celtic chants that had been in my family for generations. As I did, I started drawing with my finger. I called the element of Earth. The gold of my magic stayed in the air as I drew, leaving a shimmering pentagram in my wake. I moved clockwise, drawing the pentagram for Air to the East, Fire in the South, and Water in the West. All four pentagrams shimmered as I left the boundary and sat down in the middle of the circle.

Striking a match and lighting the candles, I said:

"Spirits, Mother Earth, hear me now.
What is lost, I wish to find.
Help me stop being blind.
Direct me to who I seek.
By Fire, Air, Earth, and Sea. So mote it be."

Blowing out the match, I set it aside and picked up the mortar. Nestling it in my lap, I started picking herbs from the jars and crushing them to as fine a powder as I possibly could. Lifting the t-shirt, I dropped it into the cauldron, then lifted the pitcher of saltwater. As I poured it over the t-shirt, I chanted:

"By Fire, Air, Earth, and Sea.
By the bonds of friends, I wish to see."

I repeated it three times as I poured, making sure to space out the water so I would have enough. Then I sprinkled the herbs into the water. I stayed silent as I put the mortar aside and wrapped both hands around the cauldron, staring into the water. It was still and dark, not showing me anything. I spat into it.

"By Fire, Air, Earth, and Sea.
By spit and sweat, our bonds are met.
Let me see Nadia Trueman.
So mote it be."

I repeated this three times as well, then I waited, not taking my eyes of the content of the cauldron. For a long moment, nothing happened, and I watched in growing despair as the globule of spit dissolved and disappeared into the water. Just as the last of it dissolved, something in the deep of the cauldron rippled. I blinked, afraid my eyes were playing tricks on me, but the ripple grew until it touched the sides of the cauldron. Inside it, I saw what I was looking for:

Nadia. She was looking up at me, her eyes wide and her lips slightly parted in wonder. Her usually thick, black hair was hidden beneath a silken shawl I'd seen her wear a few times in the morning when she couldn't be bothered to do her hair.

The view changed, and I was pulling back until I could see all of her. She stood leaning a little forward, her left hand reaching out, the fingertips seeming to touch some kind of surface between her and me. She was dressed in a t-shirt that reached to the top of her thighs and hung off one shoulder. She wore nothing else and combined with the hair; I guessed she'd just woken up.

I waited for her to move. With the original version of the spell, we watched in real-time. The hope was that this spell would copy the original, but maybe the connection between Nadia and me wasn't strong enough? Maybe I was seeing her the moment she became lost?

As I was about to pull back and break the spell, something moved behind Nadia. Until now, I'd been so focused on her that I'd forgotten to look around her. Not that there was much to see. She was standing in a grey nothingness. There was no clear floor, no walls, and no ceiling, but multiple strange frames littered the background. Some up where the ceiling should have been, some down below where the floor should have been, and they were all different. Some small and round, some huge and square.

The movement caught my eye again, and I tried to focus on it. Something was flickering behind Nadia, but my eyes kept slipping away. Like I wasn't able to look directly at it. But what could do that? A spell? A power? A spirit?

I tried and tried again to watch the thing that moved, but I couldn't focus, couldn't see any clear details. It looked humanoid. That I was sure off. And it was moving, which meant I was looking at this in real-time, like with the original spell. So why wasn't Nadia moving? I returned my attention to her and tried to see any sign of movement, but it didn't even look like she was breathing.

My eyes snagged on her hands. They were just as still as the rest of her, but they were... wrong, somehow. Almost like I was watching them through water, the color bleached out of them, and their connection to Nadia's arms a little crooked. And were those cracks running between her fingers? Not like her skin was dry, but black lines, like when a mirror cracked.

Jake said my name and I jumped, having forgotten he was there. I glanced at him before looking back into the cauldron, but the vision was gone.

Sighing, I lifted a finger to tell Jake to give me a minute before I stood and started undoing the circle. Staring with the pentagrams and moving counter-clockwise until they were all down. Then I bent and put my fingers on the chalk-circle, smudging it as I went. I could feel the pop of magic as I released it.

The moment the circle was down, Jake reached for me, and I let him examine me.

"What happened?" he asked when he was sure I wasn't hurt.

I glanced at the cauldron before telling him what I'd seen.

"Does that ring any bell?" I asked when I finished.

Jake dragged a hand over his face and stared into nothing for a moment. "I think so. 'tis... no, 'tis been too long. Give me a minute to look it up."

I squeezed his shoulder and let him sit down on the couch. As I cleaned away the tools of our craft, I kept an eye on him. His powers weren't dangerous, but he could get lost in his own mind for hours if not careful.

Witches don't have sons, as a rule, but as with every rule, there are exceptions. Jake was one of them. Until just a few generations ago, it was normal for a witch's son to be killed, because witches believed their presence somehow weakened the magic of the females in the line. If a son was allowed to grow up, however, he was called a chronicler. Their job was to keep track of witch history, spells, languages, and much more. They got this role when it became clear that they could form their own form of covens. Two men born of witches, but of completely different bloodlines, could make a blood-oath, and in so doing, they shared a mind. Not living through each other, but learning everything the other man knew.

Today, witch's sons were given to the closest chronicler to be raised. Jake's line, the Johnsson-line, was seven generations old, and one of the longest ones documented. It was normal for the boys to take the blood-oath when they turned ten, and in doing so, absorbing all the memories of their line until that point. Jake would do the oath again when his adoptive father was dying, learning everything he'd learned in the meantime. Jake was a wandering library.

Every chronicler had their way of handling the flood of information. Jake took the library comment a step further, and put all the information into ''books''. He still remembered a lot of it. Like the languages and general witch lore. Even things he learned completely new, stayed in his mind that way. A magic form of photographic memory. Obscure knowledge, like what I'd just seen, was easier to ''forget'', and so he had to ''look it up'' whenever he needed it. He called that Reading, and it was what he was doing now. As I watched, his eyes were running back and forth, as if he truly was looking something up in one of his many books.

I shuddered and finished cleaning up before I filled Midna's food-dish and sat down at the kitchen table. Pulling the notepad and pen to me, I started drawing what I'd seen in the cauldron. Hoping it would give me any more clues.

My art skills were far from good. Jake had tried teaching me, but in the end, I was better at sketches without details, so that's what I did now. I started by drawing Nadia, trying to capture her pose and the way her fingers touched something between us. I wrote a few notes on how her face looked, then tried to draw the many shapes I'd seen behind her. They ended up as blurs, but I wasn't focusing on them. Instead, I kept thinking about the other shape, the thing that had moved. Something was tickling the back of my mind, but I couldn't put my finger...

It became clear so fast I gripped the pen so hard it dug into my skin. Cursing, I changed my grip and flipped the notepad to a clean page and started to draw.

The thing that had moved behind Nadia had been hard to focus on. Like my eyes wouldn't land on it, but something had stuck with me. The hands. I hadn't noticed when I looked at it, but now that my mind was focused elsewhere, I remembered. The hands were brown and elegant and had a ring on one finger. A gold band with two diamonds and a sapphire. The shape had been too far away for me to have been able to see that detail clearly, but I trusted my luck, and it was telling me I knew this ring.

It was the same ring Nadia always wore. The heirloom from

her grandmother. But the shape had worn the ring on the wrong hand. Nadia always had it on her left hand, but the creature, for it must be a creature, a spirit, wore it on the right.

I flipped the pieces of paper back and forth, looking at the small circle I'd drawn around the two sets of hands. Nadia had still worn her ring in the vision, so how could the creature wear it as well?

As I tried to figure this out, something else about the shape came to me. It had hair. I turned back to the original drawing and hurriedly drew on the shape of dark bangs and hair falling past shoulders I hadn't seen but guessed where there.

When I was done, I started flipping the pages back and forth again. The hair wasn't Nadia's, so where did it come from? Was it the hair of the creature?

A hand touched my shoulder, and I jumped.

"Witch on a cracker," I cursed and turned to look up at Jake. He was leaning over my shoulder, looking at my drawings. "Find something?"

"Yes," he took the pieces of paper from me and lay the first one on top, the one with Nadia. "I found that," he pointed just over Nadia's shoulder. "That's the Hall of Mirrors."

"The what now?"

Jake straightened and went to the counter. He filled the boiler with water and found two bags of tea from a jar on the shelf. The smell of chamomile and lavender rose in the air.

I waited, letting him make the tea and gather himself. He was always tired after his readings, and it took him some time to gather his mind and control all the memories. It was like with my luck. When he started using his power, it pushed back, wanting to be used even more. It was almost like an addiction.

When the tea was ready, he brought the cups to the table but didn't sit. Instead, he found a packet of chocolate chip cookies from the miscellaneous drawer.

"I didn't know we had that," I said.

He smiled a half-smile. "That's because I hid it. If you knew we had it, we wouldn't have it anymore."

I stuck my tongue out at him and grabbed the pack from his hands when he came close enough. Opening it, I snatched the top cookie and stuck it in my mouth before I put the pack down on the table. Jake dragged it closer and took a cookie, but he didn't eat it. Just kept turning it in his hands as he looked at the drawing.

"From what I found, there aren't many old legends surrounding mirrors. There are some modern tales, of course, like Bloody Mary, and there are older traditions, like Jews covering the mirrors in their house when someone dies, but nothing about mirrors kidnapping anyone."

"So *Alice and the looking glass* don't count?"

"Maybe Lewis knew something we don't, but none of my line has encountered anything like it before."

"But you said this was the Hall of Mirrors?" I brushed cookie crumbs off the drawing of Nadia.

"Yes, for that I know of. My dad encountered a spell a few years before he got me that could turn mirrors into doorways. 'tis a really old spell, originally written in Latin, and it required a gold mirror."

"Gold?"

"Romans made the first whole figure mirrors out of polished silver or gold. As far as dad knew, they couldn't use the silver mirrors for this kind of travel, which would explain why the spell as good as disappeared in the early 1800s."

"And why is that? For those of us not with a whole library in our heads?"

He finally took a bite of his cookie and chewed it before answering. "Because the modern mirror was created then, and it used mainly silver."

"And silver is a cleansing metal, so magic won't stick to it for long."

"Precisely."

"But if that's the modern mirror, why are we seeing this now?"

"Apparently, we use other metals to make mirrors these days. Mostly aluminum." I tilted my third cookie at him in an ''I understand''-gesture, and he went on. "According to dad, the spell would make a doorway out of a full figure mirror. When a witch stepped into the mirror, they emerged in what they called the Hall of Mirrors. Apparently, one could see all the mirrors in the world there. One could either spy on people through them or even step through another mirror as a doorway and emerge wherever that mirror originally stood."

"That's a neat trick. Would save me a lot of gas money!"

"There were dangers, though. Like the spell had to be cast on the mirror from our side of the doorway. One could not cast the spell inside the Hall of Mirrors. So if someone broke your mirror while you were inside, you couldn't make a way out on your own. And the magic there somehow made it easy to get lost. And there was something about not staying there for too long, or it would claim you. No one in my line has traveled there, so I don't know why that is, but the dangers were real enough that the Romans only used the spell when they absolutely had to."

I stuck my tongue out at him and pushed the last piece of my cookie into my mouth. "But," I said before I lifted my finger, asking him to wait for me to swallow. "If Nadia is in the Hall of Mirrors, and she's been there for hours, we have to go get her."

"Yes. The most important question, however, is how did she get there in the first place? She's not a witch, so how could she have cast the travel spell?"

I tapped my fingers on the drawing. "I think Nadia was touching the mirror," I said, turning the drawing and pointing at the fingers of her left hand reaching out. "So whatever did this, must have pulled her through somehow."

Jake looked at the drawing for a long moment before he sat back in his chair and pulled both hands over his face and through his hair.

"Maybe 'tis an Ungaikyō?" He said in a low voice, then continued before I had time to answer. "No. That's a cursed mirror, and it doesn't have the power to pull someone into it. It just reflects you in a disturbing way." He pulled his hands through his hair again. "Were there mirrors facing each other?" I shook my head, and he sighed. "So not a ghost portal. The mirrors were broken, but most likely it happened after Nadia was taken."

"The mirror in her bedroom wasn't broken," I said in a hurry. "It was on an old vanity."

Jake nodded. "It probably had a silver backing, which means this spirit can't use it. Did it break the other mirrors to avoid anyone following it? Maybe when it had first used the mirrors for transportation, they could be used again? I don't know. There isn't enough information for me to draw a good conclusion."

He looked at me then, his eyes big and lost. He wasn't used to not having the answer. Even if he didn't want to use his powers to gain things, he always knew it was there when needed, and it failing him now was something completely new.

I reached over and took his hand. He stared at our intertwining fingers like he'd never seen them before.

"It's ok," I said. "There are many things we don't know, after all, and we just have to deal with it as it comes."

"But there isn't supposed to be any new things," he said, sounding like a small boy. "That's why we have the Veil."

I squeezed his hand. "But even with the Veil, things slip through the cracks. This spirit might be one of them. Or maybe it was created here."

"How?"

"There's magic everywhere. Maybe a witch did it? Or it might be the result of enough focused energy. If it's in a mirror, I think the last one fits. How many people use a mirror every day to pretty up? How many looks in a mirror and aren't happy by what they see? All that energy would eventually lead to something, and I think that's what we're seeing here."

Jake was nodding along. "That makes sense," he finally said. "I think I will send a message to some other chroniclers as well, to ask if they know anything. Even if they don't, they should know that this could happen."

Squeezing his hand, I stood. "Good. Meanwhile, I'll go after Nadia. I'll need that travel spell."

Jake stared at me like I'd lost my mind. "There's no chance I'll talk you into waiting for more information, is there?"

"Nope."

He sighed. "Fine, but you're not going unarmed. We don't know enough about this spirit, so you're not going in there like that."

I looked down at my work clothes. Wool leggings and a t-shirt, a light jacket above to keep the worst of the wind out.

"Fair 'nough," I said. "I'll go change."

8

Not knowing what I might meet inside the Hall of Mirrors, I thought it best to prepare for anything. We witches had dealt with spirits for generations, binding them or weakening them, so we had our tricks. One of those was iron and salt.

To carry the substances within easy reach, I wore a set of old cargo pants. The pockets were big and deep so that I could fill one with salt and the other with iron shavings. The extra pockets could hold other implements of our trade, like vials of potions and ground herbs.

I didn't have anything special for my torso, so I pulled on a black tank-top that wouldn't get in the way, and went into the hallway. There, I tied on my oldest set of Doc Martens and pulled on my leather jacket. It had a tall throat when zipped up and gave a hint of extra protection.

Lastly, I opened the hallway closet and pulled out a baseball bat. Its shape was rough and not smooth as one would expect, but the grip was worn down.

Jake's adoptive father, Baldwin, had cut the bat out of Alder wood.

In Celtic mythology, the Alder fought at the front line in the war between the trees and the otherworld. While the Alder was mostly used in witchcraft to balance energies, it held battle energies if needed. That's why Baldwin had given us this a few years ago, in case we ever needed to fight against something more substantial than ghosts. We hadn't needed it so far, but we had practiced with it. It did wonders against old plates or car windows. Now, however, it felt right to bring it with me.

I headed into the kitchen, where Jake waited. I'd almost forgotten about Midna but found her now lying under the table, just shy of Jake's feet. Her trust in him warmed my heart.

"If things don't go well," I began. "The contact info to Nadia's family is in my bedside drawer. Together with the info for my other clients. You should let Midna stay with people she knows."

Jake looked at me for a long moment before he stood and wrapped his arms around me. "You'll come back," he said and kissed the tip of my nose.

I bit the tip of his. He chuckled before pulling away and turning us both to the table.

Two bags stood there, and I started filling my pockets with the iron shavings and salt, one in each and taking care not to mix them. Jake had also found a couple of vials, a piece of nylon rope I didn't even know we owned, and gardening gloves that looked completely new.

"Gloves?" I asked.

"You're going into a mirror. Mirrors have sharp edges when broken. Better safe than sorry."

I nodded and dusted iron and salt off my hands before grabbing two vials. "I'll take the acid, but I don't think the stun or fog potions will help any."

"Why not?"

"Stun needs skin contact, and I'm not sure this thing has

any."

"It has hands."

"Nadia's hands, so it might not work." He shrugged. "And the fog will blind me as much as it, and we don't even know if it has eyes!"

Jake looked away but didn't argue. For half a second, I considered taking the vials even if I wouldn't use them, but I left them on the table. Finally, I pulled on the gloves.

Stretching my neck until it popped, I turned back to Jake. "Let's do this thing."

Jake opened and closed his mouth a couple of times before he looked away. Instead of saying anything, he grabbed the piece of paper lying on the table, took my hand with his other one, and led me into the hallway. It held the only full figure mirror in the apartment.

As I looked at my reflection, I realized it was one of only two mirrors in the whole apartment, and both had been here when Jake bought the place. I'd never noticed before, but we both avoided mirrors if we could. Maybe it had something to do with the silver? Or was it just a witchy thing? An old instinct that neither of us could explain?

Letting the thought go, I let my magic go as well, and watched as my eyes turned from blue to gold. Jake stood just behind me and met my gaze. I nodded, and he looped the end of the rope around my waist and tied it in place.

"I know the rope probably won't let you go as far as you want, but please don't unknot it. As long as you have it with you, you'll know where to go to get back, or I can pull you out when you've been in there for too long."

I turned and wrapped my arms around his shoulders. "I'll be fine," I said and gave him a quick kiss, encouraged by our preparations and the information we had gathered. "It's just a spirit. A new one, but how hard can it be?"

"If it slipped through the Veil, it will be stronger than our usual ghosts."

"But it would have to be tiny to pass through an opening in the Veil, so it stands to reason it's not too dangerous."

"You're small but deadly."

I grinned. "True, but that's because I'm special." When I kissed him this time, I held it a little longer. "You worry too much."

He growled. "You don't worry enough."

Before I could answer, he grabbed the back of my head and pulled it up. Our lips met. He kissed me with an adrenaline-fueled hunger that sent sparks of heat running down my back to settle low in my belly.

"That's not fair," I panted when he pulled back.

"If it brings you back to me, I don't mind playing dirty."

For a split second, I considered dropping this entire quest and pushing him into the bedroom, but I couldn't leave Nadia in there any longer. Her, or the owner of the hair I'd drawn.

With a sigh, I stepped away from Jake. He let me go, dragging his fingers and hands along my waist and shoulder as he did. Even with my leather jacket between us, his touch warmed my skin.

"I'll be back," I said in my best Schwarzenegger impression.

Jake rolled his eyes, but his smile was strained. I pretended not to notice as I stepped to the side and let him cast the spell on the mirror. The spell was in Latin, which he spoke fluently – even if it was a dead language. He and his dad had whole conversations in Latin, and both Jake's mom and I hated it when they did so – and that was it. I watched as he spoke the words and touched the mirror, and I saw the moment the magic moved from his fingers and into the glass. It was like a ripple on a calm lake, but nothing else changed.

Jake stepped back, and I took his place. As Jake lifted the rope, I reached forward, and my hand passed into the mirror.

Shooting a grin his way, I stepped forward and let the cold surface envelop me.

9

For a heartbeat, there was nothing around me. No light, no sound, no temperature. It was like I was in a vacuum. Then I took another step forward, and the world exploded in a pale light. I had to blink multiple times before my eyes grew used to it.

The world I'd stepped into was just like the one I'd seen behind Nadia. It was an almost white grey, with no sign of a roof or walls or even a floor. I stood on nothing, surrounded by shapes. All the things I'd seen behind and around Nadia were mirrors, and they came in every shape and size. Some were small and round, others huge and square. Some even had intricate golden frames.

Turning, I took a step back to get a better look at my own mirror. It was huge and wide, just like the original back in our apartment. Through the mirror, I could see Jake and Midna. Midna lay by Jake's feet; ears pulled back and tail around her back paws. Jake stood completely still, clutching his end of the rope. I could see both of them breathing, so I was watching in real-time.

I waved, but Jake didn't react. I tried again, but he didn't even blink, so I grimaced. When that didn't get a reaction, I made lewd gestures with my hands. Still nothing.

"Jake?" Almost before I'd finished the word, I snapped my mouth shut so hard my teeth clicked painfully together. My voice had been loud and echoing in the otherwise completely still world.

Glancing around, I made sure no-one or nothing was drawn by my speaking, then I stuck my hand through the mirror.

Both Midna and Jake jumped. I grinned as I waved at them and gave a thumbs up. Jake gave a thumbs up in return, but his brow stayed furrowed in worry. I pulled the hand back and turned to the rest of the world.

Ok, how to find Nadia? If the Hall of Mirrors showed every mirror in the world – or at least the mirrors that could be affected by magic – maybe the mirrors lay in a kind of grid that could compare to the real world? That would explain why the mirrors both above and below looked liked copies of the mirror I'd stepped through. Those were the mirrors into the apartments in our building.

Swinging the bat to rest on my shoulder, I guessed at the direction Nadia lived in and started walking.

I was afraid movement would make me sink through the nothingness, but I stayed on the same level, and somehow I seemed to move more than my steps should account for. When the rope around my waist tightened, I wasn't completely surprised to see that I was almost twenty meters away from the mirror I'd come through, even if I'd barely taken ten steps.

I turned and looked around. There was no sign of Nadia or the creature that lived here, and I was out of rope. Should I go back and find more rope? I didn't think we had any, and it would take time I was sure Nadia didn't have before we could get more.

If I untied myself, Jake would be angry at my recklessness,

but I believed what I'd told him. There were no huge big baddies in our world anymore. Even those that slipped through the Veil were small and easy to deal with. And if this thing was created here? Well, it would still be weak. It took a lot of magic for something to come to life, and even more for it to grow strong. Especially if it was a result of gathering energy, and not an intentional creation. Even if it was that, I was sure I could beat it. I had luck on my side, after all.

With a sigh and already preparing a speech for when I got back, I untied the rope and let it fall to the ground. I kept glancing back as I walked away, however, making sure it stayed where I'd dropped it.

When I was sure it wouldn't slip down through the nothingness, I focused my attention ahead and started walking faster.

It was easy to understand how one could get lost in here. For every step I took, I covered the length of three usual steps. And if I looked at a mirror on another level and thought I wanted to go there, I instantly started walking upward to be on the same level as it, or the same going down. There was no way of telling what level I was on, or how far I really was from my own doorway.

When I looked back, I couldn't see the rope anymore.

That realization chilled me, and I stopped where I was, thinking. I had to be careful, or I would become lost. Another story used to scare witch-children. Turning around, I looked for a landmark, and tried to remember how many levels I'd gone up and down. I thought I was just one level too high, and I noticed three round mirrors bound together. Ok, so that mirror would point me in the right direction when I needed to get back.

As I turned to look around, I noticed something else. Someone stood a little up and to my left.

"Hey! Nadia!" I called and started running; any earlier concern forgotten in my joy of finding her this fast.

Within seconds, I'd covered the distance between us, and I realized that the girl wasn't Nadia. This girl was smaller and wore a pink dress. As I got closer, I saw that she wasn't a girl at all, but a young woman around my age. She was of Asian heritage, maybe Chinese, and had the most beautiful black hair I'd seen in forever. It was straight and shining, with no sign of any split ends, and reached to her lower back. In front, she had bangs.

It was the bangs that brought me up short.

The creature in the mirror had bangs as well. And black hair.

I walked until I was side by side with her, and that's when I noticed that her hair was wrong. It looked beautiful from afar, but close up, I saw that it was faded into a dusty grey that didn't match the rest of her coloring. And it was filled with black strands going every which way. No, not strands. Cracks, like in a broken mirror.

I froze, staring at her hair. Just like Nadia's hands. That's when I noticed that the woman wasn't moving. She hadn't moved since I saw her.

"Hey," I said, my voice only shaking a little. "You ok?"

She didn't react. Carefully, I stepped until I stood side by side with her and used my mouth to tug off the glove on one hand. Even as I reached two fingers forward to check her pulse, I knew I wouldn't find any. She was leaning forward, her face almost pressed to the surface of her mirror. If she were breathing, there would be condensation, and I didn't see any sign of it. But I still had to check, had to be sure.

My fingers found the point where her pulse should be at her throat, but I didn't let them stay there for more than half a second. Her skin was cold, hard, and smooth. Like glass. She was made of glass.

Even as I stood there, staring, I noticed one of the cracks in her hair spreading over her ear. Instantly, the ear got that same dusty color as the hair.

I took a step back, shaking my head. How could this be happening? How could she be frozen like this, cracking? She had been a person once, not so long ago, so how could she be made of glass now? And what kind of creature had the power to do something like this?

Not a creature, a small voice whispered in my head. But the Hall of Mirrors.

Jake said something happened if we stayed in here for too long, and now I knew what that something was. You turned to glass yourself, and for some reason, you started cracking. Or maybe the cracking was an effect of the creature that lived here? That is somehow took those elements?

I turned away from the girl, swallowing bile as I did so. I wanted to help her, but I didn't know how. If I went back to Jake, he might figure something out, but what if it was too late to do anything? What if I could still save Nadia if I left this girl behind?

With a last shake of my head, I located the three round mirrors and hurried in their direction. Stick by a landmark, and I wouldn't be lost.

I'd almost reached the mirror when I saw something heading toward me.

10

The thing moved in fits and starts, and I had trouble watching it. It seemed to blend into the surrounding greyness, and only a few things on it made it possible for me even to see it. Its hands that were Nadia's hands, and its hair that was the hair of the girl I just left behind. But also something else. It had eyes now, and those almost violet eyes were focused on me.

I met the gaze and tightened my grip on the bat.

"You!" I called, my voice echoing off the many mirrors between us. "Why are you doing this? What do you want?"

The thing kept moving toward me but didn't answer. Maybe it couldn't answer without a mouth?

Grunting in sudden irritation, I started forward, spinning the bat as I went.

"Where is Nadia?" I called, but it didn't answer that either. Instead, it seemed to mirror the way I walked, and its movement became a lot smoother. "Who's the owner of those eyes?" It blinked but didn't answer.

I gripped the bat with both hands and started running. Screaming in righteous fury, I lunged for the spirit. Just before I reached it, I saw why I hadn't been able to see anything other than its hands and hair and eyes. Its body was made up of thousands of shards of mirrored glass. I saw my own furious snarl reflected in its broken chest as I drew closer.

I swung the bat, and it smacked into the creature's shoulder. The sound of glass breaking and scraping against each other exploded around me, and I stumbled back, reaching up to cover my ears. The scraping of glass against glass continued as the creature was flung to the side and moved around itself to protect its hurt shoulder. It took me a moment to realize the sound was it screaming in pain.

"Listen," I said, panting for no good reason. "I'll leave you alone if you release the people you've kidnapped and don't do it again."

The sound stopped, and the creature turned those stolen eyes my way. They were narrowed in rage and hurt. It was strange, seeing those eyes in the reflection of my face, broken as it was by all the different shards making up the creature's head.

I took a step back. "That's how you do it, isn't it? You're reflecting the things 'bout people you like, and when you do that in this world, you somehow steal that attribute from them?"

The creature, the reflection, didn't answer, but it did push to its feet. My eyes jumped to its hands, Nadia's hands, and the ring that was worn on the wrong side. Because everything was on the wrong side in a mirror. It was just a reflection.

I was so lost in the thought that I didn't notice as it lunged for me, glass shards moving into an inhuman shape as it did. It hit me in the chest, and I was thrown backward, the glass trying to envelop me.

Covering my head as best I could, I spun with the fall. Shards snagged on my leather jacket and cut through the ends of my hair. I felt them move past and around me, but my luck was just enough to keep them from touching skin.

I fell out of the swirl of glass. For a moment, the fear of falling drowned out the fear of the reflection. I slammed into the ground so hard the breath was knocked from my lungs, and I had to blink back tears as I stared up at the creature.

It gave that scraping sound again, and I wanted to cover my ears, but I didn't. Instead, I pushed up and looked around. My bat lay two meters to my side. I was about to lunge for it when the Reflection moved.

It didn't run like a human anymore but moved like a wave on the beach. Undulating forward at a fast pace, the many thousands of mirrored shards boiling around each other. Every now and again, I could see Nadia's hands and strands of the Asian woman's hair, but the eyes stayed up front.

I pushed to my feet and started to run, staying just to the side of the creature and wishing myself upward.

The Reflection was moving upward as well, and it took me a moment to realize it was heading toward the Asian woman.

I forced more speed into my legs, cursing myself for not working more on my stamina. I was already winded, but the creature didn't seem to need air the same way I did.

Beside me, the Reflection flattened out and surged forward, stretching as far as it could, trying to reach the woman ahead of me.

As my legs continued carrying me upwards, I plunged one hand into my pocket and pulled out salt. I flung it toward the Reflection seconds before it reached the woman. The salt bounced off most of the glass, but some slipped through the cracks.

The Reflection screeched.

I plunged both hands into my pockets, feeling the content

dig under my nails until it hurt. Salt and iron shavings mixed in the air as I threw it and hit the Reflection, making it scream and buck and try to dislodge the grains from its inside.

When I was satisfied it was pre-occupied, I hurried back the way I'd come. I hated to leave it, but I needed the bat. It lay where I had left it. When I grabbed it, my hands were shaking, but I didn't stop or allow myself to slow down, but skidded around and ran full tilt.

The Reflection had stopped screaming, and as I watched, it moved forward. It was sluggish, as if drunk, but it was moving.

I tried to run faster, tried to force my muscles to give more than they could, and watched in horror as the Reflection moved around the woman, hiding her from view before it started to pulse.

Skidding to a stop a few meters away, I could do nothing but stare open-mouthed as the jagged pieces of glass smoothed out and changed, taking on the proper form of a human body. The blank surface turned to tan skin, and even as it formed the face of the woman, the Reflection turned around to look at me, smiling so wide I could see the jagged pieces of glass replacing teeth.

It couldn't mirror what it couldn't see.

The thought was fleeting, and I pushed it away as unimportant.

"Leave her alone!" I called.

Instead of answering, the Reflection grinned impossibly wide, distorting the woman's usually cute face. I noticed it had kept the violet eyes and Nadia's hands.

It took a step toward me, and I hoped to see the woman left behind, grey and lifeless, but still there. No such luck. The space where the woman had been was empty, the previous occupant absorbed by the Reflection.

It couldn't reflect more than a few attributes of each person at a time, and needed to absorb them to mirror all of them completely.

Again, another unimportant thought.

"Please don't," I said as the Reflection took another step closer. "Don't make me do this."

My voice was shaking, and I couldn't quite feel my hand move.

The Reflection lunged.

I grabbed a vial from my left knee-pocket and flung it forward as I jumped back. The vial hit it right in the face with the sound of glass breaking against glass. The Reflections face started to boil.

It started keening and toppled over, pawing at its face with Nadia's hands, trying to wash away the acid now eating at its surface.

With a scream that almost drowned out the Reflections own, I swung the bat toward its head. It made contact with a crunch I felt all the way up my arms and into my shoulder. The Reflection toppled to the side, and I followed, swinging again, and again, and again. Screaming each time and breaking more and more shards as I did.

Part of me noticed that shards were falling away from the Reflection. Those were shards it could no longer use, I hoped, but I didn't stop hitting. The other part of me, the part that knew I didn't stand a chance at saving Nadia or the owner of the eyes, that I'd caused the Asian woman's death, was in control, and it kept hitting and hitting, screaming and screaming.

This world was too big. I couldn't find them without risking losing my own life.

And that thought almost broke me. I'd never been in a situation where it was me or another life. All the spirits and ghosts I'd dealt with were annoyances at best. This was something completely new, and I hated it.

I don't know how long I kept hitting the Reflection. At one point, it tried to get away, changing the shape of its body to avoid the bat, but I flung another handful of salt at it, and it stilled in its pain.

Eventually, only dust was left. I walked across it, making sure to grind any big pieces into the dust. Then I emptied my pockets over it, mixing the salt and iron in between the glass. Finally, I stepped back and pulled out the last vial of acid. It didn't contain much, but I hoped the more pieces I destroyed, the smaller were the chances the Reflection would come back.

I flung the vial into the mess and watched as it broke and spilled its content through the dust. It spluttered and hissed, and I stood there, staring until it stopped. Until there was only dead sludge left.

Tears started streaming from my eyes then, and I sniffled.

I found the three round mirrors and headed back toward my own doorway.

I didn't look through any of the mirrors as I went, even as I saw movements on the other side, and I didn't look around for Nadia or the other person that must be in here somewhere. I didn't lift my eyes before I saw the rope lying just below me. I stepped and reached the same level, then started to run, following the rope.

Sobbing and gasping for breath, I flung myself through the mirror and into Jake's waiting arms.

Epilogue

Jake went into the mirror a few hours after I got out. He wanted to look for Nadia and the other missing person, hoping against hope that we could save them. We agreed that he wouldn't stay in there for more than an hour, and I spent that entire time walking back and forth in front of the mirror, waiting for him.

He came back out two minutes after agreed, but he was fine. There was no discoloration or cracks on his person, and his skin was soft and warm as always. He hadn't found Nadia or anyone else, however, and we agreed that we wouldn't search anymore.

As he undid the spell on the mirror, I walked into the living room and curled up on the sofa with Midna. I'd cried after I came out of the mirror, and as I sat in the shower to wash away the glass dust that seemed to be everywhere, but by the time I came out of the bathroom, my tears had stopped. Now, I just felt numb.

"You didn't get any answers from it?" Jake asked for the third time since he came out. "This Reflection?"

I shook my head. "It couldn't speak without a mouth, and it hadn't reflected one yet. When it did... it didn't want to, it seemed."

Jake nodded and turned back to his laptop. He was writing

an email about what had happened to send to other chroniclers around the world. If something like this happened again, they should know about it and be able to save as many people as possible. The fact that we had done this and would help save those people didn't make me feel any better. We'd lost three lives because we didn't act fast enough, and we still didn't know why.

Jake ordered Chinese food and put on the movie *Blood and Chocolate.* It was an old favorite of mine, and I allowed myself to slip into the comfort of everything I knew and loved surrounding me.

The next day, the police called and told me they'd spoken to Nadia's family, so it was ok for me to call them. They also wondered if I knew two girls named Zi Yuan and Leah Reed. I didn't, but I wrote down the names. The police wouldn't tell me why they wondered, just thanked me for my help and hung up. I looked the girls up on Facebook. Zi Yuan was the Asian girl I'd seen in the Hall of Mirrors. Seeing her alive and vibrant in her pictures made tears fill my eyes again. Jake sat by my side when I looked up Leah Reed. I hadn't seen her before, but I recognized those almost violet eyes.

"So Reflection got three girls," I said to no one in particular as I dried the silent tears that kept running down my cheeks. I hated feeling like this. Hated that this creature, this mirror spirit, made me feel it.

"I'm sorry," Jake said and wrapped me in his arms. I let him hold me until my tears stopped.

I wanted to tell the police what had happened to the girls, but there was nothing they could do. Magic was a secret for a reason, and above all, I had to keep it that way. Nadia, Leah, and Yuan would forever be missing; their disappearances would go unsolved, their family never getting closure. I hated it.

The next few days past as normal. I was back at work, and Nadia's family had picked up Midna and thanked me for the help. Jake helped me dye my hair a strong green, and cut the tips ruined by flying shards of glass. My leather jacket was ruined, so we went shopping for a new one. Grams gave me a time and place for Nancy's funeral, and she asked me if I wanted to stay from then until Samhain, which I did. So I made arrangements with Marianne to take my clients for a few more days than originally planned. Disturbing news started on the third day; people were going missing, dogs killed in backyards and drained of blood, the cases stretching from Sky Harbour and South along the coast. I felt a small spark of shock, but was otherwise too numb to care. I went through the motions needed to survive, but I didn't feel anything. I couldn't. It felt like a betrayal of the girls we'd lost for me to just move on.

I didn't smile again before the *Jaws* theme woke me a few days later. The sound and its message a reminder that I was still alive, and that I should enjoy it. So I did.

Acknowledgment

I guess there's a lot of people I can thank for this book in some way or another.

I know I need to thank my partner. I owe them everything. Both for my falling in love with writing, but also for them standing by my side through something no couple at our age should have to live through.

Thank you for staying with me, you're my hero, and I hope you know it.

In a strange sense, I have to thank my great-aunt as well. It feels weird to thank her for getting Alzheimers, and all kinds of wrong, but the honest truth is that if she hadn't gotten sick, I would never have needed to write about it, and this story wouldn't have been born. So I won't thank her for it, but I am sending her my love and warm thoughts. Now and always.

I also need to thank my beta readers. Evelyn, Anniken, Kristina, Zack, and Courtney. Your feedback was invaluable, and I wouldn't have had the guts to publish if not for your help. Thank you so, so much!

The excellent artists at the CoverCollective.com, who created my cover, also need thanks.

This book couldn't have happened without you.

About the Author

Kima Blaze loves thunderstorms and tea, and collect feathers and owl plushies. She lives in a small house along the fjords of Norway, together with her partner and their fur-baby Kaysa. (Dog. Not cat. Kima is afraid of cats.)

She came late to the writing game, discovering it in her early twenties when sickness took hold of her life. Her partner, who has been a writer their entire life, suggested Kima write down her frustration, and she hasn't stopped writing since.

CURSE OF A NAME is her first published work.

You can connect with me on:

🐦 https://twitter.com/KimaBlaze

🔗 https://www.patreon.com/kimablaze

Subscribe to my newsletter:

✉ https://landing.mailerlite.com/webforms/landing/u6f9x4